THE HURRICANE WAKE

THE
HURRICANE
WAKE

ROSALIND ASHE

HOLT, RINEHART AND WINSTON
New York

Library of Congress Cataloging in Publication Data
Ashe, Rosalind.
  The hurricane wake.

  I. Title.
PZ4.A8246Hu3 [PR6051.S47]   823'.9'14   77–71366
ISBN 0–03–021366–5

Designer: Kathy Peck

Printed in the United States of America
10 9 8 7 6 5 4 3 2 1

THE
HURRICANE
WAKE

LAST NIGHT I woke and heard that sound again, and lay listening. I knew it was only a swooping bat—for if not, then it must be the fearsome saber practice of a samurai warrior so skilled he can shave the hairs off a blanket with curving, winnowing strokes, mincing every quarter of the unlit room.

I lay there at attention, trying to remember fear.

But the graceful samurai was wishful thinking, just another fantasy rooted in the silt of my long imprisonment. Do I desire fear? I can see that all my life slopes up to and away from the night of the hurricane. I was alive then, and perhaps only then; love and fear are bound inseparably in my mind.

Yesterday they brought a box of building bricks up to the turret. My generous brother is furnishing the village school with new equipment and somebody has thought kindly of me. In the very bottom, overlooked by my strict wardens, there was a piece of pencil. The fly leaves of my books will do for writing paper. I'll write down all that happened that night; then I can get it passed on to someone outside. But how?

I crawled in and hid under my four-poster bed a few mornings ago, to alarm him when he came for his usual

1

visit; and while I was waiting in the dust and the dark, I discovered a loose board, with a little space beneath it. I swept the droppings to one end and hid it there—my manuscript. Because I've got a plan: to tell his crime to the world, if it's the last thing I do (I know I'm ill, so it may be just that). The servants never clean the turret now; my writing will be safe as long as it isn't eaten. This place, so lonely and enclosed for me, is nevertheless teeming with life: the shingles rustling with bats morning and evening, the wainscot with rats and mice at night—free creatures that come and go. Birds nest in the eaves, flies swarm, the neat ants march through (I think I like them best: they're so orderly), and sometimes I'm visited by a big green grasshopper or a praying mantis.

I used to be afraid of a mantis when it landed, heavy and sticky, beside the lamp where Mother sat sewing. I would retreat until Nan or Father removed it. But even though it frightened me I was anxious about its fate, and wouldn't call Tom, for fear of what he might do.

Now I spend a lot of my time saving lives. You cease to be disturbed by such creatures when they are all you have, or when you think of what other things might haunt this turret.

I must not dwell on such possibilities. And now I have my writing to help me fill the long hours.

First I must try to unravel the separate strands and tell my story clearly. I feel awkward and stilted, but it is such a relief to set down my thoughts instead of having them loose in my head, lying about like live wires sparking uselessly and dangerously. I must be strict: twelve hours of storm, described in sequence. Twelve parts, carefully labeled: it must be well ordered.

Writing whenever I can, I find I'm neglecting my insects. Rescue work had become almost a full-time occupation for me, like some vestal virgin tending the vital spark, preserving what I can never create. My brother does his creating, of course, by conception; he must have plenty of little creations dependent on him by now. No wonder he needs my money.

God wouldn't let *me* conceive. He must be a just God, to disallow the monster I would produce. In my way, I thank Him; and for my sins, He condemns me to this sterile life-preserving penance: three Aves, twenty ladybirds, and four cockroaches before breakfast. I am not just a prisoner in this turret, fourteen by fourteen, but am trapped eternally in the sticky web of God's mercy and terrible patience, as I unwind a moth from the gray threads and pass it through into the world outside. Yesterday I gave my spoonful of breakfast sugar to the red ants that had come in through the jalousies; but Nan swept them all up together, hammered them with the brush, and tipped them into the dustbin. She slapped me for being hysterical, and later told my brother, she says. He hasn't punished me yet. He will be saving it, keeping me guessing, to build up my fear.

I know my lifesaving makes him wild, and now I am careful not to let him catch me at it, as it has become just another way he can hurt me. I remember all too well that terrible morning nearly two years ago when I knew there was a bat behind the picture *Hope* by Watts. I didn't have time to get it out before he came on his rounds and I prayed it would keep quiet. But he saw me watching and grew suspicious. So he found it and shook it down there and then and stepped on it, then picked it up (still vibrating) and dropped it in the wastepaper basket. I heard it squeak once more and tried not to react—he gets so much enjoyment from what he is pleased to call my "helpless flutterings." But I was hard pressed, and, as quietly as I could (I mustn't be shrill), I said: "How you must have enjoyed killing young Maurice—how very frustrating that they tied you up later on and you couldn't help in the final slaughter."

But Tom seemed to be in a good humor. He didn't hit me. He said:

"For Chris' sake, Lizzie! And what for? Why should I

3

want to do *that*? I'd got absolutely nothing from the old girl dying. But what about *you*? You didn't lift a finger to save her—and you were her only beneficiary."

"There was nothing I could *do*—" I broke down hopelessly, overcome by the bitter remorse that poisons my waking and my sleeping life. But later on, when I'd recovered a little, I remembered something he had said. I didn't take it in at first. "You were her only beneficiary."

That was the first I had heard of it. Funny how, indirectly, it took a dead rat bat to get that out of him. My words must have rankled after all.

When he came up later to lock the shutters in place—it was payday, and he would never risk my being seen by the people, in case they should pity me (as it is, they only fear me)—I said, continuing:

"So you'll have even more to gain from my death than I thought."

"I can wait," he said. "You're quite pretty, you keep me amused, and I'm still solvent, thanks to you. But when I've run through Father's money, we'll have to see what we can do about Aunt Cissie's little fortune: I'll need it if I am to put up a show and marry well. I must admit it'll be hard to find the right heiress: you've set such a high standard in looks and good company—but when you've gone quite white, when you're unattractively thin and bad-tempered—"

I caught his hand as he chucked me under the chin, and bit it hard, and he went away to tend it.

I don't like violence. I have a horror of death. I was not so squeamish before, though always softhearted, I think. I remember the time when he had two of his thuggish friends home for half-term—how big and strange and nastily attractive I found them, as I watched from a distance, awkward and pigtailed. I went through a very plain phase; it doesn't show so much in boys, I suppose—but for at least a year I didn't feel that Tom and I were the photo-and-negative doubles we were said to be: he always looked good. Or perhaps for a year I looked like a graceless boy,

4

and he *was* one, quite confidently. That was when he grew away from me, going off to school and coming back with big blond friends with khaki shorts and sheath knives and a strong musty smell. I was suddenly very aware of that smell and of their tanned, scarred knees and shapely arms —not childish sticks—and strong cruel hands. They were trying to harpoon lizards one day and I couldn't just stand by—it was so brutal, even for Tom; but he laughed and told me to run away.

Maurice saved me. Maurice was pumping water, detached, absorbed. He stopped suddenly. He knocked Tom out of the way, picked up the wounded lizard, and took it round to the veranda. There was no retaliation—only embarrassed laughter and mumbling, and then they all went off to swim. Maurice laid the lizard on a cool lily leaf and gave it water from the rain butt in the cap of an oil can. He told me to fetch a scrap of cloth from the sewing room and he bound it round the fragile, oozing rib cage.

"He may heal up with rest and cool quiet, Miss Liz," he said, "but if his insides mash up, he can't thrive, and I will kill him quick with my machete."

"Oh, give him a little time, Maurice," I pleaded, crouching by him—and I was sharply conscious all at once that he too had tanned knees and strong hands and smelled of fresh sweat from working at the pump.

Maurice—"the German," people called him—was so much a part of our everyday life that I often didn't notice he was there. He was Tom's sidekick until Tom started boarding; then he wasn't around so much, as he was attending the village school. In the holidays things seemed to change too. When Tom's friends were there, Maurice discreetly gave way; when they weren't and Tom took him up again, I realized there was a subtle alteration in status: Tom would sit and talk to Maurice while he pumped, not take equal turns with him as before. Maurice would saddle up the horses while Tom lay abed—weary with brain work, he said—and then they would ride out together. I went with them if they let me, but accepted my second-class citizenship all too readily; I was learning housekeeping from Nan and had sewing and piano practice and other "female" things. Only Tom teased and rejected me. Maurice never did. I so adored Tom that I took the kicks as gratefully as the ha'pence. And though I was envious of Maurice's favored position, I saw well enough that it was a delicate one, and sympathized with anyone who suffered from Tom's whims.

They looked good together, like the illustrations in *Huckleberry Finn*. Tom was white-haired, with the smooth olive skin of the tropical white child—no roses in his cheeks or mine. He has blue eyes and black lashes and brows, as I do—but on him, with that hair, it is almost shocking, the contrast. On me it fitted, was unremarkable. I know I had a good face when I grew into it, because he had—has. We would have been identical twins except that he was very fair and I was dark. With our Indian head-dresses on, in the early photograph on Father's desk, we are indistinguishable. Once, dressing up as two Pierrots for some silly party in Montego Bay, Tom said, "How do I look, then? Come here, mirror mirror—" to me, peering closely, nose to nose. "Oh yes. I look fine." And now, of course, we are even more alike, for my hair is nearly white.

Maurice was quite different from Tom, and a year older, though they were the same size when they were children. Maurice was that anomaly, a poor white, the last of a family of immigrant Germans who had come over to help fill the labor gap left by the slave emancipation. When I say he was the last, I mean he was the only pure German of his generation: all his aunts and uncles had intermarried with their neighbors.

He was a dark fox; his hair was thick and streaky brown, but with a sprinkling of scarlet hairs glinting along the edges. I only noticed these for the first time as I watched him bending over the lizard: I suppose his side-burns had just begun to grow. "That shows you his Other hair must be red," said Tom darkly when I pointed it out to him. I didn't understand, but Maurice seemed embarrassed, so I laid off. He was patchy with freckles in the earliest photographs of him and Tom in their frayed hats; the freckles joined up when he left school and worked in the sun all day, learning the job of head man, as he was destined to be when his father retired.

My father died when Maurice was fifteen and we were fourteen, and he died happier because of him. He had had a soft spot for the German, people said, and very early picked him out as a "front runner." "Maurice is one of Nature's dukes," he'd say to Tom; and, "I suppose you'll manage this place all right, son, with Maurice to help you."

Maurice never questioned this destiny, as far as I knew. He worshiped my father, and my sweet weak homesick English mother; she gave him Tom's old clothes—not that he was ever smaller, but it was all right for *his* trousers to be too short and his shirts to be faded and patched. And because the sewing woman always made two shirts, one for me and one for Tom, out of the Liberty lawns my mother had posted out once a year—insisting on dressing us as twins—there were days when Maurice and I found ourselves wearing the same shirt. Mine, crisply laundered and preserved by Nan, and worn half as hard as Tom's, lasted twice as long; but Maurice's faded hand-me-down was still recognizably the twin. And though I suppose we were both Tom's creatures, there were times when Maurice and I rode up through the rough grass pieces and stopped at the Halfway Tree, and he picked us oranges and peeled them with his bright sharpened-away penknife, when we felt almost free of him.

Yet how completely we accepted his dominion over us. In our games on the hillside and down in the ruins of the old Slave House, Tom was always Custer or Alexander the Great or young Lochinvar. We let him make the rules and also let him win. Sometimes I think that my imprisonment in this turret is just one of those games gone wrong, and I will wake up with Nan calling us for supper—

7

"Come, Mars Tom, untie the poor chile and wash you han',
the both of you. . . ."

But the cousins did not let him win. For four weeks
every summer, English fair play arrived: we were domi-
nated by neat panama hats and vyella shirts and good
manners. Males stood up when females came into the
room; I always shrank from creating such general disturb-
ance and would hang about the pantry or the veranda
door.

Then, our standard of living changed overnight: all at
once the dining table was cluttered with silver and slip-
pery table napkins that would not stay on our knees.
Under the cousins' directions, white lines were marked out
in the bottom garden for badminton. Our ancient gym
shoes, rusty from being used as waders eleven months of
the year, were whitened and threaded with new laces.
Meals became punctual. Classical music was put on the
Gramophone, or the cousins made their own; they all
played some socially acceptable instrument, like the re-
corder or the clarinet. Or they sang choruses and patter
songs from Gilbert and Sullivan in clear true tenors round
the piano, turning the pages for my mother. I never saw
her as happy as when the English cousins were there; she
expanded and grew pink cheeks and laughed a lot, dis-
pensing coffee from her corner under the lamp where the
moths gathered—quite the hostess, changing for dinner
and busying herself with flowers and menus and fussing
over maids' uniforms, while the rest of the year they got
by with grubby aprons.

For us children it was like being ancient Britons; the
Romans arrived for one month each year. No sooner had
we got accustomed to having clothes on over our woad and
passing the meat instead of fighting for it, than the pale
strangers would decamp, leaving only broken clarinet
reeds, a copy of *The Catcher in the Rye*, and the straight
white miniature roads of the badminton court among the
swiftly growing grass. And we would use their airmail

Observers to pack away the silver chafing dishes for another year.

I suppose Cousin Edward was special because he was our age—the youngest of them—and because he was the only one who had time for me. He was not good-looking then; Tom called him the White Slug—which was unfair, for though he was white he wasn't fat. He was fine-boned and delicate, with perpetual catarrh and he spent most of his time reading. But he would talk to me about what he read, and he drew for me pages of caricatures—I still have them—round which he would weave stories.

"He looks a baddy," he would say. "Give him an eye patch. I think he's after her money—see all those pearls she's wearing? Her name's Miss Asprey. Yes, you can *see* he's bad—with his two-tone shoes. Now for the hero—young and straight-featured and clear-eyed"—drawing all the while—"no facial hair—mustaches are for cads. He's the chap who comes to the rescue when all hope is lost, when Miss Asprey is bound and lying across the railway line. Though wounded in his left arm (it has to be their left, so they've still got a strong right arm for the damsel), he crawls the last few yards, his knife in his teeth, and cuts her bonds. . . ."

I worshiped him, but in a different way from my enslavement to Tom. Tom was my tribal chief. Cousin Edward was a pale missionary, telling tales of another world, opening up—perhaps offering?—a new life. His power was not the brute force of superior strength, of speed and animal cunning, that I had grown up to honor. His was the power of words, the suggestion of a whole different complicated civilization, where learning and manners and elegance were preeminent, where wit counted far more than whip cracking, and you could tell a man's breeding by his shoes.

Edward was an alien, but not one that bypassed our world: he dipped into it with the curiosity of an anthropologist. Whatever he inquired into he mastered, watching, questioning, drawing, reading up on it. He spent hours observing the birds that came to eat from the bunch of bananas that hung on the veranda; he knew which were indigenous, which migratory. He drew a reconstruction of the ruins, with the help of old office records and prints of similar buildings. He informed us, moreover, that there could be no dangerous snakes, even in the virgin forest of Rookoom, our dark mountain. And Tom turned this into the fiercest of the trials that were set for the White Slug.

"All right then," he said, "you can go and see for sure, can't you? And tell us if you're right when you come back. If you come back."

Even Tom grew nervous waiting at the edge of the forest for Cousin Edward to appear. I remember the heat and the noonday silence, only the flies buzzing round the horses as we waited a respectful distance from the green wall of bush. This was the true, original jungle, uncut and almost untrodden by man, choked with creepers and piled up into six volcanic peaks; an unknown mountain towering immeasurably over us, so familiar yet so mysterious. We were all too open to suggestions of mystery; most of our reading, our games, and our fantasies sprang from old stories that met and mingled with the superstitions around us.

Rookoom was the source of most local Westmoreland legend, and the pen keepers wouldn't venture far into it even after a lost steer. They came out with tales of yellow snakes coiled round the branches and wild boars grunting in the thickets. Far worse things there were, it seemed, though not for our ears—we only heard them by eavesdropping outside the bottom kitchen: the Mountain Witch (not just a bird, as people thought); Rolling-calves, the fabled black beasts with burning eyes and clanking chains; and, most terrible of all, there was the Headless Man—for he foreshadowed a death.

Waiting for Edward that day, we were heavy with our knowledge of all these things.

"He's certainly taking his time," Tom said, slapping the

10

flies from his neck. "We're going to be in bad trouble for missing lunch."

High above us in the green cliff we heard the fluting whistle of a solitaire, pure and clear. And then another.

"That's not right," said Maurice. "Two solitaires? You never hear *two*. . . ." Our uneasiness increased; we waited.

Edward came out of the forest on foot—a small pale figure against the dark curtain. He was leading his horse behind him.

"Did you hear the solitaires?" he called as he came closer. "The first one was me: I tricked it."

"Where the hell have you been all this time?" demanded Tom, who had quickly swallowed his relief.

"I found a way to the top—couldn't ride, of course," said the White Slug coolly. "Fantastic fungi. Wild-pine flowers I haven't seen anywhere else. No view up there—until I managed to climb a tree. Then I could actually see the sea, and distant land—Cuba! Quite fascinating . . . Oh, and one yellow snake, by the way, quite long, of the python family—definitely not poisonous."

Even Tom was impressed; and Edward established himself as my hero. I can see now that it had been more a scientific exploration for him than a matter of physical daring, but at the time I was dazzled simply by his courage and endurance. Not only could he draw and talk and entertain me; he was identified in my mind with the bold rescuer of the damsel tied to the railway line. I, of course, was the damsel.

The conquering of Rookoom was a typical English victory, but the most notable. The cousins always beat us at badminton and puzzles and general knowledge—their own ground; and they had this tendency, if they could be bothered with our skills, to learn quickly, once they put their minds to it. They excelled by ingenuity. Father used to drive us all in the car to the big river when the rains came down; it looked muddy, but at least it was large enough for real swimming and games. There Edward beat us all at Water Lurky, using a drinking straw from the picnic basket to swim a long way on his back underwater, unobserved, and take the "guard" by surprise.

But where natural grace or speed or endurance were at a premium, Maurice and Tom were unbeatable. Which meant Tom won and Maurice came second. None of the invaders could dive or run or limbo like Tom. Yet that was not enough for him, and he spent much of their visit defiantly playing Mowgli, sometimes with Maurice and me as attendant minor wolves, watching the cousins' activities from afar. More often I would collaborate, even just to be a linesman or ball boy, to spray antimosquito flit on their bony white ankles, or carry the jug of lime juice and make sure Edward got the largest chunk of ice.

I never saw in those days how Tom resented my devotion to my cousin. I realize now that the White Slug was too smart for his own good. Even his own brothers felt he needed cutting down to size—he was altogether too eccentric, wordy, smug, know-it-all. I saw none of this; I was under his spell. But Tom too had to admit his ingenuity and—reluctantly—his daring; it was the detachment that most rankled.

As Edward returned each summer, he grew into the tall, ethereal good looks we expected of the English cousins. He was attentive to Mother and even to Aunt Cissie, polite to Nan, and gallant with me. And I became too proud to dog him as I used to—I worshiped him silently and longed to be grown up. Only now I recognize that Tom never forgave him for taking over my mind and heart; the last time he had come out, four years before the Great Hurricane, I was still unaware of the trouble being sown; and on this night it bore fruit.

This stormy night I woke up and perceived, and started to live. For twelve hours. Tom put an end to that, and when it was finished he carried what was left of me up to this turret.

He calls me mad, and violent—but he doesn't seem afraid of me; he turns his back on me to lock the shutters or search the desk. Perhaps he thinks I have finally despaired. He's wrong: he has overlooked the one spark left in me, revenge. My revenge may be slow, but my patience is limitless, and my life is suddenly full of purpose: to bring him to justice.

He'll be surprised how thorough I am. He'll be impressed, I think, by the method in my madness.

SIX O'CLOCK

It was an evening in early August, when I was eighteen, that the great storm came; two days after I returned from my year abroad. The weather had been strange; the radio reported the birth of a hurricane far out at sea, and all that brooding day the sun shone like a small light bulb, weak and white, through high layers of cloud. It was hot, the unbreathable wet heat I had almost forgotten. I went out riding in the afternoon. When I called the dogs and turned for home—with a sudden premonition that time was running out, that I must get back—even the rush of air as I galloped along the high whale-back ridge could not cool me; and when I slowed the mare to a walk, the atmosphere settled on me, a plastic wrapping that clung even closer as I sucked it in. Now the cloud was lower, and the dead sky was yellow from rim to rim, casting a sickly twilight glow over everything. Westward, only a red graze showed where the sun would set.

The hurricane warning arrived at six o'clock. A boy brought the telegram from New Bethlehem post office; I saw him coming up the shortcut to the house as I rode into the yard, and I called out to ask him if he had any news.

"Hold dog!" he answered, halting at a distance beside a tree with a good low branch. I dismounted and gathered

15

in the two dogs. When he saw them safely at heel, he came near.

"Well come, Miss Elizabeth!" he said. "Yes'm is storm warning, same one Rita as nearly catch Cuba." He untied a piece of oilcloth and took out two thin pink envelopes. Official telegrams often came in pairs, the second a confirmation of the first.

"Thanks, Bigman," I said. "And here's something for you. I will take them on up to Mister Tom. So it's bad trouble. You better hurry back home and fix up storm boards. Walk good."

"You too, Miss Lizzie. The Lord is with us." He pulled his cap well down—it was decorated round the peak with the words I AM THE GREATEST—and ran off down the rough slope, jumping from rock to rock.

The stableboy opened the gate and took my horse.

"Storm coming, Portius," I said. "Better turn out old Rabbit quick into Pond Pasture—and then come up and help Mister Tom and me—plenty to do before dark."

"Old Rabbit can smell the storm coming, eh, Rabbit?" he said. "She give you a rough ride, Miss Liz?"

"She was jumpy—nearly shied me off in the gully. Nervous as a filly—seeing duppies everywhere."

"Them say dead people change them resting place in hurricane, you know, Miss Liz—must be a whole heap of duppy sitting up jus' ready fe go."

"Well, Rabbit didn't fancy them at all. Give her some corn for me and put her out, Portius. Mister Tom is still in the house?"

"Seem like him doing him shooting practice, Miss Liz. Anyways, I hear him up there. Is real good you get back, you know, Miss Lizzie. Him miss you bad and need you now in time of sore trouble."

He shambled off into the stables. I wondered how I should get Tom and these people organized in time, preparing the old house to meet the storm. As I passed through the gates and up the weed-choked drive, the dogs subdued and panting behind me, I prayed that my brother would be in a better mood by now; he had flown into a temper when I told him I was going riding, yet he would not come with me. It can't simply be the close threatening day that's disturbing him so, I thought; he doesn't want to let me out of his sight for some reason. Things were bad enough with Nan being so possessive, and it was a relief to get away from both of them and be alone.

The drive curved up the side of the hill into the open, leaving behind the large comfortable trees of the stable yard, the mango and breadfruit. Again I became aware of the sky, a dull gold lid closing in the breathless stillness; to the west, the spreading scarlet sunset. It was extraordinarily quiet for the hour before dark, when usually the birds were reviving from the midday trance of summer heat. This evening no birds were singing. In the distance a cow lowed peevishly, a shrill breaking note, and was answered by a nervous whinny from the brood mares' paddock. The air was as stifling as it had been all day; there was no sunset breeze to move the heavy curtains of greenery on the slope below, where the rainy season had hooded all but the tallest trees in a monstrous growth of creepers.

Only in the small changes, the weeds, the blue paint of the gate flaking under my hand, a bright patch of zinc on the stable roof, a fence removed—and in my own alteration—did I feel my long absence. Yet, during my year away in Europe, provided by a generous godmother—a year of foreign places as dazzling and different as Rome and Cambridge—"home" became just a word, an image glimpsed through the wrong end of a telescope; and from that distance I could see just how archaic it was, how isolated from the innovation and speed of life outside. Traveling back in my clever well-cut clothes, all set to impress Tom and Nan and Maurice, I felt like a foreigner: I was curious, and a little nervous, to see my native land again. But as I stepped out of the refrigerated plane, the steamy Montego Bay night, heavy with familiar smells—sweet tobacco smoke and swamps and drains and flowers that open

17

after dark—came to meet me. It wrapped me up and carried me back into the past, put me in my place. All at once I was a child in grown-up finery—the show was over. Only home was real.

Above me the dark mass of the old house cut off some of the western glare. As I looked, a light appeared in Aunt Cissie's turret: that would be Nan taking up a lamp with the aunt's six-o'clock drink. Soon the diesel engine would start up and the house would spring to life as all the lights came on at once; but my aunt could not stand the dusk, and on an overcast evening such as this she would be allowed a kerosene lamp until the electricity came on. I saw Nan's tall shape at the window, pulling the curtains across, her stiff bandanna silhouetted like a winged helmet.

As I reached the mounting block where a flight of steps leads up to the veranda, two quick shots blasted out above me, raising a crowd of screaming birds from the hillside; and an outraged peacock, poised self-consciously on the sundial, gave a piercing wail, overbalanced, and flopped heavily down the wall and into the undergrowth. Tom stood by the railing, holding his precious pistols, and as I looked—because I looked—blew on the barrels, Western style, to cool them. It was a gesture from our youth, a nod to the past, but I found it disturbing. It was not quite a joke; he was too much in the part. I could tell that he expected me to say something disapproving. So I simply handed him the telegrams.

"Storm warning," I said. I poured myself a drink from the jug of lime juice set out on the dining-room window-sill, and sat down on the bench to stretch my legs. The dogs flopped onto the cool stone flags. I watched Tom.

At eighteen my brother was strikingly handsome. Perhaps I had not admitted it before, but I think after a year away from him I was really seeing him for the first time —as I was seeing my homeland and the old house. For, familiar as they were, I soon realized that I had changed: I had stood back a pace. The beauty of the wild country-side I had grown up in, had accepted as inevitable, now seemed marvelously arranged, like the backgrounds to the Renaissance portraits or Annunciations I had admired in Florence. I had lost the innocent eye, and suddenly the textures, the contrasts and the lighting, and even the proportions of the building with its grand wooden-pillared veranda (whole tree trunks with peeling Corinthian decoration) had opened up to me. Perhaps the house itself did seem smaller; I had inflated it in my memory. Not so Tom. He was larger, and his looks were quite remarkable. Against his olive skin, the ash-blond hair was a pale casque from the straight-cut fringe down to the curve into the back of his neck; and under the fringe, his level black brows and black-fringed eyes.

There was no escaping the sad alteration in the house and yard, the neglect and seediness. It started quite slowly, I think, dating from Father's last illness, but now I could tell that it had accelerated. The tufted roofs, the court-yard, the broken panes, the unpolished expanses of cedar floor—the need for a woman's touch, I thought indulgently, until I began to see that the change was in Tom as well. Not just a "hardening eye and a loosening mouth," but the servants answering back, his office disordered and dusty, bills left unpaid, and talk of a mistress installed in the old nursery wing. "Well, so what?" he said when I challenged him with it. "My brand-new rocking horse?"

My first evening home had been strange. There was a great constraint between us; no doubt he was disturbed that I had grown up and become equal at last with him, full of experiences he had not shared, and more confident than before—arguing with him where I should have given way. He had ordered my favorite dinner; the dining table, though scabby, had been polished in my honor, and there was a bowl of powerfully scented night-blooming cereuses between the candelabra. But it was heavy going, and silences that in the past would have been companionable demanded interruption. I chattered of Rome and London and Cambridge and seeing the cousins; of Edward, so elegant now, and his little airplane—of his plan to visit the rich uncle in Florida, fly down in the uncle's little open plane, and land in the lower pasture; of the May Ball. Then I went and fetched my box of books and the records I had brought him.

As children we had always danced; it is among my earliest memories: dark rainy afternoons when we could not play outside, when one or another of a series of meek nursemaids chosen by Nan would crank up the old Gramophone in the nursery—and later, the schoolroom—and jig about with us. I can remember how the black girl would hold back and giggle when Tom tried to pull her to her feet to join us, but once caught in the music, the thin legs and arms would start to move as naturally as a bird in flight, bare feet shuffling intricate variations of the basic shay-shay on the shining boards, fingers snapping, eyes closed. We forgot the lightning and thunder as we shimmied and wiggled in her wake.

One fat sullen nursemaid there had been, who was so spectacular in action that we used to sit back and watch her, clapping out the beat and urging her on to wilder excesses. Nan opened the door on it once—Maurice was with us, waiting for the thunderstorm to pass—all of us drumming, and goggle-eyed at a slow bump-and-grind (we must have been older, nine or ten, for it was a torrid torch song, I remember, thick with innuendo, that Tom had commissioned the stableboy to buy in New Bethlehem.) Anyway, she fired our dance instructor, but she could not prevent us from commemorating her to the beat of any slow heavy record we got onto the turntable.

Now we took our coffee through to the record player in the drawing room—the only really up-to-date piece of equipment in the whole house; he played them through and we danced.

Carried by the strong beat, and absorbed into it, I felt easier, and closer to Tom. Moving to the same rhythm made more sense than chatting round in separate circles; and with my new eyes I could see he was quite beautiful when he danced. A slow sweet number started, and he pulled me close and danced on. It was then that I felt I was with a stranger, an attractive stranger. I stopped and sat myself on the window seat, sipping my coffee. I watched him swaying and turning gracefully, alone and unselfconscious: my twin brother. But I knew that he knew precisely how good he looked.

As for me, I found his closeness upsetting. I went on up to bed, but I lay listening to the beat of the music long after I had turned out the light; two days in his company, through his good moods and his bad, had not made me easy.

Now I watched him, stagily backed by the flaring sky. He lit a cigarette, then unhurriedly opened the thin envelope.

"—which simply repeats what the radio said before static took over," he said. "And this one—oh, get me some juice, will you, Liz?—is the usual confirmation." He crumpled them and pushed them into the pocket of his bush shirt. "I wonder how much of our taxes goes on officials doing everything twice—"

"But are we in the path of the hurricane, then? I thought they said it would pass north of us."

"No, there was another bulletin at four, when you were out," said Tom. "It's done another kink and is coming right across."

"We've never been in a bad hurricane, have we?"

"Something to tell our grandchildren."

"And meanwhile," I said, standing up, "what about getting ready for it? Have you—"

"Not really, no. Nan's been fussing round counting heads and stores and sending down to New Bethlehem for candles and saltfish and Lord knows what—but there's plenty of time to put up the shutters before the real blow starts."

"But, Tom, dark is coming. How can you fool around with your shooting practice—"

"My shooting practice may be just what's needed when the shelterers and the looters come swarming round,

21

sweetheart. Big winds and rain aren't the worst things that can happen in a hurricane, you know. . . . But it's all rather terribly exciting, don't you think?" He took hold of my hair and twisted it round his hand. "More exciting than jolly old Tintoretto, eh, girl?" And he turned on one of his blinding smiles.

"Stop it, Tom—you're hurting." I shook him away. "You love a drama, don't you? Something happening at last? So —let's see you in action—getting things moving. How many men are there around the yard to help you? Suppose they've all gone home to get ready for the terrible excitement?"

And where is Maurice? I wanted to ask. Now Tom was gazing up at the crimson and gold. The red graze I'd observed from the ridge had spread like an angry inflammation across the swollen clouds. When a peacock appeared at the top of the veranda steps and trailed off slowly along the flagstones, its tarnished train was almost purple, reflecting the red above. Yet the sky's change brought no brightness; it suggested not light but heated metal, and the sinking sun a blowtorch that never burned through.

"Tom? I told Portius to come up when he'd let out Rabbit and made sure the other mares were safe. But Zaccy Spence should be sent back to his mother. And the pen keepers, the ones from nearby, Frank perhaps, and Enoch—they could shut in the sheep and see about the calves on their way home. But we can't hang on to them." And Maurice? "I mean, they've got to get their chickens in and their shutters up just as we have. You'll have to organize what help there is—remember, those storm windows must be carried up from the timber shed, and they're heavy. I'll go and talk with Nan, and she can tell the others."

There came the distant clatter and whine of the generator starting up behind the stables. The lights in the house went on, and all at once the sky seemed darker, the dull red clouds boiling low and close. There was a flicker of lightning to the north and a gust of breeze riffled up

22

the valley, stirring the surface of the heavy creepers and setting the palm leaves tapping. It was just a warm feverish breath that reached us on the veranda, yet it raised the hairs on my neck. I turned away into the bright house.

Nan was coming down the stairs into the hall, carrying my aunt's tea tray.

"You get the storm warning then, Miss Liz?" Nan missed nothing; she must have seen me with the telegram, coming up the drive.

"Yes, and it's heading straight for us, so we better make ready. How is she?"

"Tricky all the day, Miss Liz, and mad crazy gone this evening. Day of Judgment, Red Sea closing over us, Sodom and Gomorrah—everything she foretell for this night. She really vex me—I have enough and more to do, and I just couldn't lef her one with the oil lamp, but have to rest with her till the electric come on. She really wild and jumpy, Miss Liz—she make me catch it too, with her talk —Lord Jesus! and plenty things to fix up still—"

"Poor Nan—you were good not to leave her in the dark; she'd have been much worse. I'll go and see what I can do. We shall have to bring her down, you know."

"I know it, Miss Liz, but I don't mention it as yet. What a business she going make! I pray just we won't have to force her."

"Let me talk a little with her, Nan. You go and tell the maids about the hurricane coming and who wants can go home, but all are welcome to stay. We have food enough? Mister Tom tells me you sent down to Bethlehem."

"Bullybeef, tin milk, match, candle, saltfish, Chinee bread—"

"But, Nan, will we need all that? It won't go on that long, surely."

"Is not just tonight, Miss Liz, is perhaps two-three days ahead you may need supply. You don't recollect 1951—we was three days and nights and no one could get through and no food left in Bethlehem—looted out—so is best to have a sufficiency, you see. Mars Tom—you stop his shooting then? And high time too, time going by—what ail that boy who can tell—" She muttered off toward the pantry, her many-layered skirts and petticoats rustling across the boards, her bare feet silent.

I knew how most people feared that sound, the swift treadless swishing. As children we were always on the alert for it. The long old-fashioned skirts and the starched bandanna—making her seem taller even than Father— were essential parts of her awesome personage. It was not just that Nan was a tartar who ruled the household and had done so long before we were born, even before my mother came out from England; it was that she was recognized to be powerful in Obeah and ruled over a wide area of fear and superstition. We did not know much about this; it was not our province and was guarded jealously from us, and even those who hated her feared her too much to talk.

We knew only of important secret errands for which she would request and be granted time off, and dark consultations under the breadfruit tree in the yard, out of earshot and beyond our stalking prowess. People would wait for hours for an audience; we children sometimes asked them boldly, "Did you want to see the master? . . . or the missis? What you come for then?" "Fe see Miss Nan" was all we got out of them. She attended all the major wakes by right; we would watch her ride off on the white mule that a boy brought for her, and we would hear the drumming and singing across the valley, or up in the hills, late into the night. "I wonder what Nan is doing now," I whispered in the dark nursery. "Sacrificing a white hen—up to her armpits in warm blood," Tom suggested.

Just how old she was and whether she was actually gray or not no one knew. No one had seen her without her bandanna. Her face was a large triangle—cut off straight across the top by the line of the kerchief—of polished pale brown, grained with a multitude of fine lines. Father used

24

to say that the high cheekbones and the light coloring showed Arawak blood—the aboriginal race that the Spaniards had killed off—and this enhanced her mystery. For she kept her distance, not as a good servant does but *de haut en bas*. My mother was terrified of her, and friends would say they didn't know why we put up with "that old sourpuss." But my father, whose sphere conveniently lay elsewhere, said, "She runs the house and keeps the children obedient and the maids in order—who can ask more?" So she ruled on, and after his death, when Mother had a breakdown and went back to England, she took charge completely, directing the big house while Maurice's old father ran the property, until Tom left school.

For us children she had been perhaps the greatest, and certainly the most constant, influence in our lives. Not one of our varied governesses made such a mark. Later, when I ran away from school, Parson Sanguinetti took me over, and what education I had was the smattering I got from him. But Nan was the traditional "mother who fathered me," much more even than my real mother; and to me—and me only, I think—she was indulgent. I was her ewe lamb, and, except superficially, I could do no wrong. She must have adored Tom, but very early on he escaped her, set himself up against her, his will to hers. They had tested and now respected each other's strength, and lately Tom had learned to use his charm on her.

Perhaps Nan was mellowing, even losing her grip; certainly the management of the house was going to pieces, and not simply for lack of money. I could see that Tom did not care; and meanwhile Nan was becoming more and more absorbed in her other role, as her age and her status of wise woman increased. In the two days since my return I became aware of a balance: Tom recognized—and feared —her power over the people as much as she did his position and his dangerous temper.

Now it worried me to see her usual severe serenity disturbed. Clearly my aunt had sensed the approaching storm, and in her Cassandra-like outbursts she could be very unnerving. With some dread I went up the twisting stairs to her room.

This room. Fourteen by fourteen.

In Aunt Clarissa's day it was heavily overfurnished, a complete Victorian boudoir, draped and swathed and pelmetted and tasseled, with ranks of dark pictures edge to edge (my *Hope,* by Watts, was one of them). The wardrobe and the ornate dressing table—good Colonial pieces, in blood-red mahogany, carved and polished—seemed to lean out into the room; and there was a single four-poster (it's still here), all barley-sugar twists and pineapples and a headboard like a peacock's tail.

Through the peephole I could see Aunt Cissie sitting on a low stool, folding and tearing newspaper doilies—Nan's patent therapy. There was a nest of scrabbled fragments around her and she rose up in a flurry of gray confetti as I unlocked the door and came in.

"My poor child!" she cried. "To die so young! This night shall be the last of our world!—*as we know it,*" she added in a stage whisper.

She was tall, the strained tallness of a crab on its toes, and the crustacean effect was increased by the wide-apart pop eyes—angled outward by a squint—that appeared to be at the very top of her tilted head; the pale hair brushed smooth by Nan offered no further horizon, no softening frame; it was parted and flattened and held by a pink plastic bow. A drooping pastel silk dress from her heyday lay in folds across her flat chest, richly pinned and shawled, and from it emerged pallid, long, angular arms of great strength, as we knew too well. Below, the fine lacy stockings ended abruptly in plimsolls—I had never seen her wear anything else.

She had taken to the turret fifteen years ago, when her father and her big brother had died within a week, from malaria. She was older than our father, and the only unmarried one; she had outlived them all, not moving from her hidey-hole. When she saw the cars arriving for Father's funeral she got very excited. "At last!" she cried. "There's going to be a party. I knew there'd be a party one day." And she insisted on dressing up in all her finery, but she still would not leave the turret; instead she sat sipping champagne on her own. She demanded champagne. ("You cannot obstruct her, Mars Tom," Nan said. "She must have her little party, even while we drink our bitter sorrow—the master won't hurt"—a typically Nan-ish ambiguity that I remember. Did she mean that my late father would not suffer, or that he would not punish us from beyond the grave?)

But Aunt Clarissa had always been more than eccentric. Nan used to tell of her carrying a mouthful of twigs about with her, "to help the birds building their nests"; and one day she had launched out from the top veranda on a carpet. She broke an ankle. She was quite harmless, I think. Once only I remember her fighting, and screaming at Father: "Why are *you* alive while *they*'re so cold and dead?"; and Nan hurrying up with the straitjacket that was kept hidden in the office (we had discovered it and borrowed it for The Curse of the Mummy's Tomb in one of our games; and Father gave us both a beating). Tom and I accepted her as part of our lives. We were brought to visit her every day as children; in my teens I spent more time in the turret with my sewing or a book, curled up on this window seat where the light is best. Sometimes I read her the sentimental novels she loved, sometimes I played her her favorite records on the Gramophone, but mostly I listened and half listened to her rambling sagas of beaux and balls and conquests and fine clothes—all fantasy, according to Nan, but food for my own romantic dreams.

She was fond of me, I'm sure: she always recognized me. She feared but depended on Nan, her keeper; and Tom she muddled with people from the past, treating him accordingly: sometimes she was haughty, sometimes grotesquely coy, often darkly suspicious. I understood from Nan that recently she had been turning more against Tom.

27

It may have been the shooting practice, which always upset her, or it may have been something in his manner—impatience or ill-concealed distaste.

"Come on, Aunt Cissie," I said. "It's not going to be that bad, dear. We'll all stick together and get by, really we will. You've been through hurricanes before—you're a hardened campaigner."

I settled her in her chair and sat on the stool in front of her, holding her restless hands still. "And, Aunt Cissie, you know that if it hits us hard it won't be safe for you alone up here." Better to break it to her gently, I thought, than rush her downstairs later.

"You may come up and keep me company, Elizabeth," she said grandly. "We don't need *them*—" (suddenly conspiratorial).

"But, Auntie dear, it won't be safe for either of us, you see. We'll have to go downstairs— No, no, Aunt Cissie—be calm." I caught the panicky hands and held them firmly; they were cold, scaly, not so much pulsing as ticking in my grasp. "Think of the wind up here, how it will roar round. It'll be very cozy downstairs—we'll make it a party—light the fire and play records, and the night will soon be over. Now I've got to go and supervise things and I'll be up again as soon as I get a chance. Are you going to finish that lovely doily? No? Well, why not sit quietly and listen to your transistor." But it only crackled with static, and she cried, "Take care! The lightning will strike you!"

"Look," I said, "why don't you sort out your treasures?"

It was usually saved as a treat, but this seemed the right moment for a little spoiling. I lifted her heavy box of jewelry down from the shelf; it was always left in my aunt's room as the safest place—the servants were far too afraid of her to venture into the turret. I left her dressing up in ropes of pearls and admiring herself in her silver hand mirror.

Nan was overseeing the clearing of the veranda with two maids: the carrying in of dogs' beds, wicker chairs, and pots of orchids and lilies. Flurries of rain were already bouncing on the flatstones, and Daisy and Lena ran about with their aprons over their heads, and dropped the bench to cover their ears when there was a bright flash of lightning. Through the thunder I heard hammering: the shutters were going up.

I looked up at the darkening sky and the ranks of hurrying clouds. Here at home there was no long twilight as I had seen in England; even on a clear evening night came quickly once the sun had set, and this evening it left only an angry purple bruise in the west, fading, as I watched, to a dull liver color. Away to the east the spread of darkness seemed brown, not blue—the sick gold light had simply muddied, grown thick, as the day waned—and now I fancied I could hear the approaching storm. It was a soft throaty roar, like surf, but steady, continuing when the mutters of thunder died away.

Still I was reluctant to go back into the house. Earlier it had seemed bright and welcoming, but now, I felt, it was more like an airless coffin, and the monotonous hammer blows beat inside my head. Suddenly I was childishly afraid; I wanted someone to turn to. As so often in the past—an old habit left lying unused for many months—I looked round for Maurice.

I had not seen him since my return, except at a distance, this morning. I'd woken late—the overcast day tricked me —and I only saw him mount and ride out of the stable yard. I wanted to call out, but I didn't. I wondered whether he was avoiding me; now that he was head man and I was the lady of the house—fully fledged, the finished article—whether he might set a measured distance between us. It was absurd—we had been friends so long. Still, I sensed that he would not seek me out; and I realized he never had. Yet he had always been available, ready to join in our escapades, unless he had work to finish. It was up to me to do the seeking.

But I held back. I suspected it was I who had altered,

and outgrown our childhood kinship, adapting myself to Edward's world. Soon—any day—he would be flying down in his little plane; he had promised. There was something to look forward to beyond this stormy night, outside the darkly circling hurricane; and I *could* hear now—through a pause in the hammering, and still distant, but coming closer—a menacing curtain of sound like a mighty water-fall. I wondered if Tom had everything under control; we could have done with another able-bodied man around. Maurice must have left early to reach his home on Green Mountain, above the highest pastures. It was a nuisance, I thought peevishly; just when we needed him.

"Come, Miss Liz—child, you getting wet through! Come now."

I couldn't ask Nan about him, for it was not for me to check up on the head man; and our companionship was, in her eyes, a thing of the past—and properly so. I turned up my face to the rain and breathed in the warm syrupy air almost as if it were my last. Then I went in, and the bar was fixed in place across the big doors.

The hall was cluttered with stacked chairs and rush mats and the sweet-scented flowers that now stood in ranks along the walls. The dogs whined nervously, hating the upheaval, the atmosphere of packing up with its threat of departures. I found their beds and comforted them; they settled down, Labrador and bullterrier together in one basket.

Nan arranged some chairs in what space there was near the bookcase, in case we should have to take refuge in the hall itself. She picked up Tom's shirt from the floor and smoothed and folded it, shaking her head, muttering crossly.

"An' is why the young master ha' fe strip down same like common somebody breaking rockstone inna roadside . . . ?"

"Now then, Nan, we'd better see what the boy managed to get at the shop," I said.

But she seemed not to hear, standing with her back to

me. She turned round hastily, thrusting some paper into her apron pocket.

"What's that, Nan?" I asked.

"Nothing, Miss Liz. Just storm warning."

"The other telegram? . . . I thought it was just the confirmation—Master Tom read it. Or was it something else? Let me have it, please, Nan."

It *was* something else; I could tell she did not want me to see it.

"Is only trouble, Miss Liz—we have sufficient trouble already." But she pulled the crumpled pink paper from her pocket and gave it to me. I read: FLYING DOWN FROM FLORIDA ON WINGS OF STORM STOP SEE YOU IN HOURS D.V.—EDWARD.

"But this is from Cousin Edward, Nan!" I cried, grabbing her and spinning her round. "He's on his way to see us! Why didn't Tom tell me? He's actually on his *way!*"

"So it seem, Miss Liz," she said, drawing away and smoothing down her layers of skirts. "Or so it say—but he will ground in Kingston for sure. Only duppy can fly in storm."

"But he could make it across the mountains before the big winds hit us, Nan. Wouldn't that be *wonderful?* Nan, aren't you *pleased?* Cousin Edward is coming!"

"That boy bring nothing but trouble, Miss Liz. Mars Tom always—"

"Oh, come now—they've grown out of all that foolishness. Why didn't he tell me, I wonder. I suppose he wanted it to be a surprise."

"Don't fool yourself, me dear—Mars Tom prefer to hush it up. Lord! You don' recall the big quarrel when them see each other last time? Oil and water won't never mix, child—I tell you for fact."

"But, Nan, blood is thicker than both," I countered.

"*Blood*, Miss Liz? Mars *Edward?* Ink, maybe, or some weak ice tea, like him always ask me for . . ." Her tone was withering. "Cold as charity, Miss Liz. He always strange and different, even from a child. Sweet mouth when him want, pretty manners, and brainy—Lord, like some old priest! But same blood as you and you brother, me love? Never tell me that."

It was quite an outburst for Nan and I was taken aback. Earlier, when we had been unpacking my things upstairs, she had admired the dress I had worn to the May Ball, poring over its pin tucks and pleating and stroking the flowered silk. "And I'll bet my Miss Liz had all the beaux crowding around," she had said.

"Well, of course we were mostly in our foursome—and it was Cousin Edward I danced with the most—" She had cooled suddenly, and I stopped.

"Is beaux I talking of, Miss Liz. Beaux is one thing; cousins is another."

"Well, I think Cousin Edward is quite special," I said lamely, and diverted her from the subject.

Now it was all coming out, as much as anything did with Nan. I realized that she saw him not just as a source of friction with Tom but as a threat, someone who might take me away; and of course, as far as I was concerned she was right. I was in love with Edward with a pure, rapturous devotion—had been since I was twelve, I suppose—and suddenly he was on his way—he'd soon be with us! I felt like dancing, but I put my arm through hers and leaned against the tall disapproving shoulder so that she should not see my face.

"All right, Nanny dear—so he's different. But he'll be welcome, won't he? On this bad night, flying through it to get back to the old home? And you'll be nice to him? For me? Come, let's see about the stores. You're right, Nan—there's enough to think about—and he may be grounded in Kingston, as you say. Now—we'll see to the breadkind first."

Breadkind was everything they called "carbohydrates" at my finishing school: bread, flour, biscuits, potatoes, yams, breadfruit, red peas. We found we were short of "English" loaves; but Chinese bread, dry and close-grained, we had in plenty, and dog biscuits—large tough

32

crackers that we loved when we were children, and used to steal from the animals' shelf as provisions for our adventures: ships' biscuits, Tom decreed, and we went through a weevil-tapping ritual before we ate them.

Soon I was absorbed in the immediate problems of a house under siege, counting heads and apportioning food for the bottom kitchen and ourselves, leaving some to be kept back for real need, like the arrival of unexpected shelterers. It was stuffy in the narrow shuttered storeroom, and now we had to talk against the rushing wind and staccato salvos of heavy rain. I discovered that we had very little kerosene and few candles; due for the monthly provision shopping in Montego Bay, we had run low. And I suspected that Nan had been letting the housekeeping go its own way; supplies like candles, which were seldom used—and so, seldom counted—had dwindled (Cookie's contribution, as she passed through, getting rice for our supper: "It seem like them all borrow, please'm . . ."). As long as the electricity did not fail we would have light. If it did we would soon run through the few candles and the oil in the two remaining lamps.

"Were there no candles or kerosene at the Bethlehem shop, then?" I asked when I had scrabbled right to the back of the musty store cupboard and come out with only a couple of gnawed night-lights.

"Clean out, me dear."

It was no time to take Nan to task; it was too late. The first huge gust struck the house as the hurricane's shifting cone caught us a glancing blow with its outer edge. We looked at one another and listened, then turned uneasily back to our counting. We would have to manage.

"Well," I said, getting up and slapping off the dust of a year's spilled flour and cornmeal, "many others need them more than us, and we must make do."

Bread, rice, saltfish, yams, coconut oil, red peas, one of the oil lamps, and half the store of candles were dispatched to the bottom kitchen. They at least had the big old wood range for warmth and cheer and to cook their food. We,

33

on the other hand, would be cut off from our store by the storm, as it was in the cookhouse along the back veranda—which would certainly be impassable when the hurricane hit us. We had only a Primus stove apart from this; many times I had tried to have a small gas cooker put in the pantry to make us more independent of cook and maids, but Father's answer—and now Tom's—was always that we would lose face if we cooked for ourselves. Even the Primus was erratic, and it looked as if we would have to rely on bread and tins of stew and corned beef for as long as the crisis lasted.

The hammering was now above us: Tom was starting on the bedroom windows. As I went back through the somber dining room, its shuttered, already stagnant air filled me with such a wave of claustrophobia that suddenly I felt near to panic. I had to breathe. I turned and ran up the narrow back stairs to my dressing room and flung open the window onto the wild night.

This was the sheltered side, which Tom had left till last. Behind me, to the north, the infernal machine was spinning closer—a giant shredder let loose on the wooded countryside. I leaned out and could see lights on in the stables and somebody on a ladder against the granary hatch. The cry of a peacock like a soul in torment reached me on the wind. I looked up at the fast-flowing clouds, and I wondered how strong a gale had to be to ground a small plane. Surely he could have avoided the hurricane itself, flown round it and come up from the south. I listened, but the distant throb was only the generator. Then the hammering started up again behind me in the house, drowning even the roaring of the bitterwood tree in the backyard.

I found Tom nailing up the jalousies in the big guest room, bare to the waist. Zaccy Spence, the garden boy, was handing boards up to him. I wanted to blurt out all my excitement and my fears; I longed to be reassured. But, remembering how Tom had put the telegram in his pocket, I wondered whether he had read it aright, and if he was playing cat and mouse with the news—it was the sort of thing Tom might do.

However, I could not ask him now, with Zaccy there, in case Nan was right.

"Tom, I think Zaccy should be going home," I said.

"He still has to round up those damn peacocks and wire up the chicken run—eh, Zaccy?"

"True, suh, I don't do it as yet."

"But, Tom, isn't there anyone else who could help you?" I asked. "I see someone is still down in the stables."

"Could be old Maurice, faithful unto death." His laugh was unpleasant. "But he would have left by now to make it up the mountain to his bachelor residence."

Zaccy sniggered obediently.

"Please, Mars Tom—" Lena was at the door. "Is Busha Maurice fe see you."

"What is it, girl? You must shout louder than hurricane, you know."

"Please—is Busha Maurice, Mars Tom!"

"Well, well—speak of the devil! Where is he, girl?"

"Him waiting at the back step, please, Mars Tom."

It was all wrong for Maurice to "wait at the back step" like a supplicant. I wondered, not for the first time, what the state of play was between them now, in their new roles of master and man.

"Tell him I'm coming," said Tom.

I followed him down. As I went I smoothed back my hair and tucked my shirt in. So—I would see Maurice now; quite inevitably, in the course of things.

On my first morning home, I was woken by his voice; he was in the office below, in Tom's place—for Tom was still in bed—giving the day's instructions to the pen keepers. I listened to his low rough voice answering the babbled questions, laughing at outbursts of wit from the hangers-on. But he had already left on his rounds when I got downstairs. I thought he might have waited to say hello—till later in the day I heard that Tom had sent him to supervise the loading of cattle on the Kingston train.

35

"And after that he's picking up feed in Montego Bay," said Tom. "And when will I see him?" I asked. "Oh, tomorrow sometime, I expect."

But I missed him again, sleeping through the dark dawn. Then, in the still hot afternoon, I thought I heard him driving cattle, and I went out riding, expecting to find him. Silly, I told myself, to think he was avoiding me. He was busy; and there was plenty of time.

Now I would see him. Good old Maurice—he'd stayed to help after all. I was glad, but at the same time felt suddenly shy and apprehensive, perhaps because I'd changed so much. How would he see me? Would we have anything in common now? And there was something else—something Tom had said the evening before—that made me realize there was a complication.

We had been talking about the property, Tom blaming its neglected state on hard times and the lonely problems of management and labor.

"Surely Maurice is a help?" I asked.

"Maurice is a rat that may well be leaving the sinking ship, sweetheart—talking about setting up on his own somewhere."

"Really?" I was rather impressed by such initiative. "Well, he has a perfect right to; and he must be a pretty good farmer by now, I should think. I can see how you'd miss him, Tom. When might he go?"

"Oh, I think he'll hang around for a while yet. The noble savage suffers from romantic aspirations, I believe, in spite of any number of dusky beauties queuing up for his harem. Like Mama's song about the magnet hanging in the hardware shop, remember? 'And all around was a loving crop/Of scissors and needles and nails and knives/Offering love for all their lives . . .' But magnetic old Maurice has set his sights on the silver churn. As I see it, he'll hang around just as long as he thinks he might have some chance with you, sister dear—so play him along a bit, eh?" Slyly, the smile all honey and almonds. "I really

36

need him to run the place until I've sorted out the finances and all the damned paperwork."

"I'm deeply sorry, Tom darling, but quite apart from the dastardly meanness of your cunning scheme, I simply could not find it within my dramatic powers to play convincingly the role you so generously offer. Alas, my affections are otherwise engaged." I took cover in the Court Language of our childhood games to hide the sudden turbulence inside me—a confusion of my need to tell someone about Cousin Edward, and a surprised alarm at the thought of Maurice, the chum, the soul mate, cast unexpectedly as a lover.

After that I had dreamed of him, not the usual dream where he and Tom and I, a three-headed protagonist, faced adventures—swam impassable rivers or crawled out on an airplane wing. This time it was a one-to-one encounter with Maurice. He was, surprisingly and quite devastatingly, in full evening dress, and he carried me up a huge flight of stairs. Then I woke up.

Now I followed Tom through to the pantry. Even in the storm and chatter I could distinguish the same voice, rough and slightly singsong—a Welsh sound, my mother used to say—that had woken me my first morning home. He was out on the back veranda, talking to the maids. Tom called. Then Maurice stepped out of the dark, out of my childhood, and into the light of the doorway.

SEVEN O'CLOCK

HE NARROWED his eyes as he came into the bright light. His hair and the sheepskin jerkin he wore, sleeveless and rough, like John the Baptist's in my illustrated Bible, were dark with rain, and he paused awkwardly on the threshold, wiping his feet on the coconut mat, before he saw me. Then he shed his humility; he stepped forward to greet me, ignoring Tom, and stood smiling down at me, holding both my hands.

All my apprehension was burned out, forgotten, in the shock of recognition: Maurice, solid and close. Strange that you can't imagine someone precisely, any more than you recall pain; however you try, it remains merely an outline, a description, words. Until the moment when he steps in through the door, to take up space, send out heat, meet your eyes. Which is why only the present moment exists—even if it exists in no more than watching the sun move across each inch of the mahogany bedhead, as I look up from my page. And I might have had him with me *now*.

Blazing Maurice, tawny and warm. I will hang the man who put out that light.

I said, "Maurice." Then, "But shouldn't you be off home?"

He said, "Too late now." He let go of my hands and

turned to Tom. "I fixed up the grain store. I'm afraid it took longer than I thought—had to nail some battens across that weak corner so the wind can't lift it." With us he dropped the broad dialect he used among the servants, but the lilting rhythm did not change. "And I got the top door boarded right across—"

"That's overdoing it a bit, surely," said Tom. He was sitting on the pantry table—a shirt draped round his shoulders, his smooth chest bare—very deliberately relaxed, lighting a cigarette, missing nothing: Maurice, tall and broad and ruddy, steaming and gleaming with rain; beyond, the maids crowding at the door; Nan, a graven image, holding the candlestick she had been polishing, and me. "Surely," he went on, "if it's ratproof it's windproof, man."

"Not draftproof—and a strong gust could get in through the cracks and lift those old shingles easy. Corn is too precious to fool about with—it's safe now. But I'll have to ask shelter for the night."

"Please, Busha—is a bad storm, you think?" One of the maids spoke for the rest, and there was a backing of "mercy on us, Lord," and "Heaven prevent," as a strong gust swept along the back veranda. It was to the German they all looked. And Tom sat and watched.

Maurice glanced at him, then turned to the anxious faces, the twittering, the eyes rolled heavenward. He stood in the doorway so that those huddled on the bench farther down the covered way could see and hear him.

"It's going to a bad old hurricane, this Rita—seem like she take one look at Cuba and don't fancy what she see. She turn back and try a bit of north coast—too many American there—make up her mind she really favor Westmoreland—is *proper* Jamaica—" There were cheers and laughter. "All right—is a big boas'y gal coming, and we must ready for her—"

"We ready, Busha—we good and ready!"

"Fine, fine—and we all the lucky ones, don' forget.

Praise the Lord you have this strong house and a good stone kitchen down there and fire and food. Enoch gone? Good. Frank and Portius? You want to get back. Thanks —you done well, sheep safe and snug and the horses happy. Here, take a cigarette—light up and you will reach home before you burn filter tip." Laughter. "Okay then, and good strong little homes thanks to the master. Mercy, is that Zaccy Spence still here? *Run* now, Zaccy—have this little flashlight fe keep off duppy. Oh, Miss Nan, you got any small something there for a good man? Here, Zaccy boy, some fancy stew-steak, Florida style—give you ma to sweet her up, we keep you so long. All right. Walk good. And you people staying on, thanks be to Mister Tom, you get down into the kitchen and board up the door and window, make up a nice fire, a good meal, and have candle by in case the electric blow off—"

Tom's voice made him turn back into the room.

"Fine, Maurice. I hope you'll be all right down there. You can organize them and control the flow of rum. They need someone in charge—looks like you're just the man." And he smiled charmingly.

Nan stepped forward as if to protest, but she did not speak. Inside, it seemed very quiet all of a sudden, the flurry of rain very noisy on the roof; the faces melted away, whispering and giggling, into the dark.

So Tom had his moment of triumph, his audience, his chosen time. He waited until there were only those who would remain under his roof and had everything to lose by incurring his displeasure; then he delivered his bolt, point-blank.

Maurice flushed a deep red brown but did not answer. Without looking at Tom or me he raised his hand slowly, yanked at his wet forelock, turned, and stepped out into the darkness.

Tom eased himself off the table. He tossed his cigarette out through the door, then closed it.

"Tom," I burst out, "you can't do that!"

"No, Mars Tom," said Nan. "Flesh and blood can bear so much. This time you go too far. Maurice is a proud man, you know, and rightly. You want to drive him off for good, eh?" Nan in anger was an impressive sight, her brows knit and eyes glaring like the carved grimace on a heathen battle shield.

But Tom laughed in her face. "Think you know him, then, Miss Wise-and-Mighty? Think he is petty like woman? Oh no—he won't leave just because I put him in his place—"

"But his place is here with us, Tom!" I cried. "He's always been like one of the family—my God, Father would have sorted you out—" And stopped, biting my tongue.

"Father has quite a lot to answer for," Tom said slowly. "After all, he is to blame for dear Maurice's aspirations. Well, Nan, off you go—I'm sure you've things to do." He opened the door with a mock bow, and she swept through, bandanna, elbows, and skirts bristling.

"Tom," I said as gently as I could over the noise of the storm, "quite apart from our need for another able man up here, just think of the situation in the bottom kitchen. You know what gap there is in status between him and even Cookie—they're going to be constrained and embarrassed closeted there with him all night."

"My dear girl, they'll love it. They all worship him and have probably, most of them, been laid by him at one time or another—he's one hell of a stud is old Maurice, your childhood chum. They're all dreaming that he'll make an honest woman of one of them one day—and why not? We all hope to marry up. There's even a word for it, 'hypergamy,' as Cousin Edward would point out. And they're no different—why, they'll fuss over him like a visiting sheik, never fear. He won't really lose face—sleep, maybe, but not face."

"What's got into you, Tom? Why do you want to slap him down like this? Why shouldn't he leave you if you don't treat him right?"

41

"*You* know the answer to that—he's got his own hopes. I told you last evening. Though he might be contented just to make free with your fair body a couple of times—"

"*Shut up!*" I hit him as hard as I could with both clenched fists and his laugh ended in a grunt of pain. He caught my wrists and pulled me close.

"Look, sweetheart, I don't want that stallion in this house all night cooped up with my sister—OK? Fair enough." He let me go and I stepped back and held on to the edge of the table. I was amazed as much by the relish as by the force of his disgust.

"Is that it, then?" I asked. "Is that why you sent him—"

"Mars Tom!" The door opened briskly and Nan strode into the room, dragging a writhing figure after her. "Look what I find hiding out in the sewing room! I pack her off home already once and she back again. Is you I blame, Mars Tom—always trouble!"

It was Tom's current girl friend. She stood now with some dignity, smoothing down her straightened hair into a kiss-curl on her coffee-brown cheek. She was quite expressionless, her soft incurious gaze moving slowly about the room, as though she was so accustomed to being the center of attention, even of disturbances, that she was bored by it. She was lovely.

Her dominant feature was her mouth. It was both large and delicately molded, a tight, ripe, thin-skinned fruit, bulging from a small sloping face that was simply the setting for it; her neck and body, the stem to carry it. Her eyes were flat, painted onto her smooth mask at a gentle slant; they were well shaped but muddy in color. From her brown suede arms, braceleted, dangled a large handbag. Her breasts pushed out the thin satin shift, vibrating, unsupported. Her feet, forced into the vertical on the highest of heels, were small bright hooves; they were placed to throw her body into a gawky graceful model stance. But the mouth was the reason for all, and I gazed in fascination at the complicated symmetry of its points and curves. It

42

looked too elaborate to use, a showpiece like those swans and castles carved in ice cream and served up at banquets. But when she smiled and spoke and licked her lips, you could see it was supple, highly evolved, sophisticated, prehensile, tough.

I did not know where Tom had found her, perhaps in town. If so, I was sorry for her, marooned here in this wild old house for the sake of an untender lover. I knew she had been turned out before my arrival—part of the spring-cleaning operation—and imagined she had been sleeping down in the maids' house and lying low. I was sorry for her, but curious, and envious too. I could see she must be very attractive to men.

Now Nan was giving her her marching orders, the harangue stiffened by biblical threats, with special attention to the details of Jezebel's last moments. Tom did not say a word, just lounged against the dresser, looking beautiful and fed up. Perhaps he was finished with her anyway, and was leaving Nan to do the dirty work. I interrupted long enough—shouting over the howling wind—to establish that the girl was not to be turned out into the night, but should go down to the lower kitchen until the hurricane had blown over. When Nan shut the outer door behind her, Tom did not wait for more; he turned and sulked off into the house. Like a stooping hawk, Nan picked up the aunt's supper tray; then I was alone again.

It was a scene that clearly had been played before—often, maybe. I realized that Nan had much to fear from Tom's mistresses, and as for marrying up, might not one of them actually become *her* mistress? It was not impossible, though—I thought—unlikely, for Tom had always talked of marrying late and well. He still does, and may already have selected an American heiress, though he would have to finish me off first. I can see his oil princess accepting his fitful charm and the broad acres, however ruinate. But not the crazy white-haired sister in the turret.

And Nan can see herself as housekeeper to such a princess, I am sure: there will be lots more money to play with, more servants to rule. Otherwise, little would change—she would be indispensable and in charge. On the other hand, a nubile brown girl, and one bright enough to trap Tom into marriage, would quite displace the Faithful Retainer; keeping house and holding the purse strings would be precisely *her* field of operation, and Nan would be put out to grass. Without the background of the big house, she would lose the edge she had over other wise women and become just another clever pensioned-off brown lady, like any postmistress or schoolmarm—long on experience, short on charisma. Small wonder she was tough on the girl with the lips.

I was talking in my head to Edward again, escaping for a moment from the din of the rising storm. He was the only person who was interested in *everything*—or rather, interested in finding words for everything, which was how he had first beguiled me. Edward. Coming nearer each minute, flying through the rain and wind. As a huge gust rattled the doors and windows, I imagined what it might be like up there, the wind butting the airplane about. It was a long haul in an open plane; and even a "rich man's toy," as he called it would need refueling. Crazy marvelous Edward—I knew he would make it, just as he conquered Rookoom. He would walk in—we might not even hear the plane if the wind was roaring like this—and pull off his gloves and say, "Fantastic cloud formations up there . . ."

Then I realized I had not yet spoken to Tom.

I found him nailing up the jalousies in my dressing room.

"Tom," I started, "that other telegram—"

"Oh, hand me the new pack of nails there, Liz," he said.

I could not tell him while he was hammering. He probably didn't read it, I thought. Or it was only a trick, hiding it from me. The point was, Edward was coming.

"Okay," he said, "now, one more lot of shutters you can help me with, and I can do the boxrooms single-handed."

I nearly said, Why not let Maurice help us?—but I wanted to keep him sweet. I waited until we had maneuvered the heavy boards into their slots, and then I lit two cigarettes, gave him one, and said:

"Tom, did you see the other telegram?"

"I only glanced at it, I suppose. I thought it was just the usual—"

"Didn't you see it was from Cousin Edward?" I said.

He carefully put the spare nails back into the box and picked up the hammer before he turned to me.

"No. And what has Cousin Edward to say this fine sunny evening? Anyone for tennis? Or perhaps there's a hunt ball you absolutely mustn't miss? Perhaps he could fly you over for it and back all in the twinkling of an eye. Well, go on, startle me—" I hesitated. Even a furious outburst would have been better than this bored cold inquiry.

I said, as evenly as I could, "Better than that. He's flying down from Miami tonight—'on the wings of the storm,' it said. And landing in the bottom pasture, I suppose, as he always planned to."

"Well, forget it, sweetheart. He'll be grounded when he stops to refuel in Havana or Nassau."

"But if he flew well round it and came up from the south—"

"He'd be grounded in Kingston."

"But the telegram was sent off at midday—why, he could be here before the winds get strong—he could be here any minute, Tom. He could still land in gusts like these, couldn't he?" I had to shout because of the shuddering of the windows and the lashing of the bitterwood beyond.

Tom just smiled as if this were his answer. I hated his triumph. I turned away and laid my forehead against the cool spiral of the bedpost, terrified that I might cry. "I know he'll come," I said fiercely at the dark wood, and the vehemence of my breath clouded it. I drew an *E* before the mist faded—a quick spell in a tight corner—and faced Tom. "I know he'll come. You'll see. He'll just walk in and take off his flying goggles and say—" My throat was too tight and my eyes prickled and I left him quickly, but he called after me in the strangled Oxford accent he reserved for the White Slug:

"A bit blustery, what? Anyone for badders? . . ."

"Edward will come," I repeated, locked in the bathroom and burying my face in a wet flannel. I believed in Edward—I had to believe in something. "He'll come all right." And I willed him to. Rain hit the window like a handful of gravel, in an onslaught of wind that made the room shake, and I wondered suddenly if I should not be willing him instead to play safe. Think of a small plane in this . . .

But I thrust the thought away and went to change out of my riding clothes. I knew I still had rounds to make downstairs, that I must go and see how the maids were. But it would be good for morale if I changed, like any other evening, and did my face and brushed my hair. No need for a gracious skirt or anything fancy; I put on some black linen trousers and a white silk shirt and a big ring. I was dressing to receive Edward: he cared about things like changing for dinner.

The good manners that so charmed Aunt Cissie hadn't been entirely for show, but were part of an ingrained formality—and Nan was wrong, I felt, in confusing it with coldness. When he involved himself in the Slave House games, he usually introduced a formal element into our rough-and-tumble sieges and kidnappings, our races to the Pole, or to the peak of Everest, or Darien, our Death of Caesar or Wedding of Pocahontas, our Fall of Prometheus or Breaking of Batman. At that time Tom mocked continually; he would groan and roll up his eyes at the new routines. But when Edward had gone, they were quietly co-opted and absorbed. "This is where I raise my arms slowly to the setting sun—no, you just kneel on either side of me. And stay *still*." Or, "No, Liz—you don't simply *die*—you've got to do the Dance of Death, ending with a low obeisance here before me. . . ."

As for Tom and Maurice, they wouldn't notice how I looked, though Tom himself seemed to be taking more trouble with his own appearance. He was much more vain now. Maurice was always the same. Actually, I thought, Maurice is quite good-looking—bigger, and more striking, and much more confident. He *had* changed. I wondered what he would think of my new soigné look; he mightn't have a chance, of course, shut away in the bottom kitchen. What would he be doing now—the center of an adoring crowd of females, as Tom described? I hadn't even thought of him as a Man before. I could see very well why they liked him. Would he try to get his own back by seducing Tom's girl?

Absorbed as I was in Edward, wrapped up in his danger, his fate, in our future, I kept finding the present more real. My mind's eye kept wandering back to dear old Maurice, and to Nelly—almost as if I were jealous.

The noise in those upstairs rooms was deafening now, and the very ceiling seemed to shake under repeated blows from the strengthening wind. It sounded terrifyingly near, only inches beyond the high white-painted rafters— all those tons of force and miles of darkness. I peeped in at Aunt Cissie; she was eating her supper peacefully and seemed untroubled by the din. So I let well enough alone, and went along to the back stairs, checking windows as I passed. I found that someone—probably Nan—had lighted a fire in the drawing room. Now she was in the big pantry, feeding the dogs and getting our meal together; so was the cook, wearing an old anorak of mine and a sou'wester. She had managed to keep the stove going in the top kitchen long enough to reheat the curry she had made us. But when she opened the door to go back for the rice and vegetables, the wind roared in, tearing at the tablecloth, bowling the empty baskets about, and bringing with it a wet ragged hen that squawked and flustered wildly round the room, took off, and landed on the top of the dresser, sending several cups crashing down. It was quite a shock and a shambles, and Cookie was shaking all over. I sat her down and gave her a nip of rum.

"But, Nan," I said, "the fowls shouldn't be loose now—surely Zaccy, or Portius—"

"Seem like him don' fix them quite secure, Miss Liz," said Cook. "The peacock them all inna them house, but fowl, I don' know—I hear more than one cry and complain—from out the cookhouse window, when I warm up the food. But Busha Maurice down there now, I believe. I see him light and think it was duppy and then him call out 'Cookie'—Lord Jesus what a night! What going happen—"

"Some duppy!" I said. "We could do with more handy duppies like that." And my spirits rose, for he wasn't sitting snug with Nelly after all, but quietly working away, making ready for the storm. "Listen, Cookie," I said, "you go off to the bottom kitchen now and we can manage the rice and things. I'll take the old hen down now."

I went to fetch an oilskin from the hall, and when I returned, the cook and the wet hen had gone from the pantry and all was peaceful.

"Maurice take poor Cookie down to the others, Miss Liz, and catch the fowl for us again."

"Thank God for Maurice," I said. "Well, the bottom kitchen is the safest place, they say—with those thick walls, and set into the hillside. I wonder about us, though, Nan, if the roof goes. We really catch the wind up here."

"Maurice say is the bitterwood tree he most mistrust, say Mars Tom should chop it down long time since."

"Look, Nan, I don't know about my brother's plans, but I want to see Maurice. We've got to prepare for the worst, and it sounds as if he's the most useful person around here, if things get rough. Do you think they really need him in the maids' kitchen?"

48

"Lord no, Miss Liz. Them have everything—snug as bug —and Lena boyfriend stay behind anyway; he ask me to ask Mars Tom for shelter. So them have a strong man down there will guard them."

"Fine. Well, don't you think Maurice's place is up here with us, then?"

"Yes, Miss Liz—and so I tell Mars Tom. You hear me." Yet she seemed almost truculent.

"What is it, Nan?" I said. "Maurice is a good man, isn't he?"

"Boy and man, Miss Liz, good and fine. A good worker, good with the people them. Mind you, is like any young bullcalf, messing with women—all the time—this last year, I tell you, Miss Liz, him and Mars Tom together! Lord Jesus—no girl safe! But Mars Tom is Mars Tom—he have a kind of right, you understand me. You must remember Maurice blessed by the master's favor always, but even your good father, Miss Liz, can't make him an equal to Mars Tom and youself."

"But, Nan—"

"No, Miss Liz. You see, he have pretensions, he suffer from overweaning ambition. Just remember him is poor white, Miss Liz. See him hand how them rough—and how him smell like working man, and remember. He can't never be like you people, no more than myself can be. Still. I will fetch him."

She did not wait for my answer—if I had one. Father used to say, "Discrimination is hardest to shake when it's halfway up the ladder." But I wouldn't try to reason with her; I guessed that she, like Tom, was chiefly troubled about Maurice and me.

I went and sat down at my desk in the drawing room, to receive him in the manner Nan would see as proper. Business as usual. But when she showed him in and closed the door behind him, I got up and poured out two drinks. He raised his glass.

"Good to see you back, Elizabeth," he said. Not "Miss Liz."

"Good to see you," I said. "Rough outside, is it?"

"Beginning to be."

The fire was burning well in the cut-stone fireplace my father had put in for Mother on their first anniversary. Not many houses boasted such an extravagance. There were few nights in any year cold enough to justify it, and since our mother had gone away to the nursing home in England no one had bothered to light it. But now it blazed brightly, giving the long shabby gracious room a new dimension, a focus, and a neat stack of logs lay ready warming beside it. Over this Maurice spread his sheepskin jacket to dry, and I watched him in the firelight, his intent face, his able hands—hands that were indeed rough and ingrained with tractor oil, one knuckle bleeding from the chicken wire; and, standing by him with my glass, looking down at the wide shoulders, the torn red shirt, I could smell the muskiness and sweat of a long day's work. The moment came back to me when we had crouched side by side over the speared lizard—everything clear and detailed: the veins of the lily leaf, the curve of his bare knee on the stone, the tender, direct look from under the red-brown brows, considering my pain, estimating my strength. "If his insides mash up, he can't thrive, and I will kill him quick with my machete." It was the moment I had first noticed his physical reality, his body, and with it went that alarming power—entirely masculine—to dispense life and death. Women are built to carry and preserve, but men can originate, and destroy.

As I stood, watching—remembering the lizard, and wondering if he ever thought of it—he picked a wood louse out of a log before it went onto the flames. He set the bug down safely among the unused kindling and stood up, saw me watching, and smiled.

"My good deed for the day," he said.

Now that his hair was nearly dry I could see how

tawny gold the sun had bleached it, though it was still dark underneath. The roughness, the streaks of dirt, did not disguise his good looks.

I gazed too long. I lowered my eyes and said:

"So—we must talk storm strategy."

But he went on looking. "You've grown up very nicely, Elizabeth," he said. "Quite a little dazzler. Got the old country at your feet, I'll bet. It was fun, was it? Tell me."

"Oh—there was so much! I just wish Tom and you could have had a bit of it. *Italy*, Maurice—and *London*! And how I wish I could have shown you off at the ball in Cambridge—no one could dance like you two. They don't know how."

"I bet you showed them, though. Goodness, Liz—but wasn't it hard to leave it all and come back?"

"Oh no. This is a sort of paradise—Cousin Edward used to call it that, didn't he? I'll always come back. And it'll always be the same."

"Until it actually falls down. Me, I don't like to watch it go to pieces. Maybe *you* can get your brother to see what's happening."

"I think that between us three we might return it to its old glory," I said, watching the fire.

"I hope so." But there was a sudden reserve in his voice. When he spoke again I understood. "And I hear from Nan it's going to be 'us four' any moment now. She said your Cousin Edward was flying down to see you—in this storm. He must be mad."

"Tom says he'll be grounded when he stops for fuel, before he gets this far."

"Then he'll be here by tomorrow evening, Liz—don't worry. He always led a charmed life. It'll be funny to see him again after, what, four years?" He put down his glass. "All right. We must think about how to hold this rickety old fortress of ours."

"Yes, Maurice." I went over to the desk and sat down.

51

"And Nan thinks you're worrying over the bitterwood tree."

"Tom should have let me fell it months ago," he said. He crossed the room and stood behind me, leaning on the back of the chair and looking over my shoulder at the list of preparations I was ticking off. I could feel his warmth, and the weak rum punch seemed to trickle through my knees. He went on in a level voice, still close behind me:

"A big limb came off last November and it's been lopsided ever since. He said he would take off some branches on the house side to even it up, but it never got done. I blame myself. Now if it falls it's likely to fall this way—depending a bit on the turn of the weather. Tom said the wind would shift round as the storm center moved closer, and by the time it was at its worst, it would carry the bitterwood down the hillside. But what a gamble!"

"And if it falls against the house?"

"The roof goes on that side. If we're lucky, just the turret; if it's the main roof, the whole lot may lift off once the wind gets in."

"What then?" I twisted my chair round, preferring to face him, and he moved back a little and sat on the arm of the sofa.

"Then, well—we move down to the bottom store. The final stronghold. Your father always called it that. Like the maids' kitchen, it's built into the hill—goes back even deeper. We'd be safe there."

"And do we need to get it ready somehow? What's down there now? I thought it was hardly used."

I had never liked the bottom store; it used to terrify me. But sitting there, poised and sophisticated, and two feet away from Maurice, I felt I had put away childish things.

"There are bananas ripening," he said, "and some big cans of oil—coconut oil, bought in bulk way back. There's a couple sacks of corn and the straw they use for the fowls—and rope, and wire; crocus bags, empty oil drums piled up. Not bad. I've been and had a look around, tidied it up a bit. The door is stout and sound; I took the padlock off, and we can bolt it from the inside."

"And we get down to it through the hatch in this floor?"

"Yes, that's the way. We wouldn't be able to go outdoors at that stage—it'd be murder. That's why retreating to the bottom kitchen is out."

"Yes, I see. So the bottom kitchen is safe for the maids?"

"Like a rock; set down low, and the roof's good—I only mended it last month. This—" he glanced up "—is the only roof I'm not happy about, but I thought it was better to fix the corn store: we can always shift out of here—say, into the hall—but the corn has to stay put."

The long drawing room was one of the extremities of the rambling house; it had two weather sides, and its roof sloped back some way before the upper floor of spare rooms and dressing rooms rose out of it. Even with a sound lid it was one of the house's weak points—as a fortress—because of the two large windows flanked with jalousies that looked north and east over the best view: two large thin curtain walls, difficult to reinforce, fronting the weather; a promontory from which the hillside dropped steeply away into the valley and the bottom pasture. Where Edward will land, I thought.

But already, when the gusts persisted—and the rain was hard and heavy at the moment—the jalousies let in fine hissing feathers of water. We started shifting the tables and chairs toward the center of the room.

"It's beginning to show its teeth," I said. "I want to do a last round outside before it's too rough. Tom's still battening down the boxrooms—perhaps you'd better help him."

"I'm going to, when we've been round—I don't think he'll pack me off at this stage. But first I'm coming with you."

"Thanks," I said. "I'll just see Aunt Cissie's all right."

I left Maurice in the pantry, filling and lighting one of the storm lanterns, while I went up to my aunt. Through the peephole I saw Nan playing Beggar My Neighbor with her. She caught my eye and nodded me away. In the turret room the shutters were already closed and latched; it is the only place in the house where they are built in, folding back into the deep window embrasures. An embattled watchtower.

Now the huge gusts came more frequently, successive waves giving no time to breathe. Between the onslaughts of wind and rain the house was strangely quiet, stuffy and stale and dumb. In each room, the clumsy boards were plastered like so much adhesive tape across nose and mouth, with the bright electric bulbs burning everywhere, frightened eyes determined to stay awake. I longed for air. When Maurice opened the pantry door on the storm, we plunged out into it as though giving ourselves up to a great breaker whose curling top was too high above our heads to see. Out in the backyard we looked up and watched the clouds tearing across an improbable moon. The last of the sunset had not quite left the sky; and the road, the limewashed stable walls, the moonflowers fluttering on the wall of the drive, a dishcloth left out on the clothesline—all held on to the dying light. Then the distant roar came toward us like an express and crushed us back against the wall of the house, soaking and blinding us and blotting out the moon. Maurice steadied the clattering lantern with both hands, then nodded toward the back veranda, and we ran, heads down, into its comparative shelter.

"I want to go and see the maids first," I shouted.

We edged round the corner and down the open steps, and banged on the door of the ironing room. Lena's boyfriend let us in and we went through into the long smoky kitchen.

"Good evening, everybody," I said. There were many more faces than I had expected, several of which I did not know at all; two or three children, a mother with a baby and perhaps half a dozen besides; bundles brought in by shelterers and hangers-on, a pile of breadfruit picked to save them from the storm, a goat, and a basket of chickens. Nelly was sitting with the maids; she was busy buffing her fingernails. The cook's son Henry-Esmond had a ukulele.

"Come then, H.E.," I said. "Give us a tune." But he was too shy. "Everyone all right? No one sick, or hurt? Good. You seem fine in here—warm and well off and plenty company. You have sufficient food and water?"

"We going have a whole heap of water outside, Miss Liz." Laughter.

"True enough. And spare nails and boards? Fine. And you good people taking shelter for the night?" I looked toward the outsiders.

"Pleace'm. If you and the young master permit us."

"If Cookie and company have room enough, you're welcome. Each must mind for all in times of trouble—share and share. And God give you all a good night." A chorus of "Thanks, Miss Liz" and "Glory be!" and "Lord bless the young missis." They weren't afraid of me then.

I turned away, rather envious of the party spirit, the warmth and cooking smells and noise and camaraderie. Maurice had been standing behind me; I looked up at him and said:

"*They're* all right, I reckon."

"And you," he said. "Just right—set them up proper, made them feel good."

"Words are cheap, Father used to say. But I'm surprised you could bear to leave them—it's not going to be half so jolly up there, you know."

"I'll be just where I want to be," he said. "I could have got home, but I didn't want to. And don't worry about Tom. He'll come round. He's got to make a show of strength sometimes, just for the record."

"I suppose so," I said— but I avoided his eyes, remembering Tom's own reason: "that stallion," he had called him; and Nan's "Lord Jesus, no girl safe." "Okay—fine—I think we may need you, Maurice. Now—once round the outside."

He opened the door and the wind pushed us backward. It was no stronger but somehow steadier, more purposeful, and walking in it was like wading upstream. The rain now was only a fine needling. Maurice led the way down past the outer kitchen door; it was boarded across on the outside, and I held the lantern while he looked up under the eaves. He nodded and we moved off, trudging slowly through the lashing grass, past the great portal of the bottom store, lit briefly by the moon between clouds. It looked sinister and forbidding. As children we always used to run past it, a dungeon door with only a small slit window set into the thick wall beside it, like a single suspicious eye. I prayed secretly that we would not be forced to take refuge there.

We followed the narrow fenced path hugging the hill between the tall cliff of store and drawing room piled high above us and the tops of the surging trees below; crossed the drive and took the steps leading up to the office window, where we stopped to wire up a small side gate we found banging; then circled the house looking for chinks that might show a weakness in our defenses. The great bitterwood tree stood at the corner of the backyard, raging and creaking as the gale bludgeoned it. I could see that if it fell its full length, its top branches would catch the turret or the main roof; but falling the other way, it would lie down the slope and hardly touch the stable yard —and certainly not reach the outbuildings.

At last we came round the corner onto the big veranda, into the very teeth of the wind. I staggered and Maurice caught me, laughing down at me and shouting something I couldn't hear. The great torrent of air was stupendous, an invisible power of such magnitude that I felt not merely small but gone, annihilated in its huge violence. We stood out on the terrace beyond the pillars, under the open sky, holding on to the railings to steady ourselves as we gazed up into the primal chaos above us.

Up there, towering clouds piled high and were ripped to streamers in seconds like a speeded-up film. To the north and over toward Catadupa, the air and the land merged in inky blackness, but under the rusty western sky the middle distance was a heaving battlefield where the forest bowed and thrashed and roared. While we watched, a tall coconut tree at the edge of the bush, outlined against the open pasture, bent double, whipped back, doubled up again, and snapped off like a straw.

Suddenly I felt the terror of it, and our helplessness. What was there to save us? Not even in a sound modern building would I have felt secure on such a night. But here we were trusting ourselves to an archaic, run-down shell of a house just because it was home; set high on its hill, elegant, vulnerable, neglected, it was an anachronism almost untouched by progress and change.

I shivered in my thin oilskin and hugged my arms round me as I leaned back against the veranda railings and gazed at the crazy beautiful old building. I felt Maurice wrapping his heavy sheepskin round me, and gratefully I pulled it close, without argument. He did not seem to feel the cold; his hands were warm when he took hold of my wrist and held up the lantern so we could look at my watch. Nearly eight o'clock.

And then, over his shoulder, I saw at the top of the house a lighted window, still unshuttered, and a figure silhouetted in the bright oblong, watching us. It stayed quite still for a long moment and I could make out the big claw hammer in one hand. I suddenly caught the impression of a prisoner in a high room, trying to get out. Then a shutter moved across the window frame and the light went out. A prisoner walling himself in.

Maurice had not seen, but he saw my face in the light of the storm lamp. He turned round and looked up. Now the house was all in darkness.

"What was it then?" he asked, staggering as the wind caught him. He pulled himself back to the railing beside me. "What was it, Liz?" he said close to my ear. I shook my head.

"Nothing. Time for supper."

EIGHT O'CLOCK

THE WORDS were lost in the storm. Maurice took my chin and turned my head so that our cheeks were touching.

"Word don' catch, please, missis," he said softly, his mouth forming the words against my skin. Again I shook my head, more slowly, and he rocked with me, cheek to cheek.

"I said, 'Nothing,'" I murmured. "I said, 'Time for supper.'" And I pulled back.

Maurice put his arm round my shoulders, and leaning together, and backward against the weight of the wind, we walked and were blown across to the corner. By the time we made it to the cookhouse veranda, keeping close to the walls for fear of flying slates from the roof of the dairy, and hurrying past the roaring bitterwood, we were soaked and battered. We saw how the black water in the big catchment tank tossed and broke over the edge, sluicing down the hillside, and there was a large piece of slate set like a razor in the turf; it wasn't safe to linger. But Tom was there before us when we burst into the warm quiet pantry.

He was helping himself to curry from the hotplate. He had changed into black Levis and a dark shirt, and somehow his dry clean clothes, his neat hair shining under the light, gave him a commanding edge over us—sodden, bedraggled, panting. He watched us pulling off our muddy boots, and I caught his eye and he smiled, quite unruffled —very alert and cool. Without comment, he put down his plate, picked up the hammer from the shelf, stepped over to me, and hooked Maurice's sheepskin jacket off my shoulders. He let it fall to the ground. It was a simple gesture of distaste.

"Well?" he said brightly, returning to his curry. "Everything tucked up, then?" He spoke to me only, and behaved as though Maurice just wasn't there. Always the first stage in Tom's elaborate process of forgiving, it was a good sign.

"The maids seem to be in good spirits," I said, and helped myself to some food. "They've got quite a party going down there, with music and followers and friends. All very cozy—one big happy family, and probably mostly family, at that."

"That's right," said Maurice. "Cookie's other son, and Lena's boyfriend and his sister and brother-in-law I recognized. They seem to have brought a lot of food with them. And that bottom kitchen is as tight as a drum."

"No doubt they will be too before the night is out," said Tom.

When he had finished eating, he lounged against the door, tossing and catching his two silver bullets. They were his worry beads. He had cast them long ago as a Christmas present for our father. They had taken three silver florins—his saved-up pocket money—and long patient heating in a homemade kiln; they had reposed in splendor, couched in velvet, on the big office desk, honored but forgotten, until after the funeral. Then Tom went and reclaimed them; now, as far as I knew, they never left his person. He was forever fondling them, and this kept them as bright as the day they were cast—brighter, for now they were polished smooth. When he stood about, tossing and catching them, the resonant click got on my nerves. I wondered if Tom was as calm as he made out; but as he watched Maurice and me bent hungrily over our food, his expression was one of detachment touched with indulgence, as though we were a pair of gerbils.

I finished my curry. "I'm going to dry off in front of the drawing-room fire," I said, but it was really to escape that lofty scrutiny.

Tom had always had in a high degree the gift of discomfiting, with or without words. I had discovered self-consciousness—as distinct from mere embarrassment—when Tom brought his school friends home for the first half-term. How I looked forward to that long weekend. His absence had created a huge hollow in the center of my life, and I learned painfully that being ignored by someone who is *there* is no kind of preparation for his removal. How I anticipated—as I believed—his every whim and need for that weekend; finding and setting out his favorite books, polishing the bagatelle board, stitching up his old Sam Browne with twine and a bodkin and Portius's help. I currycombed his pony till it gleamed like the bagatelle board, and tied a ribbon in its tail. I even—impulsively —put flowers on his dressing table.

Was it the tall tough friends he had around him? Either he would have been different anyway or they made him so; there was no telling whether it was the way the gang laughed over the books by his bed that made him instantly outgrow them, or whether he had already left them behind.

He did not even look at the Sam Browne. Sam Brownes were out; narrow alligator belts and sheath knives were in. He whisked the ribbon out of Bonny's tail and stuffed it in his pocket without a word or a look. Bagatelle was kid stuff—it was poker, now—and the flowers were dismantled and dissected during a discussion on sex, punctuated by guffaws, and I was shooed away. Worse, far worse than any of these, was Tom's scrutiny of me on arrival, and after the formal introductions on which our father insisted. All eyes were on me suddenly, as Tom said, in a new, hearty voice:

"Well, and how are you then, sis? Just the same I see—still biting your nails. Ah yes"—expansively—"it's good to get back and find nothing's changed around the old home. . . ." That moment was the start of self-consciousness, of hideous, agonizing visibility: Tom's eyes on me, estimating my weak spot, measuring me for my shroud.

And now those eyes under the ruler-drawn brows could tell me other things—different, but as discomfiting: how my wet shirt and trousers clung to me. Maurice, I realized, disturbed me in another way, and I was sharply aware of how my body felt—alive, blood racing, cold rain, warm hands. With him I had not once thought of how I looked. But Tom in a moment reduced me to seeing myself as he saw me; and I told myself, as I so often did, that it was just part of being twins. Perhaps, I thought, we are unnaturally—no, uncomfortably—close.

"So if you'll excuse me—" I said. I made myself rinse off my plate in the old stone sink with deliberate care as, in silence, the two men watched me. Tom lit a cigarette and stepped between me and the door as I turned to go. He cupped my chin in one hand, and took the cigarette from his lips and put it between mine. I did not want it, but it was quicker, simpler, to accept. If he had to make his small possessive bullying gesture in front of Maurice, let him. The night ahead, I thought, as I closed the door on them, promised enough stress and tension to relieve even Tom's boredom, without my creating a tiny scene of symbolic rejection for him.

I threw the cigarette into the fireplace in the drawing room and looked round. The pool in front of the shutters had spread, and rain was dripping through the roof steadily in two places near the far end. We could not stay in here—that was clear. It would have to be the hall, now; and Aunt Cissie must manage without the cheerful fire I had promised her. Soon, judging by the torrent of wind that battered round the house, we would have to bring her down, but first there were carpets and pictures to save from the creeping flood and the driving spray.

"Tom!" I called, but the noise drowned my voice. "Tom!" I threw open the pantry door. He and Maurice were standing at either end of the big table; Tom was white and Maurice was red.

"Here, would you two come and help—" I said quickly. "The drawing room's getting the full force of it—things to move—"

Maurice hurried past, stepping round me with exaggerated care. I pushed the door shut for a moment. "Look, Tom," I said. "It's going to be a long night—"

"You're telling *me*?" he said, stubbing out his cigarette viciously. "And couldn't be too long for that jumped-up Jerry—" He snatched at the door handle.

"Tom, what have you been saying?"

"Nothing, sweetheart. Only asked if he didn't have a watch of his own, that's all."

Tom had observed us from the upper window, seen us close together by the veranda railings, bending over my wrist, and, instead of flying into a temper, he had decided to play it cool. But he hadn't been able to resist the pleasure of making sure we knew he knew, and had picked on Maurice. I was filled with the heat of indignation.

"Ooh! Hot little flushes—" cried Tom gleefully, leaning close in the nose-to-nose gesture of our childhood; and the two fierce eagle's eyes ran into one. I could smell the cleanness of his shirt and the rum on his breath. I ducked away and he opened the door, leered over his shoulder, and was gone.

I took the dipper and scooped up some water from the earthenware jar that stood in the corner. I drank some and wiped my face with a handful. It was cold and pure from filtering through the porous dripstone above. All the tank water had to be boiled; this was the cooling system, and the slow steady plopping, echoing in the jeroboam—as much part of home and childhood as the grandfather clock—soothed and comforted me.

This was no time for scenes or sulking. As I dried my face I wondered whether such antagonism had been open before—or was my arrival to blame? What was certain was the approach of a new enemy, whose power and persistence called for some unity of opposition.

For the moment at least they were united in carrying the cumbersome sausage of rolled-up carpet from the drawing room to the hall. I moved chairs so they could lay it along the wainscot, and then we went back for the pictures. The tempest howled round the northeast corner and struck the curtain wall so hard that the louvers of the jalousies seemed to flutter and gape as the rain sprayed through. We piled the long sofas and armchairs against the back wall, near the fireplace, and covered them with tarpaulins. We draped the bookshelves and tables with polythene weighted down with stacks of old magazines —it was not good, but it was better than nothing—and I carried in my two favorites, the illustrated *Idylls of the King* and Mother's Dulac *Arabian Nights*, with its leaves of tissue over every picture (I still have them with me; indeed, I am writing now on the large mauve endpapers from the Doré). And we rescued the playing cards, and the games box, and my precious folder of drawings, my own and Edward's; Tom gathered up the records and Maurice carried the clock and the glass dome of stuffed birds.

We came back to deal with the fire, and for a moment we stood, all three of us, in front of it, enjoying its bright embracing warmth—for that moment together, like the old days. That's the lovely thing about a fire: you all look into it, instead of at one another, and sharing it is a sort of contact. I can remember that driving along side by side in a car was the same—easier to talk when you are looking together at the same prospect, not isolated, each hiding behind an observed face.

"We needn't put it out," said Maurice. He spoke very

quietly after all the shouting and hustle of the last ten minutes against the tumult of the storm, and we only heard him because we were close, shoulder to shoulder in the hearth.

"The chimney cowl must still be pretty good," I said, "there's hardly a drop coming down—" and I squatted and gazed into the incandescent coral and crystal caves at the heart of the fire. Tom crouched down by me and said, "Smaug's lair," and glanced at me, and I smiled in agreement. Then Maurice, above us, said, "Or Mount Doom, waiting for that ring . . ."

Had Tom forgotten—didn't he know—that I'd lent Maurice *The Hobbit* and the *Ring* books? Tom stood up, reached for the soda-water siphon, and aimed it at the fire. There was an explosion of steam and ash that made me gasp and fall back, coughing. Then it swept off up the chimney in the strong draft, and all that remained of our enchanted caverns was a heap of sodden cinders and the gnawed log, hollowed into a frail brindled arch like the stomach of a stray dog.

"Oh, *Tom!*" I cried. "*Why?*"

"So much for magic," said Tom. Maurice said nothing. Tom picked up the whisky decanter in his other hand and held them both high. "Here's to the magic that really works!" he crowed above the wind, and left the room, swinging them on either side.

We turned our backs to the hissing pool of ash. I felt ashamed of my twin brother—even though there was "only Maurice" to see, and the sort of Tom-ish behavior we had grown accustomed to as children. But, more than that, I was cast down, quite unreasonably, by the swift and total destruction I had just watched, of something so beautiful, so indisputably alive. I felt the press of storm against the thin curtain walls, and the old house shaking, and the chill taking over the long sad room with its shrouded furniture huddled at one end.

Then Maurice put his hand on my shoulder.

"Be all better in the morning, you know," he said. "Remember Parson's wise words: 'This too will pass.' " He ran his hand up under my hair and rubbed my cheek gently with his knuckles, just as I had seen him cosset a horse or a cat; and like a cat I pressed my face against them and nudged and was comforted. More than comforted.

I said quickly, "I must go and get the aunt down," and I followed Tom.

He was in the hall, stretched out with a drink beside him on the wicker sofa. His holster belt was hanging over the back: it was all wrong for the pistols—far too Wild West, too raw and bright—but he liked it, and they fitted in it well enough. He squinted down the long barrel he was polishing briskly and said without looking up, "I told Nan to get the old girl down."

"I think she'll need persuading," I said, starting toward the stairs.

"You leave it to Nan, sweetheart. Relax, have a drink. Come on—she'll cope. She hass vays of making her valk." Then, speculatively, gazing at the ceiling: "I wonder how our fine young friend next door would have made out if he'd stayed on in the old fatherland-*über-alles*—would you fancy him all kitted up in black leather SS gear, Lizzie?"

"Do you *always* think of him as a bloody Jerry? Why should that bug you so? I wonder. The way you go on about him, it sounds a bit as if you fancy him yourself—" But he shouted me down.

"*Christ*—you have the blasted nerve—! After letting him—"

"Shut up, Tom!"

There were noises on the landing, and Nan's skirts and the aunt's plimsolls appeared at the top of the stairs. We could hear voices, one loud and firm, the other high and shrill, but not what they were saying.

"Let them *be*, Liz!" Tom snapped.

Aunt Clarissa came down the stairs gingerly, delicately, like a spider testing a web. She did not seem alarmed, only suspicious; and the sidelong glances of the pale popping eyes were not fearful, rather, cautious—even crafty. She was in all her finery. Nan said she had flatly refused to put away her jewels, and she had changed into another, longer, droopy dress, this time of oyster-colored satin, cruelly grand and bare about the bony chest and arms. These were clothed instead with necklaces and bracelets, the ropes of pearls and the family garnets chinking against chunks of paste, colored beads. And above, around all this, she had draped a long white feather boa that had seen better days. Moth and rust had corrupted it, judging by the shape and color, and little fragments of it fluttered away in the wake of her imposing entrance "Down the Great Staircase—the Cynosure of All Eyes," as she had so often described to me.

"Oh, *Aunt!*" I cried, loudly, over the wind's roar. "Aunt Cissie—you do look lovely!"

"Jesus Christ!" said Tom, leaping to his feet. "What does she think it is—Queen Flaming Charlotte's Ball?"

A chair had been set out for her in the center of the room, a tall, rather uncomfortable high-backed Italian chair, all heavy carving and cut velvet, the best the hall had to offer. We called it Siege Perilous: it was just like the ones at the Round Table in our book of King Arthur and His Knights, and we used to sit and wait on it by the office door, as children, when summoned by Father, to be punished or praised or simply to recite our lessons. Now I wished we had brought through one of the soft easy chairs from the drawing room, so she might relax. But as soon as she took her place in the Siege Perilous I realized it was the right choice; grandeur, a sense of occasion—not relaxation—was what Aunt Clarissa required. It was patently an important chair; and she sat up very straight and tall, and gathered her boa about her. Now I could see that her hair was newly brushed, caught back flat and hard as usual with a plastic bow, but it was diamanté this time, and below it the hair had been fluffed out on either side in a pale frizz. Nan had really excelled herself.

"Thank you, Nan," I said when we had settled the aunt

and placed a small glass of rum and water on the table at her side.

"Ah—the cup that cheers . . ."

She never admitted it was rum or that she liked it. To drink was always "just observing the decencies" or "keeping body and soul together." The aunt's social chat was a net of inappropriate clichés; her doom talk was battier, but more original.

"I bring down her pink cardigan as well, Miss Liz," said Nan. "She refuse to wear it and hide up her party clothes—"

Aunt Cissie was plucking at my sleeve.

"Someone *special* will be coming to the party," she said coyly. Then, with one of those unnerving switches of mood, she jerked to her feet and cried out, high and clear: "Yea I tell unto you: little Edward will outstare the lightning and do battle with the Prince of Darkness in the Valley of the Shadow—"

"Never mind about Edward now, Auntie," I said, retrieving her blue velvet reticule and settling her back in the chair. But Tom had chosen to ignore the outburst, inscrutable behind yesterday's *Gleaner*. I could hear Maurice hammering in the drawing room, nailing up the jalousies.

"I tell her, Miss Liz, as a diversion merely—she always sweet on the boy's English manners—"

"But he will come! Out of the eye of the storm will he step forth—"

"Well—yes, Aunt Cissie, that would be fun. It'll be nice to see Cousin Edward, won't it? But let's hope he's spending the night in some lovely airport, with a café and lots of magazines, and coming on tomorrow."

"There will be no tomorrow, my child. The Lord has torn it from His calendar!" The shrill insistent voice ceased suddenly on a panicky upbeat; but then she sipped at her rum as if the subject were closed. I knew it was not, and would start up again when least expected; it was hard to ignore, like a bird scarer set to go off at random.

"What we need," said Tom, emptying his glass, "is some good music."

The fury of the hurricane had risen to a continuing thunderous roar. It seemed to press remorselessly, not just on the house but on our very skulls.

Tom went back to the drawing room and returned with the record player.

"We can't move the loudspeakers," he said, "but we can get a certain amount of volume out of the cabinet amplifier."

"That'll be wonderful," I said, eager to encourage. "But, Tom—nothing too wild—couldn't you compromise with some old favorites, say Cole Porter? Or *Highlights from Showboat?*"

"Pete Fountain will have to do," he said shortly.

Nan had gone to the pantry to make coffee, but it was Maurice who carried in the tray.

"Henry-Esmond is here," he said. "He's come up from the bottom kitchen—seems like they have run out of nails after all. I'll see him back down again and get some more crocus bags: we haven't nearly enough for all the cracks where the water's coming in."

"Take these wretched animals with you while you're about it," said Tom.

Our arrival in the hall had woken and excited the dogs, and with the sound of the record player they started whimpering again.

"They only want a bit of attention," I said. "I rather like having them around." And looked forward to their solid wordless company in the long watches.

"Well, they get on my nerves. Liz, they'll be far happier in the bottom kitchen. Take them down, Maurice."

Maurice whistled and the two dogs ran and leaped against him joyfully. "Come on then," he said roughly, "you'll get a whole heap of lovely tidbits down there, you and the goat between you." He took a packet of nails and went, the dogs gamboling behind him. Nan would let them out through the pantry door; and in the lee of the hill, the way to the bottom kitchen was comparatively sheltered.

I got up; I wanted to catch H.-E. and ask how things were below.

"Sit down, Liz!" Tom called out. "Stop chasing him, girl."

I felt the rush of protesting anger, the rising cry, "It's not *fair!*"—motto of childhood—but stopped myself.

"I'm only getting Aunt Cissie the book I brought her from England," I answered quickly over my shoulder, my face burning. I rummaged through the carrier bag of diversions that I had collected for her, and found the big glossy "pop-out" book of Cinderella.

"You see, Aunt," I explained, sitting on the arm of the tall chair, "here's the royal palace to set up, and Cinderella's kitchen, with a table and a broom. Here's the pumpkin coach, and all the white mice changed into horses: they're a bit tricky—Nan and I will help you. Then here are all the people—stiffer cardboard, you see—and then *pages* of clothes to dress them in. And you just pop them out, like this, along the dotted lines." It had been quite a find, for Nan would not let her have scissors, and had trained her actually to dread anything sharp. Perhaps it was better so; nothing, not a knife, not a pen, not a pencil. They protect me just the same way.

Aunt Cissie's popping out the royal palace was far more restful than her normal repose, when she endlessly fiddled with her beads and her boa, or fumbled in her blue velvet bag for a handkerchief or powder compact or her silver hand mirror. I picked my way through to a chair by the bookcase and lifted down one of the big faded red *Punch*es.

I knew and began to accept that the night would be full of waiting, of patiently killing time; there might be bursts of activity, even moments of urgency, but perhaps the greater strain would be the long gaps between. I turned over the pages and read the long wordy captions under groups of bustled beauties and suave hairy men, aproned fishwives and rude urchins and old gaffers. I found cads and heroes in plenty, and Miss Asprey, to the life. I thought of Edward, then and now; I used the yellowed pages he loved so well, and the smell of the binding—painted inside the covers with darker stripes of bookworm killer (one of the recurring tasks of our childhood)—to bring him back to me. And he kept forming, under my eyelids, as a pale spectacled child; the new tall elegant version I had encountered in England somehow eluded me.

Yet it was only six weeks since I had seen him and danced with him at the May Ball. He was off to America the next day. His official girl friend—official in parental eyes, I knew—was waiting to whip him away in her sports car, so it was a hasty farewell, but as romantic as a girl could wish—magical fleeting moments in the pearly dawn at the end of a marvelous party. Edward when serious looked rather like Rupert Brooke—the flower of English youth, tall, fair, and willowy. And without a trace of catarrh.

"I shall be with you early in August," he said. "Without fail."

"Undoubtedly?" I asked. It was a recurring word in all those endless dogmatic arguments with his friends, one of whom had been my—official—partner.

"Undoubtedly," he said, and smiled; and he bent and kissed my cheek.

We could hear the girl friend calling. "Buck up, Eddie, or the car park will be *jammed!*"

"I'll come," he said to me, and left.

Now he was on his way. I tried to imagine him in the cockpit of his plane—but still he was just as small and pale, with goggles instead of spectacles, leather-helmeted, braving the storm.

Even the beloved ghost could not keep out the present. The raging of wind and rain, and Tom's music burst-

71

ing through it in waves, kept bringing me back to reality, to the herded furniture round me in the harsh overhead light, and the wicker chairs and garden tables suddenly looking tattered and panicky, upended, all the loose bindings and cobwebs exposed. A big oval looking glass on the wall over the side table was hung too high to reflect the muddle, too high even for human use unless we stood tall; this had been at the firm request of a stern Scottish governess who suspected Tom and me of vanity, and it had never been moved down again. Round the rest of the walls and up the stairs hung the trophies of our father's years in Africa; the largest, above the front door, was a massive buffalo head, black-horned and white-skulled, with cavernous eye sockets where Maurice had once found a young bat. (Where *was* Maurice?)

At the far end, near the office, stood the big grandfather clock. It had grown eccentric through neglect since Father died, and could only strike twelve. We found this too much, every hour on the hour, and Tom had invented an ingenious method of silencing it except when it was relevant; so now, on the hours from one to eleven it only churred and coughed—sounds that this evening were covered by the storm. Close to me, too close, stood the ranks of orchids and lilies; they seemed garish, waxy, funereal, the sweet scent almost tangible, so that the high room became a treacle well, a jam jar like Nan used to put out for the hornets. Now we were the trapped insects. I turned back to *Punch*. But I found that I didn't want du Maurier's dapper gentlemen: suddenly I wanted Maurice.

"The clothes are not right, Elizabeth. And I don't like the noise; it's all wrong for the ball." Aunt Cissie was cross and querulous, so I showed her that the fairy godmother's gown was no good for Cinderella—far too big, so she would not be able to dance. "But the hurricane keeps blowing the palace over and the poor girl has nowhere to go, with the flood creeping nearer and the rain of fire and the Angel of Death—"

72

"Oh, come, Aunt," I said. "There's no flood or hurricane in here. You just haven't bent these sidepieces, see, so that it stands up."

Tom was watching, standing behind her chair, refilling his glass.

"So what's become of the jolly chum, eh?" he said loudly.

Aunt Clarissa jumped in alarm, dropping her Cinderella doll.

"Who are *you*?" she said crossly, rounding on him. "And don't you know he's a *prince*? And he will take her away from all this in his airplane and they will fly over the mountains and over the sea—"

"Yes, Aunt," I said quickly. "So why not dress up the prince next, and I'll get some music ready for the ball."

"Silly old bat," said Tom. "Nan's been filling her head with nonsense."

"Tom, can't you find her some dance music?" I went across to the record player and he followed.

"Didn't answer my question, did you, sweetheart?" The whisky was making him overemphatic. "Reckon your chum Maurice has decided to stay down below after all, like I told him to in the first place. Know what? *I* think he's discovered my little Nelly down there and figures she's more his speed." I felt a wild unreasoning surge of jealousy at the thought of Maurice and the brown girl with the beautiful mouth. "He won't be back, old dear. And good riddance . . . Yes, and by what right, might I ask, do you countermand my order and get him up here with us, anyhow? Since when—?"

"Look, Tom, both Nan and I felt we needed extra help up here; there's far more to contend with, if the roof goes or the bitterwood comes down."

"Oh—he's been on about *that*, has he?"

"I asked him to work out some sort of strategy, supposing things got bad—you were busy—and anyway he knows this house better, structurally, than either of us, what state the roofs are in, and so on. He's a useful man, Tom. And

73

it was crowded enough in the bottom kitchen as it was—" I heard myself taking refuge in excuses. "No—to tell you the truth, I felt safer with Maurice coping—" But Tom simply reached out and turned up the volume to full.

The pantry would be a refuge. I opened the door, and there was Maurice.

He was standing with his arms full of sacks, while Nan clucked over his wet clothes and the pool of water he'd let in. Even here the backlash of the storm was fierce. It slapped and plucked at the door and drummed dismally on the tin roof outside.

"No one pass that way again this night," said Nan. "Mop it, boy, and remove that sacking out of here. No room to turn around, with all the grocery and the puddle and the supper thing them all about—Lord Jesus what a night."

Maurice and I stood smiling at each other, letting it all flow past—an assignation on a traffic island. Then Nan paused for breath, and I took my eyes away and turned to her.

"All right, Nanny dear—I'll take the sacks, and Maurice will mop, and everything will be lovely."

"Don' you touch those old sacks, Miss Liz—is Maurice one can carry them, and is Nan will mop up the little water. And is Nan will fetch down a dry shirt for the poor wet boy there—Lord what a business! What a heap of fuss and fuddle . . ." Nan always looked just as fierce whether taking a stand or giving way, but I could tell she was almost as relieved as I to have him back.

Tom, however, might not be so joyful, and even less so if the German appeared in one of his shirts.

"Oh, Nan," I said, "I have a old shirt of the master's in my sewing basket that will do."

"But you tell me you saving that up to make youself a pretty nightdress, Miss Liz."

"Never mind that," I said, very conscious of Maurice watching us. "It's too big, anyway."

He followed me and dumped the pile of sacks in the wide tiled passage. "I need some of these for the drawing-

74

room windows," he said, "then I'll bring the rest through to the hall. Keep the shirt for me, Liz; I'll get this done first." But he didn't go. "Everything all right?" he asked. "Got your aunt settled?" I nodded. "Been missing me?" I nodded.

"You took your time," I said. "Tom reckoned you'd discovered his girl friend down there."

"Poor little Nelly . . . Why, Liz—you been jealous for me?" He stepped close to me and turned me to face the light. "Jesus—that's made my day!"

I shrugged him off. "Just didn't want to lose a good strong useful man on a night like this," I said, turning back at the hall door. I didn't fool either of us.

"Maurice has brought up a load of sacks," I told Tom. "He's blocking some of the cracks in the drawing room, and I think we ought to help. Nan can stay with Aunt Cissie."

"She keeps on about music for the damn ball," he said. "I tell you straight: it's either Mantovani or me—you can't have both."

Poor Tom. I was so happy that I felt expansive and I saw suddenly how lovely and how lost he was. Graceful and fair with dark angry eyes—a smoldering Adonis in a room full of junk and the horns of dead animals. He should be on a chaise longue with a mandolin and a rich beautiful widow, or lounging against a gaming table in Monte Carlo. Then he would look right.

"What are you smiling at, dammit?" he said. "I suppose *you're* all right—Maurice for now—instant comfort—and Cousin Edward for the morrow, and the best of British—"

The lights flickered suddenly and then were bright and steady again. Nan hustled in; Maurice followed. "Did you see that, Mars Tom? You think the lights going off already?"

"Where have you got candles and lanterns, Miss Nan?" Maurice called urgently over the screaming wind.

"All right, now: one proper oil lamp already in here, I

bring down from turret." It was there on the side table. The lights winked again. "Lord Jesus! The big candelabra, them and the storm lamps in the pantry, I going fetch them right now. I will just take this one candle in case dark come on me."

She opened the door leading through to the pantry, screamed, and dropped the candlestick.

"Lord Jesus God Almighty what is this?"

Beyond her in the doorframe we could see a hooded figure, huddled and small—a shiny black mound with eyes. And a mouth. It opened wide and out came a thin terrified cry:

"Light! Light leave us!"

"It's only Nelly, Miss Nan," said Maurice, who was nearest the door. He bent and picked up the candle. "What is it then, Nelly girl?"

Tom pushed past him. We heard a yelp of pain as he grabbed the girl and dragged her into the hall under the bright overhead lights. She stumbled on her high heels and whimpered while he jerked away the oilskins she cowered under. He shoved her into the center of the room, where she teetered and fell to her knees, babbling words we could not make out.

"Stop it, Tom!" I shouted. "Leave her alone!"

His hand was raised to strike her, but Maurice caught it from behind. He was hampered by the candle he was holding, and Tom twisted away from him, ducked forward, and struck the girl across her face. She bowed double, rocking and moaning. I got between her and Tom. Maurice had him by both his arms now, and Nan was calling out, "Hol'im! Hol'im!" The aunt was laughing hysterically, and over it all the storm raged and the music played.

"What's wrong?" I asked, holding the girl's thin shaking shoulders. "What happened?"

"Lord Jesus—the light!" she squeaked. "The light them! You don' see them flick and flick? Them going *die*, I tell you! Lord preserve we all—"

76

"But, Nelly—listen to me—" I had to shake her to make her hear. "We have candles and lamps. There are lots down in the bottom kitchen—didn't they tell you?"

"Electric going leave us in darkness—we all going *die*—mercy on us—we all going—"

"No, Nelly." I made her look at me. Poor lovely thing—she was a mess, her stiffened hair on end, her blue eye makeup streaked with tears; the wonderful mouth was fishlike, wet and gasping. "Not darkness, Nelly," I said, "just different lights—candles and lamps."

"Candle can't keep out this dark—Lord Jesus!—no way! Electric only have the power—"

"Let her go, little fool!" Tom was free and pulled at my shoulder. Turning my head, I saw that his fit of temper was fading; he was panting still and there was sweat on his forehead, but the blind rage had left his eyes. Maurice stood close, but I motioned him away.

Nan too could see that the fit was over. She stood before him, her face carved in lines of distaste.

"You is a violent man, Mars Tom. Lord Jesus, only trouble!"

Tom ignored her; he was still spitting words at Nelly.

"Bloody little puss-face! City gal! Leave her, Liz—you won't make her understand. The only candle she ever saw was in a clip joint—'cheat-lighting'—right? 'Colorful,' eh, colored gal? Only wild country people use lamp and candle, eh? You *stuck,* gal—you shut in with the wild people now—have fe make do without you fancy city lighting. . . ."

Maurice had turned off the music, and Nan calmed Aunt Cissie and got her back to her chair. I managed to raise Nellie from the floor, talking to her quietly under Tom's shouting. She still trembled and cowered away from him.

"What going become of me?" she moaned. "Going die in the darkness far from me home—"

"Stop whining, woman! Is you boast to you friends about big house and white lover boy—is *you* chase *me*—"

"Shut up, Tom," Maurice cut in roughly. "Quit bully-

77

ing the girl. She's here now—who chased who you can work out another time." He put his arm round the narrow silky shoulders, and I stood back, fighting down a sudden hatred that was too like Tom's. "Hush up, Nelly—finish your crying now," said Maurice. "You foolish to run from your friends downstairs—they maybe tease a little but all good people. All right then, you can stop up here and make yourself useful—if that's okay with Miss Elizabeth." I nodded dumbly. "You can clear up the pantry for Miss Nan. Go wash you face now." He pushed her gently in the direction of the cloakroom.

"Don' lef me alone, Busha!" She clung to his arm. "Darkness will come and catch me." Tom's back was turned; he was pouring himself a drink.

"I'll go with her," I said. "The lights seem all right now, but let me take the candle just in case." Anything to stop her snuggling up to Maurice.

As I waited outside the lavatory for her, I studied myself in the looking glass over the basin and wondered if *I* was pretty. I turned away quickly; I was surprised at myself. It almost seemed I had fallen for Maurice, after all these years. He had become—or I had discovered that he was—extremely attractive. He's just a flirt, I told myself; I've met his sort. I've coped with Italians like that. But why so possessive then? Because we somehow belong to each other. Have we always?

Outside the cloakroom window, the roar of the wind through the bitterwood tree was like a crowd on its feet.

And Edward? Don't I belong to him? Yes. He's my destiny. And I've seen it now, Edward's marvelous world that I'll share. He's my future. So—this is just a little adventure along the way? It must be, I suppose. But somehow it didn't feel like that. For I didn't *feel* fickle. I felt alarmed.

Nelly took time repairing her makeup and her hairdo. I remarked that the lights seemed to be all right—no more flickering—but she did not want to talk. The fear in her eyes was slowly soothed away by the stroking finger-tips; lotions restored the tear-streaked slopes of the small pert face, roses bloomed in her cheeks, and shiny mauve lipstick was painted expertly on the lips. Catching a glimpse of myself lurking behind her, I wished I were more tanned, better groomed, more sensual-looking—especially that. I wanted, quite suddenly, to be luscious and curvy; to be myself, but as spectacular as Nelly, so that he would not look at her, would not let his hand linger on her satin hip as he comforted her. Almost furtively I put a comb through my hair and tucked in my shirt smoothly, carrying the fullness round to the back to make the most of my small breasts. This was the silk shirt I had chosen for Edward's arrival. Remembering guiltily, I sent up a brief prayer for him. Earlier I had felt my concentration sustaining him as he flew through the night. Now I prayed simply that he would be all right without that auxiliary lift.

"Okay?" I smiled brightly at Nelly, took the candlestick, and led the way out.

In the hall Nan had set out the lamps on the side table, with matches beside them. The aunt was in her chair. Tom had put on another record; he stood by it, listening and sipping his drink. He did not even raise his head as we came in. Maurice wasn't there.

Nelly sat down in a wicker chair, her handbag in her lap, her face serene.

"Busha gone for the sacking, Miss Liz," said Nan. "And I recall I leave the other big candelabra in the storeroom, fixing fresh candle into it." She turned to fetch them. Maurice appeared at the door with a pile of sacks.

"And there's the big stand-up torch in the office," he said.

"That's mine," said Tom. "I'll get that."

He moved toward the office door at the end of the hall, picking his way between obstacles. The lights dimmed again. The storm was so loud over the music that it took me a moment to register the flattened, trailing notes. Then the lights and the tune picked up, seeming somehow more bright, more hectic and shrill than before. It was a saxophone solo, I remember. Nelly was crouching, with her face in her hands. We all started forward again, like a film that had broken and been mended in mid-reel: Tom to the office, Nan to the store-room, Maurice carrying in the sacking, me toward Aunt Cissie, who had stood up, knocking her glass to the floor with a splintering crash. She squinted up at the ceiling, rigid with doom, crying:

"The Angel of Darkness is coming! He is drawing nigh!"

This time the lights did not flicker. They went out, and the music died.

Though I had always known this might happen, I had not tried to imagine it. The darkness was complete, the blackness of a nailed-up box from the inside; and the noise of the storm—I thought I was learning to endure it. I was wrong; for suddenly there was nothing else, and it was as frightening as—as being buried alive in my own coffin, and then that coffin thundered upon by the fists of a thousand screaming devils. How the house ached and shook, how every beam seemed to cry out in pain and fear—because of the dark. In the absence of light, life was insupportable.

All in that first black moment. Then I heard Nelly wailing, and the aunt screamed something—it sounded like "Hide!"—and I thought I heard or felt her fall. I crouched and reached out for her, and cut my hand on the broken glass. Then Maurice struck a match, found me, and pulled me toward him. He saw the blood, and the match went out. I found I was kneeling on the sacks he had dropped and he was holding my hand up, to slow the bleeding, I suppose. I felt his other arm supporting me, and I felt his breath and his wet hot mouth as he sucked the wound.

I felt it all very clearly: the pain, the rough sacking, my fear and my need, the impulse to comfort that brought

80

him to me, and the impulse—electrical? as swift as that—that traveled from my licked hand to my loins. And then I saw, brilliantly lit, his rough bowed head, my bleeding hand hiding his mouth, his eyes staring into mine, reading and reflecting the admission there.

But it was Tom's powerful cigarette lighter that froze the tableau, for him, for us, forever.

NINE O'CLOCK

MAYBE THAT WAS the moment in which my brother decided that Maurice had to die. I don't know, I only saw Tom's face fleetingly; but even in that turmoil I felt a shiver of pure terror that was nothing to do with the howling dark. The hatred I glimpsed was implacable. It would not pass with the hurricane nor disappear in the morning light, and I feared for Maurice.

He raised his head but did not let go of my hand. He picked a chip of glass from the tip of his tongue and said: "Give us some light here, then—it's quite a bad cut."

Then Nan came through the door, preceded by the glow from the big branching candlestick she was carrying. Tom's lighter snapped out, and with the brightness beyond I could no longer see either his face or Maurice's.

"Lord preserve us!—What happen?" Nan cried out, and real life started again. It had been only a few seconds of suspended time. Now I became aware of Nelly's shrill crying over the roar of the storm; of the smell of whisky and lighter fuel; of my aunt's absence. She was nowhere to be seen.

"Aunt Cissie!" I called out. "Nan! Tom! Is she all right?"

Nan put down the candelabra and hurried past us.

"Come, Miss Cissie dear—don't hide from Nan."

The aunt was crouching behind the wicker sofa, still clutching the prince. "The Angel has passed over," she announced flatly, in a clear newscast voice, rising to her full height. "It's all right, men—it was one of ours." I was so relieved I even laughed; I'd anticipated hysteria, or even a fainting fit—she hated the dark.

But Tom had not so much as turned his head to see.

"You can let go of her now," he said.

Maurice did not release the firm pressure on my upheld wrist.

"Here, Liz," he said, "take over and squeeze it here, hard. The bleeding's nearly stopped. I'll get the first-aid things from the office. And the torch, while I'm at it. Cheer up, Nelly girl." He patted her shoulder as he passed her. "See the candles? We'll have the electric torch soon as well. Keep it high, Liz."

"How touching!" said Tom—he almost spat the words—but Maurice was gone. "A human tourniquet, in two easy movements. And for my next, The Little Boy and the Dike, a heartwarming story of endurance, of holding on alone in the dark—well, not alone exactly—"

"Stop it, Tom!"—it was he who was hysterical. "Bring the light here and help me—there's glass everywhere."

Holding my left wrist hard, I struggled up off the sacks and got to my feet. The cut, I found, was long and jagged, in the heel of my hand, but it was clean and the bleeding had slowed to a trickle. Tom turned away to the side table to light a cigarette. "Jesus Christ, woman," he shouted at Nelly over his shoulder, "quit that bawling!" He lit the oil lamp and its soft radiance, so steady after candlelight, filled the room.

"That's better," I said, and felt my pulse settling. "Will you give me a drink, please." He poured me some whisky and handed it to me without a word or a look. Nelly was quiet. Nan was on her knees, picking up glass. "You need more light for that, Nan," I said. "There'll be splinters all over the place, underneath— Here's Maurice with the torch."

83

Aunt Cissie let out a wail of horror when she saw the broken glass. She drew up her knees and huddled in the chair. "The bright swords of the Philistines are all about us! See them glinting—there!—and there!" I hurried to calm her—foolishly, for my bloody hand scared her even more. "And look!" she cried. "The Prince is wounded!" In picking him up for her I had smeared him, and her alarm was not over me but the cardboard doll.

"Come, Aunt, it's only a spot of my blood—he's all right. Here, Nan, can you take over? Wipe this off and settle her, do—"

Maurice was down on his hands and knees. He said, "I've got all the glass up now, Miss Cissie. No more swords anywhere, see?" Nan was straightening out the aunt and wiping off the Prince. "Sweet Lord Jesus! Only trouble, always trouble." And I stood back, helpless, pressing a sodden handkerchief to my cut.

Nelly, hunched over in her chair with both arms wrapped tightly round her handbag as though it were her only hold on the bright sane world she had lost, looked round fearfully at the darkened room. Tom, holding his glass and watching, did nothing to help; but when Maurice opened the first-aid box he said sharply:

"Nan! You fix Mizz Liz's hand here, please. It must be bound up properly."

Nan's eyes rolled toward him in the light, surprised, exasperated—and then knowing. Maurice was an expert at treating anything ailing, from lizards to laboring mothers, and we were all well aware of this; we could see, moreover, that Nan's hands were already full. But Tom did not want Maurice bandaging my hand.

"Yes, Mars Tom—is I will do it. No, Miss Cissie, you must wait, and sit quiet till I come back."

Nan's first aid was, of course, just as expert, but rougher; I could remember—and I was sure Tom could—how as children we dreaded her ministrations. So often then they had seemed part of the punishment for some wrongdoing:

iodine was meant to hurt, because you shouldn't have been climbing that roof, or riding so fast on the road.

"It will have to probe, me dear," said Nan with suppressed glee, bustling and peering and getting out her spectacles. "It don't look good at all—is discolored, you see—too dark altogether."

"That's just the blood that's dried, Nan."

"Come! Don't pull away like that, Miss Liz! Rest still while I find my needlebook. . . ."

"Miss Nan, I think no foreign matter remains in it," said Maurice. He had swept the floor now and wiped up the pool of spilled drink; returning, he read my anguish from across the room. "You see, I got some glass out of it already." At this, Tom picked up the torch and strode off toward the pantry. "It only needs some iodine now, I think, to sterilize it. Miss Nan—?" She was freezing him over her spectacles. "Really, Miss Nan. I wouldn't be teaching my gran'ma to suck eggs, you know—not *me*, Miss Nan."

She melted a little; Maurice did not have much truck with deliberate charm, but when he put himself out he could be very persuasive.

"If the hand fester then is you guilty," she said darkly. "Smart Busha—know everything, like all the young people them," she muttered, and gave the cut a few brisk dabs with her swab. Soon she was absorbed in measuring and cutting lint and gauze and choosing a worthy bandage; she loved it all. "Hold still, Miss Liz—that's my good child. . . . Should rightly have a stitch into it—I don't want my Miss Liz having no disfigurement—hold still, me love—on her pretty hand. . . . And no smart Busha German can tell Miss Nan 'bout bandage. 'Glass take out of it already'—hunh! Is so *him* say . . ." and more, but she had two safety pins in her mouth. Maurice and I watched her and each other, across her winged bandanna. Once I looked over at the huddled figure of Nelly in the wicker chair, so still I thought she must be asleep. But her eyes

85

were on us. I wondered what she was making of it. Her careful makeup might, after all, have been for the handsome, kind young Busha.

I couldn't sort out my own feelings. I didn't want to; there would be time for that. Some seven years, as it has turned out. I was still tingling from the electric shock of that passionate yet practical gesture, the sudden contact that reached me in the fearful dark; and I felt my body was not just vulnerable but treacherous, responding to comfort with desire. Yet I smiled to myself (and he was smiling, with a streak of my blood on his chin) over his cool-headed handling of Tom. Pressing the racing pulse to slow the blood, eminently reasonable but—sweet Maurice —self-defeating. "The human tourniquet, Tom called you," I said across Nan's mumble.

"Must get that into my references," said Maurice, glancing down to hand Nan the scissors, and returning his eyes to mine.

"There's water driving in under the pantry door," said Tom abruptly, stepping out of the dark. "It needs some sacking, and it must be much worse on the weather side, especially upstairs."

"You'll have to do another round of inspection," I said. "I can't help much with this—" ("Hold still, Miss Liz!")

"Okay, Maurice," Tom said. "And take some nails as well."

"I've got to finish the drawing room first," said Maurice.

"Okay," said Tom, "but get on with it." He threw himself down on the wicker sofa and reached for his glass.

A sudden parrot call came from the great chair: "Tommy's turn to go! Tommy's turn to go!" The aunt's utterances always carried excellently, even in a storm.

Tom sat up and looked round. No one caught anyone's eye, and no one spoke. "Oh well—if that's what you people feel. Fine," he said. He didn't move. We were very busy, holding or snipping or putting things away in the battered Red Cross box. "After all, it's my house," he said. "I might

as well see it's done properly—since you're all so—" No
one agreed or disagreed, and the howling of the gale filled
the pauses and spoiled the punchline. He finished his
drink, stood up. and snatched the torch from the table.
Then Nan said:

"Have the storm lantern, Mars Tom; oil more plentiful
than battery." She went to light it. I looked up.

"Are there more batteries?" I asked.

"*Are* there, Nan?" asked Tom. "*You're* in charge of supplies, for God's sake."

"No, Mars Tom—don' come with that. I look after the
storeroom things them—and is true, as I tell Miss Liz, we
run low and due for a big shopping Friday. But battery—
never. Office business, like nail and wire and battery, is
for Mars Tom one to buy. Is Mars Tom one who know—
not Nan, no, sir. Never."

"I'll have a look," said Maurice, and took a candle with
him.

Nelly uncurled. She moved her chair nearer the light,
found an old magazine, and started flipping through it. I
envied her detachment. She seemed to accept the situation, adapting to it with the suppleness of a cat—safe and
uninvolved. It would be difficult to find ways to make her
useful if she could not venture out of the steady lamplight.
Since his outburst Tom had virtually ignored her. At least
she was calm—he was the jumpy one now. I turned to him.

"Not that we'll *need* the torch," I said; I felt morale was
at rock bottom. Yet our vigil had barely started, for it was
only nine-thirty, and the long stretch of the night was still
ahead. A line of poetry came into my head: *Finish Lady:
The bright day is done and we are for the dark. . . .*

Tom spoke again, rushing into the vacuum we all felt.

"Well, I don't know what the flap is about—I don't give
a damn *what* bloody light I have with me. And since it's
me who's doing the job—" He took the bag of nails, the
hammer, and the sacking, picked up the storm lantern,
and started up the stairs, and the swinging light made the

horned shadows rock crazily across the wall. He disappeared into the gloom, and then the glow of his lantern faded too and was gone.

I thought of what it would be like in the big upstairs rooms now, with only the small pool of light, and the storm leaning more heavily on the house and fingering through the cracks to get a hold; of how it felt to be ganged up on—as he saw it—left out, to go and eat worms. No. I was projecting myself there (Tom never let himself be humiliated) and in the terms of childhood. We had left that behind. Maurice, indeed, had always been older than his years; so much had been put upon him. And I'd changed, I knew, in my time away. Meanwhile, had Tom ever grown up? Physically, yes. But there were times when his mind seemed like nothing more than a deep stagnant pool reflecting his own face.

Now something was disturbing it; Maurice and I were no longer just his creatures, governed by his fickle love, competing for his favor. He'd lost his hold on us, it must appear to him; and yet, I thought, as I listened for his footsteps through the roaring of the storm, how wrong he was. I still doted on Tom—I was part of him; it was this, with Maurice's loyalty, that had forced us into an alliance years ago. No, I said to myself, Tom shouldn't be jealous.

(Like so many illusions, it sprang from the wish that everyone should be happy—so busy was I living my short life. So leisurely now, with nothing to watch but a fat fly bumbling about near a web.)

I heard him overhead and wondered if he was safe. If the chimney blew down and came through, if the bitterwood fell—

Then Maurice came back.

He had stuck his candle into the band of one of my father's old hats he had found, leaving his hands free for the paraphernalia he had collected. He was crowned with light, like some hero in a Florentine frieze. I couldn't see his face, but when Nelly clapped her hands like a child he pirouetted for her. He sounded triumphant:

"No batteries, but look—everything we need to make glims! Well, nearly. Miss Nan, how are we off for coconut oil?"

"Plenty coconut oil, and youself did tell me an abundance down the bottom store."

"Of course there is. *You* remember glims, Miss Nan? My father told me how they were used in the war when kerosene ran out—"

"Remember glims? Like it was yesterday, child. Remember glims, Miss Ciss?" They had assembled the coach and horses now and sat back admiring the effect as the aunt drew it gently to a halt in front of the royal palace.

"Trit trot trot . . ."

"Miss Cissie? Those little lights we used to make in the war—"

"We used to drive out in a coach and four," said the aunt.

"That's right, Aunt," I said. Actually it had been the old buggy from the stables.

"No kerosene, no gasoline," said Nan. "And glims. You remember the little lights we make then—little floating lights? She always think them so pretty. . . ."

"How do we make them?" I asked her. "Do we need bowls? Or jam jars?"

"Anything like that, Miss Liz; and a little piece of tin and four piece of cork and a hole with a bit of wick thread into it down into the oil, and then water beneath."

"You used to use the lids of cigarette tins—that right, Miss Nan?—back in the days when they used to come in tins."

"Not the lid—no, sir: too heavy. The piece of shiny tin *under* the lid—remove with can opener."

"Well, any used cans will be out on the rubbish heap," said Maurice, "but I found a sheet of stiff foil the master had for patching buckets and dustbins, and some shears—

89

it'll be quite tough to cut, but I'll do that bit, and you ladies must chop up these corks and tack them on. Hammer, three-eighths tacks. So now we need some rags that will do for wicks, and jars, and the coconut oil."

"*We*'ll find those," I said.

"And while you're getting them I'll go round this floor and check on cracks." He gathered up some sacking, and his illuminated hat disappeared in the direction of the schoolroom.

"Fancy making glim! Lord, Miss Lizzie, how history run round the other way and met up with you again! Remember now, Miss Ciss me dear, the little lights?"

"That young man had a halo," said Aunt Cissie rather crossly. "He must be very good."

"Oh, he is, Auntie," I said.

"Don' fool youself, child—that young Busha is not a saint—no, sir."

"I want a halo," said Aunt Cissie, querulous. "Why can't *I*—"

"Maybe, Aunt, if you're very good, he'll let you try it on and you can see yourself in the big looking glass. Are you going to set up Cinderella's kitchen now? Nan, you better stay here, and I'll find the jars and things."

"With that poor hand? No, Miss Liz. I fetch them now. You drink your bit of comfort and rest quiet awhile." We both looked toward Nelly, who had made no move since Maurice's entrance. "Come then, girl," Nan called, "come carry fe me." So I sat down by my aunt and cut up corks with Maurice's penknife—the one he used to peel our oranges with—while Aunt Clarissa popped her way round Cinderella's kitchen.

Nan and Nelly came in with a tray of jam jars and went back for the oil, and there was almost an atmosphere of harmony. But I felt restless. It was more oppressive now, for there was not even the music to compete with the storm's ranting. When they returned, I said I would find some material for the wicks; I left Nan supervising Nelly as she half filled the jars from the water jug—hurricanes make strange partnerships, I thought—and, my candle held high, I set off for the sewing room.

Passing along the tiled passage, far from windows and outside walls, the noise of the wind seemed far away; but I went through two more doors, came into the little cubbyhole next to the drawing room, and suddenly I was on the weather side.

My candle flattened in the draft. I put my hand round it and stood it on the floor where the big dresser gave it some protection. The broad top was glistening with water, wetting my hands as I gripped the edge to get a purchase on the stiff top drawer. I held my fingers to the light, and they were smeared with a thin green porridge. Now I could see it spraying through the cracks in the jalousies: a scum of emulsified vegetation from the maelstrom outside, lying on the window ledge like a puddle of green blood. The force of the wind scared me, and the room shook as its strength increased, each onslaught worse than the last; yet, each time, any greater force was unimaginable. And any sort of conclusion to such a progression—

I pulled the rag drawer down onto the floor and burrowed through it by the light of the candle. Fortunately, it was texture, not color, I was after—something to suck up the oil: capillary attraction, as Father had taught us, when the damp from our bathing shorts had mysteriously crept up our T-shirts. An old T-shirt would be just the thing; I found one, and a torn vest—Who on earth wore vests? I wondered. It could only have been shed and left behind by one of the English cousins. I wondered where Edward was now, and if the storm was beating on the plate-glass windows of the airport café. I wondered what Maurice was doing, and if he would be pleased with my assorted rags, and if he was thinking about me. Perhaps he was back in the hall. I pictured him bending over Nelly, instructing her in glim making, showing her the best way. . . .

It was difficult getting the drawer back with my bandaged hand, hurrying now, driven as much by my own

91

green-eyed monster as the one that panted at the window. When I had done, I held the candle high, sheltering it, and looked round. Nothing was really suffering from the filtering spray; the sewing machine was in its case, the faded gold sign of SINGER glinting through the spattered green. There was nothing I could do and little in there to come to harm. I went out, closing the door on the howling beast, and I wished I could feel more like a fearless white hunter. But *it* was free and wild, rattling *our* little cage.

Maurice opened the door as I reached the hall. He said, "I was coming to find you—catch you alone—" He took the candle from me, blew it out, and was pulling the door behind him, but we could hear Aunt Cissie calling me.

"I can't stay," I said, stepping past him. I could smell and feel him in the dark. His hands were on my waist, his mouth against my hair. But the light came through the strip of open doorway, my aunt called again, and I had to go.

"See me in my halo, Elizabeth!"

She was transformed. Father's floppy felt hat with the candle stuck in the band was now on her head, hiding the scraped-back hair and shading the mad popeyes. The light fell instead on her glittering beads and jewels; even the scrubby feather boa looked white and lush in the gentle glow. "Hold still, Miss Cissie—mind it don' fall and burn you," said Nan, hovering round her. Nelly sat at her table, cutting corks with Maurice's penknife, one manicured finger laid along the back of the blade. I wanted to take it from her. But Aunt Cissie called again.

"See me, Elizabeth, in my glory!"

"My, you do look good in a halo, Auntie!" I said. "Really lovely! And now you really are my sainted aunt! —straight out of one of those gorgeous gilded Christmas cards in your scrapbook."

"Now, Miss Cissie, you must take it off—you see, the candle burning down and might catch."

92

"I want a halo for Cinderella," said the aunt belligerently.

"Here, Miss Cissie, try this on her." Maurice had started cutting rafts for the glims. He took one of the tin circles across and carefully taped it behind the head of the cardboard figure. The aunt was enchanted, tilting it from side to side so that it flashed light.

Nan watched with pursed lips, intensely possessive about her charge.

"Mind you don't cut yourself on it, Miss Ciss, and then come running to Nan to make it better."

"It should be okay, Miss Nan," said Maurice. "I put some tape around the edge as well."

"Why don't we dress Cinderella properly and stand her here by the lamp so you can see her?" I said. "We want you to help us with the glims, you see, Auntie."

Nan was happier when she had the aunt back under her thumb, tearing the vest into wick-sized strips. She sat Nelly on a stool beside her, to roll the wicks. The girl was as compliant as she was calm; she did not even seem put out by the eccentric old lady. We blew out one lot of candles to save them; and Maurice and I sat at the side table, making tin rafts. The others had the lamp (and St. Cinders propped against it): two pools of light in the big dark room, and the storm howling outside.

"This is how it was when we were small," I said, "before the electricity. Cutting and gluing in the schoolroom while Nan sewed—or the drawing room; we had to be tidier there. But I used to be afraid of this room; no light from a lamp ever reached all the dark corners. And the horns moved when the light moved."

"I used to believe they came alive at night, after you told me that," said Maurice. "I always tried to get away home before dark so that I wouldn't see. But I still worried about you."

"Did you? And the buffalo really *did* look alive that morning you found the baby bat—remember? How something moved in the eye socket, and I said, 'It's watching! Its eyes are following us round!' You were very brave, we thought, climbing up and putting your hand in—"

"Only after Edward said, 'Don't be silly, it must be some small creature, like a bird.' He was always right, and I knew it."

We talked quite softly, heads close, handing and clipping and tacking. I didn't fear the storm now. The hall felt very solid after those minutes in the sewing room. It had no windows, just the two big doors, one each end, which usually stood open all day and were closed at night or when the rain was blowing in. There was a tall window, heavily boarded, at the top of the stairs, and we could hear the wind shake and suck at the shutters. But I did not even miss the music, with Maurice there.

He stood up and took a pile of rafts over to Nan. "I've made a hole for the wick, see—but tell me if it's too small." When he came back to the side table, he stood looking down at me.

"I ought to go up and help Tom, I suppose."

"Have a drink first and then go—you haven't stopped all evening."

He topped up my whisky and poured himself one. Then he sat down and leaned forward, cradling his glass. He was still wearing the dark red shirt, and his eyes were the color of whisky in the light.

"I love you, Liz," he said quietly.

"I must get that shirt for you," I said, getting up; "it's only over here—"

"And you know it," he said, pulling me down again. "Just drink your drink and look happy or old Nan will be over to see if I'm troubling you."

"You are," I said. "Have been all evening."

"That's nothing, sweetheart." He said it so differently from Tom: Tom's was a tough guy to his moll, but this was a tender, relishing sound. "You've been troubling me all my life. But I'm not going on about that—or the future, whatever it brings. It's now—between us: you feel it too—don't fool with me, Liz. God, I wish I could touch you."

He glanced across at Nan. Aunt Cissie was helping to roll the strips of vest into thin sausages, and Nan was feeding them through the punched tin. Nelly was out of sight beyond them on her low stool. Maurice reached for my hand below table level in the dark and laced his broad fingers between mine. "Bird in the hand," he said.

"A port in the storm?"

"That's right—and maybe I'm no more than that to you, Liz. But you can't pretend it isn't there, even if there's no future in it. For Chris' sake!—" he hissed, leaning toward me in the candlelight, his tawny-fringed eyes drawing me in like sea anemones to eat me alive. "And this is on top of the closeness we've had all our *lives*! It was all there, Liz—it's just caught fire, hasn't it? Admit it."

I could not think with his strong hand locked into mine, the fingers caressing, the warm weight of it on my knee. I felt again the treachery of my body, and now it was subduing my thoughts completely.

I struggled against it. "Edward—" I said. "He's coming here."

He did not stop caressing my hand; he reached out and put his rough right forefinger across my lips, just for a moment, and I closed my eyes at the power of the touch. "Yes, I know," he said softly, insistently. "But does he make you feel like *this*?"

I opened my eyes and drew my traitorous, collaborating hand away.

"Well—no, but he—"

"Look, Liz," said Maurice sternly, standing up and leaning over me, "you worship that character. When you've finished, come back and be loved by me." He softened again. "I know all about worship, my love. You can't live off it. You get hungry. And Lord am I hungry right now." He stood between me and the rest of the room and pulled me firmly to my feet. He stroked my neck slowly once, twice. I quite simply ached for him, and at last he kissed me—not long, not hard, but thoughtfully, absorbed, tasting, marking me for his own.

The hammering was above on the landing, not in my ears, and we both looked up to where my twin brother must be reinforcing the shutters to the top-veranda door. Then Maurice licked his lips and smiled. "Now I'll go and help," he said.

"Look at the fairy lights!" came the aunt's penetrating call. Nan had lit two of the glims and was carrying them toward us. One was sputtering; Maurice took it and held it up.

"They're good, aren't they?" he said. "But this one's wick is too near the water. A bit more oil—"

"And when the wick burn down it have to pull through again, I recall," said Nan.

"They're marvelous, Nan," I said. "They'll see us through the night." Maurice turned and looked at me, and the small flame between us fizzed in his irises. Then he took a candle and disappeared up the stairs. I heard him cross the landing and go into the spare rooms.

Suddenly the door to the passage opened. Tom came in.

"Goodness, you startled me!" I said. "I couldn't think who it was—I heard you upstairs a moment ago—"

"Ah! The hammering. Yes—well, I'm down here now." I felt that he was obscurely disappointed. "Where's Maurice then?" he asked, reaching for the whisky.

"He went upstairs to help you—we thought you were still up there."

He smiled fiendishly. "Aha!" he said, and I realized with a start of revulsion that he had meant us to. I looked at his feet. He had changed into his ancient, silent gym shoes. Chaperoned we might be but the noise and the gloom had created a new kind of privacy, one that my brother did not trust.

"Oh, Tom! For God's *sake*—" I said, angrily. But I was more alarmed, and by my own thoughtlessness: to dally with Maurice on a night like this and Tom in such a mood —when he could so easily have observed us. It seemed that

Maurice had melted my wits as well as the marrow in my bones.

I saw Maurice's light coming back down the stairs and turned away. "We've been very busy making these," I said loudly over my shoulder. "Come and see."

"Oh, there you are," said Maurice. "What do you think of the glims, then?"

"Fine. Better than nothing, certainly. Well done," Tom said grudgingly. "I see you've got Nelly working, at least."

"What about upstairs?" I asked. "Everything all right? A lot of water coming in?"

"No—pretty good on the whole." He threw himself back on the sofa. "The spare rooms are getting it, of course, but the shutters seem firm enough."

"I'm sorry I didn't get up sooner," said Maurice, and as I handed him his glass I was careful not to look up. "I've had another go at everything down here . . . the drawing room's the worst. And I wanted to get these lights made before the candles ran out—coconut oil is the one thing we've got in plenty."

"Shall we do without the candles, then?" I said. "They're burning down so quickly. We don't really need them now, do we?" Four glims were lighted and burning well.

"Okay," said Tom, "but we should keep the lamp going—for little Nell and Aunt Cissie's sake." His sudden thoughtfulness was no surprise: glimlight provided too much cover. But Nelly looked relieved about the lamp, I thought—though it was hard to read any real emotion in that flowerlike face.

The pretty brown girl bothered me no longer, I found. From behind her magazine, she watched Tom or Maurice, ignored by both. I turned away, took a glim, and went back to my chair beside the bookcase. It was a small gesture of independence from both of them; moreover, I wanted to be alone, and this was the nearest I could get to solitude. Here I was still within helping distance of my aunt, but too far from Tom's sofa to talk across the hubbub of the storm. Louder than wind or rain was the singing in my blood. I felt so violently alive, it was only with a conscious effort that I sat still. I picked up my year-old knitting.

Close by, the faded *Punch*es admonished me. I could not face them now. I felt more cut off from Edward than ever before in my life—even those long evenings when I played his favorite records and copied his drawings, trying to imagine (when I had calculated Greenwich Mean Time) what he might be doing at his English school. Not thinking of *me*—that I had accepted; *that* didn't cut me off. Only my own inability to think of him could ever separate us. But aren't I? I cried silently. I squeezed my eyes shut and conjured him. His face eluded me. I tried to put it together like an Identikit. Fair soft wavy hair. Light green eyes, with lashes—rather fair lashes. A slightly aquiline nose, thoroughbred nostrils—always pink from catarrh when he was small. The mouth was difficult; I could see it talking, but it would not stay still and be defined. Then it did—and it changed and became . . . I opened my eyes and picked up a stitch. Think of his voice. "Don't be silly, it must be some small creature, like a bird—" A well-delivered imitation of the clipped accents, but the singsong lilt gave the imagined speaker away.

He was sitting on a roll of matting near Aunt Cissie, leaning into the lamplight, mending the wire handle of the old storm lantern. His back was toward Tom, and he was facing me—only had to look up to meet my eyes across two yards. He did. And beyond his head Tom sipped his drink and smoked and watched me. I bent to my knitting. The hurricane roared and battered ceaselessly, numbing, isolating.

Tom got up, prowled about, and sat down again with a gun-sale catalog.

The night stretched ahead of us, behind us, round us, an immeasurable chaos. I could not imagine it ending; I couldn't even remember silence. Yet there seemed no hope of growing accustomed, being bored, sleeping through it, for its violence demanded attention. I was keyed up, five senses working overtime, no respite.

Watching, covertly, the brown hands in the lamplight bind and weave, I felt linked to them by a finer silver wire, my hands to his hands—the puppet master who could move my body so. And there were wires to my heart and lips and neck and thighs as well. Spider and fly. Fisherman —tight lines—fine sharp hooks into my tenderest parts. I was very conscious of the tautness, and when his eyes played me nearer the waiting net, the sharp tug in the guts, slow bleeding. If he decided it was internal mash-up I was suffering, I mused, would he kill me quick, with his machete? . . . and then was dismayed at the muddle of love and violence in my musing. It's just this night, I thought; I've got the storm mixed up with this thing between Maurice and me.

"Passion" seems a simpler way of putting it, now—but it's a word that only works in retrospect, just as some verbs are always intransitive. Not that I thought in words at all.

And now there are only words.

"Moonies are better than fairy lights. They stay still, you see." The aunt muttered and sang most of the time, but every now and then she would make some announcement in a piercing voice that even Tom could hear. Nelly's slanting glance slid over to her and back to her magazine.

"Is that right, Miss Ciss? Well, is you know best," Nan answered automatically, threading a needle. Then, rousing herself, "But come now, me dear, moonies is much harder to catch than glims—"

"You have to know how," the aunt said owlishly.

Moonies were what we called glowworms. Glowbeetles, really: they were hard and black and clicked about in your hand when you picked them up. Tom and I used to read with them under the bedclothes; two or three in a tumbler, five or six inside a handkerchief, we reckoned, produced a very acceptable wattage; in fact, you could read with a single moonie if you pointed it at each word in

99

turn. I glanced across at Tom, but he was observing the rise and fall of his silver bullets.

Suddenly he leaped to his feet. "Christ!" he said. "It's terrible without the music! Only wind and the sound of bats in the belfry—"

"Get your guitar," I said. He shook his head, and started pacing, as far as he could, up and down between the piles of obstacles.

If I could have some music, I thought—any music—to divert my mind from the roar of the wind and the rain, from the shudder of the windows and the creaking of the shutters, from my aching hand, from the hands weaving the silver wire, stroking my neck . . . I thought of Maurice and me—he must have been fifteen, and me fourteen—the day we discovered a strange piece of music together. The cousins had come and gone, I remember, and I was missing Edward badly. Maurice was whitewashing the passage that day, and he asked me to play him a tune. It was because I couldn't bear to sully Edward's *Tannhäuser* that I turned the record over. "This is called 'Liebestot,' " I said.

We were both mystified by the slow unfolding semitones. Maurice stood quite still; then he put down his brush, and we listened, right to the end.

"What's it *about*, Liz?"

"I don't know," I said. "*Liebe* is used in letters. 'My dear Stoat—' do you think?"

When we'd finished laughing at our joke, we took down the fat red book on opera that the cousins used, and we found and read the story of Tristan and Isolde; of King Mark, whom they deceived; of divided loyalty, of love and death. We played it through again. I think we'd both been aware of the passion and sensuality of the music without trying to define it. But Kobbé spelled it out. It was like eating an apple and suddenly seeing we were naked. Early the next morning I woke and heard the distant echo of those first six magic notes used as a whistling

cattle call, somewhere up on the ridge above the morning mist. . . .

"*Christ,* I need that record player—" said Tom, smashing down his glass on the tabletop. "We're going to fix the
generator—Maurice? What about earning your keep?"

"If you please," called the aunt, "I don't like any discussion of money. It's so common."

"Shut up, you silly old scarecrow! *I'm* talking. Maurice"
—standing squarely in front of him, intercepting our line
of vision—"get your things on, we're going to fix that
generator."

Maurice stood up and set the mended lantern on the
table.

"Look," he said, "you can't leave the women on their
own. And anyway it'd be madness to go out in this—
there'll be zinc sheets and slates flying about—"

"Well, of course, if you're *scared,* I'll go alone. I couldn't
care less, quite honestly, if that's—"

"Tom, be sensible," I said. I got up and went over to
them. "Tom, it's not a question of being scared, now; it's
too late to go out there."

"And whose bloody side are *you* on then? What's going
on here, I'd like to know—?"

Maurice said, "Nothing's going on." (That's what
Tristan said to King Mark, I thought.)

"Tom," I said, pleading. "Don't go. I can't let you,
Tom—it's too dangerous."

"And whose skin are you so worried about, sweetheart?"
he said, his voice suddenly low and cool again, his fierce
eyes hooded. Now he was really angry; I knew the signs.
His tone would have seemed almost conversational if he
had not been gripping my upper arm, his nails digging
in. I feared this quiet fury more than his explosions:
banked down, it was far longer lasting.

"Oh, *Tom*—" I put my arms round his neck. "Both
of you, of course—"

"Well, and aren't you the lucky one!" he said, detaching me coldly. "An *embarras de richesses*, as Cousin Edward would say—but you'll have to wait a bit longer for *him*. Until Doomsday if he's fool enough to fly in this. Come on, Maurice—*if* you're coming. And don't look at *her* for an answer, Jerry-boy—" Again he cut off Maurice, forcing a confrontation. "Are you going with me?—or are you scared?"

But Maurice didn't answer. There was a new sound reaching us from outside, through the rage of the storm. We all heard it and lifted our heads, listening. It was a loud cry, the cry of many voices.

TEN O'CLOCK

THE SOUND came again, ragged, multiple, whipped away by the wind before words could form. Aunt Clarissa fluttered up, uttering sharp breathless squawks of hysterical laughter, shedding feathers round her; she took refuge behind the chair, her hands clutching the carved wood as if it were some high perch, and only the bristling white boa and the startled eyes were visible above.

Nan did not go to her. She was standing tall and rigid with horror. "Duppy call!" she whispered, and I only heard because I was beside her; then loud and clear: "We hear you, Dead People! Leave us now and rest in peace!" Nelly threw herself onto the floor and blocked her ears.

The crying reached us again, nearer and stronger. It seemed to come from the veranda outside the big front door; less animal, more human, now, and a broken-backed, half-formed word emerged: "Shel-ter!" or maybe "Help-us!" And then loud knocking.

"That's no duppy," said Maurice. He went over to the door, but Nan rushed and clung on to his arm.

"Don't open, Busha! Evil Spirit can cry and knock, you know."

"Hush!" said Maurice pressing his head against the

wood. The knocking again, rapid and desperate, and the calling voices, one above the rest: "Shelter—beg shelter!"

"That sounds like Lord Penn from across the Line," said Maurice, "and there are women too. I'm letting them in."

"What, in *here*? But it sounds like a whole crowd." Tom had to shout above the hammering and calling and the roaring of the wind.

"You *can't* turn them away, Tom," I yelled.

"They can go round to the bottom kitchen."

"Whatever you do you've got to let them in here now," said Maurice unbolting one side of the door. "Come, put your shoulder to this or it'll blow right open. Nan, shield the light!—never mind about the glims. Let's have the torch on, quick."

Nan held the oil lamp firm; I switched on the big torch and set it on the floor, and joined Tom on one side of the great double doors. Then Maurice lifted the iron bar from its slots; the weight of the storm leaned on us all three, and we shouldered it and eased our side ajar. A torrent of rain and leaves and whipping twigs tore past us.

The first man fell through the door and into the beam of the torch. The next came in on hands and knees; then two women—we only knew by their high wailing—slithered through together and fell in a heap. I pulled them firmly to one side—it was easy enough now with the floor awash—then I crossed through the wedge of wind and water to reach the protection of the closed wing on the other side, where I would be able to grab hold of the fugitives as they came and make room for the next. As I did I had a glimpse of the world outside the house.

I saw it as it must have been in the Beginning, when light moved upon the face of the waters, and the darkness comprehended it not. Enough faint radiance came through the careering clouds to show how fast they moved. That was the sky; and the land was part of it, only the texture was coarser lower down, where the dregs of chaos were stirred. A huge onslaught of wind came upon us, and what actually sped past, at close quarters, along the length of the veranda, was a glittering wall of chrome and green like a phantom express train. Out of it, as into a different dimension, crawled the shelterers. They humped and slithered up over the top of the steps and across the flagstones to the door.

It was only a glimpse, recollected in this enforced tranquility, a brief vision like a gap between two tunnels. Then I was behind the solid wing of the other door, helping with bundles, more wet bodies, a baby, some chickens, a last crawling, falling fugitive; and then we forced the door shut and barred it. It was still again.

Outside, the wind and rain screamed—venomous, cheated; a pack of demented Furies. In the hall we lit the candles and the glims that had blown out, and looked around us. Pools of water, twigs and leaves, even small branches, and the sluggish scrum of huddled bodies. Gradually they uncurled and began to peer about. Panting and wailing gave way to words. We stood back to let them recover, nine or ten adults, as far as I could see, and one baby. Slowly they sorted and settled themselves on rolls of matting, or crouching on their haunches, picking through their scattered wet possessions, talking a little, breathing more evenly again.

"We can't move them on, Tom," I said. I glanced round at the aunt behind her chair; Nelly had crawled over and taken cover beside her, still clutching the handbag. "There's room for them in here." I looked from him to them. White and dry, wet and black. Meaningless contrasts. Helper and helpless. "Let them stay."

He nodded, and stepped over some bundles to the nearest of them.

"You like a dry cigarette now? Pass them around."

There was a little animation at this—smiling and nodding, and match flames lighting up intent faces. It had been a perfect gesture, and for a moment my twin brother was gentle and handsome: the "before" picture of the young Lucifer, Jehovah's pet.

105

"I'm going to brew up some tea, Miss Liz," said Nan. She had coaxed the aunt back to her chair and given her two jelly babies from the sweet jar to calm her: one was tucked into her cheek, the other was having a ride in the coach. "If you could work the Primus stove for me, Miss Liz." Nan did not trust the Primus. "And you, girl—you can help carry." Nelly made a face, but got up and followed. We took a candle—glims do not travel well—and went out to the pantry.

When we returned with a big enamel can of tea, Maurice was squatting down by two of the men, talking to them. He stood up and came to help us.

"Can I mix a shot of rum into this?" he asked. "I think they need it. They've come from over the Line. All their homes have gone, and the Big House was the nearest shelter—quite a journey on a night like this. One of them is hurt—caught by a falling tree."

The Line was the northern boundary of the property. There, beyond the very English-looking (my mother said) dry-stone wall, the small holdings started and straggled as far as New Bethlehem and beyond. They had been wrested from the bush, as originally our farm had, by dint of fencing and felling and clearing over the years. Each piece of cultivation, each family's ground, supported that family, with some to spare for selling on market day in Anchovy, or distant rich Montego Bay, twenty miles away. Sometimes they made extra doing piecework for Tom, and this is how Maurice came to know one of them, Lord Penn.

(Now I remembered him: he was the one who had been christened Penelope. Parson Sanguinetti's predecessor, a notoriously vague, cultivated man, was asked for suggestions before the happy event, and offered "Ambrose or Penelope." It only came clear after the actual christening, when Penelope had been given his name, that his parents thought "Ambrose" must be feminine, short perhaps for "Ambrosia"; and the preacher of course hadn't known the sex of the baby in his arms—"Who nameth this child?"

106

So my father stepped in and saved the day with a glowing account of the career of William Penn; and the family added "Lord," more as an intensive adjective, just to make sure; but his name on census papers was still Penelope. A big man, now, stooping with the weight of huge bunched muscles, he would have been a surprise to Ulysses.)

"What about their children?" I asked. "I wondered why there was only that baby."

"They were advised to leave them all at the school-house in Bethlehem," said Maurice. "It's stone, you know, and right next to the church where a lot of people will be spending the night. But for this lot, the Big House was closer—the hurricane has probably done much more damage where they've come from than further on, towards Sweetwater and Maggotty. They're just a handful of unlucky ones—they joined forces when they found themselves without a roof—not a family, you see—well, a man and his mother over there, and a pair of brothers; but mostly not knowing where their families are."

"No wonder they look so lost, poor souls," I said. "But at least they won't be worried over their children. I'm going to get some blankets from upstairs."

"Let Nan go."

"No—she's got enough to do, brewing up, and keeping an eye on Aunt Cissie," I said. "What's more, as the aunt would say, It's Lizzie's turn to go."

He made me take the storm lantern he had mended. He lit it for me, and came as far as the back stairs. "Tom is busy controlling the rum bottle," he said, and took me in his arms.

"I must go," I said with my remaining breath.

"Well, this should keep you going," he said.

"I must go," I said. "They need warming up more than I do."

The back stairs were narrow and steep, a friendly white tunnel that had seemed so huge and high when I was small. Starting up it at last, weak-legged and dizzy, I was glad of an errand that would give me time to cool down. The stairs led to the nursery wing, and on the landing there was the big linen chest.

Up here, the storm was alarmingly close. I took out a stack of folded blankets—the thin, mealy, striped ones I remembered from those nursery days—and two tartan rugs we used for picnics. I could carry them all, balanced precariously, or make two trips. The wind's force seemed to bow the shutters above me: could it still be getting stronger? I wondered, and decided to take them all at once. But the back stairs were clearly too narrow and steep for such a load, and I did not want to throw them down, for there were unexpected pools of water everywhere now. So I set off through the dressing rooms and spare rooms toward the front stairs, deliberately choosing the weather side in order to check on the windows.

It was more frightening than I had expected. I had not heard before just how terribly the main roof groaned under the onslaught, nor how the driving rain roared, pounding against the windows like surf. Indeed, it was more like sea than air out there; Poor old tub, I thought, God bless her and all who sail in her. I felt the blankets slipping and stopped to secure my hold, letting the lantern, hooked up in one finger, stand down for a moment on the broad sill. As I did, there was a deafening crash against the window—so close that I lurched backward—and a loud splintering of breaking glass. A high-flying branch of some size must have been blown against it. The wind screamed in through the gap, whistling between the shutters; and the lantern flame flapped wildly and went out.

Instantly I was thrust back and down into the worst of my childhood fears: I was alone in the dark. And, as then—when once on the big staircase, watched by the horned heads, my candle had died—I was paralyzed with fright, and could neither go on nor go back. I felt like dropping the blankets on the floor and burying my head in them.

Then something brushed against my shoulder and there

was a sharp tap and then another against the glass close beside me. The indescribable horror of something trying to get in at an upstairs window turned me to ice. Again the soft touch on my shoulder.

I let the blankets go as I hit out at it wildly. I found myself clutching the blinds cord with its wooden acorn, swinging in the strong draft. I knelt down and gathered up my load, feeling blindly for it, and made myself reach out for the lantern—concentrating on the image of Maurice's hands binding the wire loop of the handle, remembering his face as he bent to light it for me. I hooked it back on my finger and set off slowly, making my way through the hideous roaring dark, in the direction of the landing.

The storm filled my head. It breathed down my neck. A shape moved somewhere ahead of me in the blackness, and I stopped. It stopped. Then I saw a glow; the door was open, and the light in the hall below filtered through to me faintly round the intervening corners. And when I had passed the wardrobe looking glass, I came out at last onto the wide landing. Someone had reached the top of the stairs and shone the torch on me. It was Tom.

"I thought I heard a crash," he said. "Are you all right?" He took the rugs from me and tossed them to the floor, and held me tight. "You're not allowed to leave me!" he whispered fiercely.

"I was only getting these blankets—" I said, coming out of my nightmare.

He laughed and said, "Yes, well, just let's keep it that way," and he let me go, and together we carried down the tumbled heap. Now that I think about it, that was the last time I went down the stairs. As things are with me, I suppose I am too weak even to try.

The hall was a strange sight from above. There were the two big rings of light from the branching candlestick and the oil lamp, and a cluster of glims on the side table where Nan was ladling soup into mugs. In the gloom beyond, inseparable from the jagged reefs of furniture and flotsam of sacks and bundles and clothing spread out to dry, crowded the huddled survivors of the wreck. The light glinted back from eyes and teeth and bottles, from a tin mug, and a couple of machetes by the door.

I could see they were talking more now, mostly among themselves. They answered Tom's or Maurice's questions, and accepted soup and bread from Nan, with a few mumbled words. But mostly they passed the dark bottles, stoppered with newspaper bungs, from hand to hand, uncorking and tilting them to their lips, without comment. I found it strangely oppressive to have a silent crouching beast with many eyes watching us from the border of our lighted camp.

Thinking the blankets might be an excuse for contact, I went over with them, but Nan took them from me and set down the pile on the edge of the encampment. The watching beast heaved and shifted and rippled as it digested them.

"Let them be, Miss Liz," said Nan, taking my arm and turning me away. "It don't do to busy with people in trouble. Just give and turn you back—them feel better this way."

I went over to Maurice, who was pulling the glim wicks through with a pair of pliers. Nelly leaned against the table, watching. She seemed to have transferred her attentions entirely to Maurice now, and I saw that rare phenomenon, feline devotion, in the slanting eyes. I stood near him, on the other side, and experienced again that sudden warmth. I did not need to touch him—just to see him, to be close to him. Perhaps it is Time's proverbial healing that nowadays I cannot summon his image at will, but the cure is sabotaged by dreams that wake my sleeping blood.

He only glanced up from his work, but his eyes took in the whole of me. His eyes are better than Edward's, I thought, and realized with a shock that I had not thought of Edward for a long time. Earlier I had felt not only excitement over his coming, but a sort of responsibility to guide him through the storm. How would he manage without me?

"You all right?" asked Maurice softly, under the noise of the tempest. "Seemed long without you—Tom or no Tom, I nearly came up to help."

"Might have taken even longer—"

I saw him smile, intent on his task; his tongue slid along his upper lip. Beyond him Nelly shifted her stance. She could see his face but not catch our words. I raised my voice a little. "I was fine," I said. "Just a bit scary up there—a branch bust into the window near me and gave me a start. The gale force must be quite something to carry that size— Everything all right down here?"

"Pretty quiet."

"It's almost as though they're in shock, isn't it?"

"Well, a lot has happened to them, you know, Liz. Just getting up here must have been a nightmare—and then they wake and find themselves in all this splendor."

"Splendor?"

Nelly had drifted away, back to her magazine and her stool beside Aunt Cissie.

"It is to them. It's like Buckingham Palace for luxury and, say, Westminster Abbey for size, in their eyes—not that I've ever seen either. They'll relax when they've got used to it, and then, I expect, they'll sleep."

"I shouldn't think anyone could sleep tonight," I said.

"Sleeping would be a waste of time for me," he said, very absorbed in trimming a stubborn wick; then abruptly he raised his head and looked into my eyes with such a violence of love that I felt it hit me like the heat from a furnace door. He bent over his work again, his fingers glistening with oil. "And I don't think," he went on, almost to himself, "that watching over your slumbers would be enough for me now."

"Hey, Maurice!" said Tom roughly, coming up behind us. "Answer this one: if *they* can travel a mile under these conditions, why can't *we* walk a couple of hundred yards

111

and back? It's not as if our helpless womenfolk are still without company; they've seven strong men to guard them —strong enough to get here—and three other women."

"Fair enough. But remember, there are more hazards in crossing a stable yard than in making your way across pasture or through bush. Until they came near the house, there was no business of flying zinc sheets or slates or electric cables. Getting down to the generator, you're going into the thick of it, and your chances of—"

"Is why dem call you 'poor white,' eh, boy?" said Tom, broadening his accent. "Is 'poor yaller' sweet you better! And what Miss Nelly going t'ink of big boas'y Busha when she see—"

"Tom! Maurice!" I said fiercely. "For God's sake, don't quarrel now—we'll only *survive* together. And what d'you think all these people are going to make of you two bickering? You've *got* to stay calm and keep their confidence in you—don't you see that?"

"Oh, they can't hear—any more than we can hear them," growled Tom.

"But they can *see* you, Tom, you're in the limelight You've *got* to behave."

He put his hands into his pockets and lounged elaborately against the table. " 'The young master caught in a rare moment of relaxation in the hall of his gracious home' . . . That better, sweetheart? Now, as I was saying, Maurice old chum"—he was doing his White Slug voice now, at once clipped and fruity—"what about the blooday generatah?"

"I'll go with you," said Maurice.

And then I realized that they would; I couldn't stop them.

"But first," Maurice went on, "I'm going to take the woman with the baby, and Nelly, down to the bottom kitchen. If we can still move about in this, I reckon, they can manage the short distance along the back veranda— though there wouldn't be room for all of them down there. Yes," he turned to me, "Nelly would like to go back, she says; she's got used to the funny lighting. And there's little joy for her here. So—"

Still I argued, but nothing I said would dissuade them from going. Not that there was much to say; I had to be very careful with Tom, for any concern on my part would be seen as fear for Maurice.

So I tried to put a brave face on it. I wrapped the baby in a blanket, and I was sorry to see it go; as with the dogs, I had rather looked forward to cosseting and diverting it through the long waiting hours, cooking up something pappy for it, being allowed to feed it on my knee. But it would be safer down below. I provided the mother with oilskins. Nelly shrouded herself under the black water-proofs in which she had arrived.

Maurice was waiting in the pantry. He pulled away the sacking and opened the door. Even on the lee side, the wind and rain, spiked with harsh shreds of vegetation, smote our faces. When Nelly stepped out into it, the mackintosh, its sleeves flapping like a spaniel's ears, ripped out of her clutching fingers and vanished. She squealed with fear, but Maurice did not let her stop. The last I saw of her she was huddling inside his yellow oilskin with him as they ran, heads down, behind the mother and baby, toward the bottom kitchen.

Tom reached past me and slammed the door shut.

"Ever so cozy they looked," he said, smiling happily and drying my face with a tea towel. I said nothing, nor did I resist. Torn as I was by the sight of Nelly enfolded—and at that moment I would gladly have given away a whole night's shelter for five minutes alone in the storm with Maurice—I did not want to ruffle Tom in any way. On the contrary, I should be pleased to have a moment's quiet with him. Firmly I dismissed the enviously imagined warmth, the smell of the familiar shirt, the brown neck and protecting arms—my new world—and concentrated on my brother.

113

"Tom," I said—I would try once more—"*must* you go down to the generator? We're all right as we are, with extra lights now and enough food—"

Tom had his back to me. He was hanging the towel meticulously on the rail, smoothing and straightening it. He seemed not to be listening.

"Please, Tom," I said, touching his shoulder.

He turned round and his eyes were extraordinarily bright, glittering with suppressed excitement, almost amusement.

"Jobs for the boys! Jobs for the boys!" he called flatly, in Aunt Cissie's announcing manner. For a hideous instant I thought of inherited madness. "Oh, Liz—I'm just *bored*!" he said with a sudden radiant smile, which switched over my shoulder to embrace Maurice as he burst in through the door. He leaned back against it, panting and wet, and I reached out for the towel. But Tom caught my wrist.

His smile, no less broad, was fixed and bright.

"Well done, Maurice! Noble stuff. But I expect little Nell helped keep out the cold. . . ."

Maurice looked at me—standing there by the sink, still anchored by my brother's bullying grip—and the tawny eyes told me everything that he could not say. Tom observed. His fingers tightened cruelly.

I twisted round to face him, trying to short-circuit the dangerous current; and I heard my own voice, low and very businesslike, offering him my heart for supper.

"Why not let one of the others go down with him, Tom? Why should you have to risk your neck? You don't *both* need to go—I mean, Maurice knows how to fix the engine, don't you, Maurice?" I half turned, but Tom had both my wrists now and pulled me close to his chest.

"Didn't hear me the first time, did you, sweetheart?" he hissed. "I'm bored to death. I wouldn't miss this for anything."

"Stop it, Tom!" I cried out. "My hand—"

Maurice stepped over and took Tom's arm, but not before my twisted wrists had forced me to my knees.

"Poor Lizzie!" Tom whined. "Of course—the poor cut hand! Didn't Superman kiss it quite better then? Beg . . . beg!"

Maurice jerked him backward.

"Go on—*beg*!" he yelled. " 'Please, Tom, don't make Maurice go.' Go on—that's what you *wanted* to say."

"Oh, come on, Tom man," said Maurice roughly, avoiding my eyes. "Let's get moving. Sooner the better— it's blowing worse all the time you're messing about in here."

"I'm right there with you!" said Tom, following him through the door. "Just try and stop me." And he blew me a kiss.

Oilskins were in short supply now. "You have this," said Maurice. "I'm happier with my old jerkin." Looking cheerful for the watching company in the hall, I helped Tom into the yellow waterproof. Maurice borrowed one of the machetes in case they had to hack their way through to the engine house—by now there would be trees and creepers down everywhere—and Tom went into the office to collect the tools they would need.

For precious seconds I clung to Maurice in the darkness of the passage. He was leaving me so suddenly, and I felt, for some reason, that it was momentous, and I was unprepared.

"Take care and come back," I whispered.

"I will, I promise," he said, and kissed me.

Tom was ready with the torch by the big door, and three men unbarred it and held it for them. It would be safer to stay on the weather side of the house as long as they could, since a hurricane made any building a heap of potential missiles. They stepped into the slipstream, staggered, ducked out into the roaring dark, and were gone. The door was fastened back, the great iron bar put across.

And then began the most terrible waiting of all.

Even now, long after, in the turret, I nearly could not bring myself to write of it. I have put it off for days, wasting precious passing time. (At first I thought that writing would kill time. I still do—especially in those long hot afternoons when it seems to stop altogether. But sometimes—increasingly—that frantic whisper pierces through my head: *Just how long do you think you have?*)

Now I must do it. I must be clear and precise and orderly, about facts, about sensations.

I sat by my aunt and knitted like a blind machine, trying to feel nothing except the wool creeping through my fingers and slotting between the needle points, programmed to distinguish only purl and plain. The aunt had got round to the ugly sisters, one fat and one thin, whom for some reason she called Nelson and Eddy.

"Don't you mean Abbott and Costello, Auntie?" I said once, and even my voice was metallic, cutting brightly through the noise.

"No, dear," she said quite sharply. "A singing couple. You can always tell by the headdresses." The tone was crushing; I turned back to my knitting. It was ten-thirty. Only ten-thirty.

What had happened to me? Was this being in love? But that was for Edward—I thought. Since the age of twelve I had always considered I was properly in love. It was the dawn of sensibility; until then I was as unconscious, as unthinking, as an animal—fully aware, but lacking the powers of association and reflection. My amazement was at the beauty round me; it only struck me then because I tried to find words for it. Edward it was who named, defined, compared the elements of my wild world; and the point at which I decided I was in love coincided with my own need to communicate.

To begin with, it was simply a feeling that I would burst if I couldn't hold on to the sunset—keep it *somehow*; by describing it, like painting it, I might make it mine, perpetuate it a little. For seeing Beauty was also seeing that it would pass—Parson's aphorism cut both ways. Poetry helped—it had caught and held the passing moment—and taught, as some music did, how to accept and endure the "dying of the light."

If in the midst of this delicate state, balanced between destruction and elation, hell and heaven, you hear someone say, "I know exactly how you feel"; and if he takes your hand, leads you into the chaos, passes you the clue he holds, shows you some pattern in the whirling particles, and says, "Isn't it marvelous?"—you'll fall in love with him. Edward, pale, bookish, catarrh-ridden, had done this for me. Not that he ever bared his soul; he had come through that emotional awakening, had suppressed and channeled it (or he would not have survived an English public school), had reduced it to an acceptable formula. Somehow he understood my state, while being neither female nor wild, and—amazingly—took pains to bring some order to it.

I still think that if life had gone on Edward and I would have married. Yet even now I cannot capture and define—as he had taught me to do—Edward the Husband, or Fiancé. Or Lover. The grown-up cousin of my dreams I found when I went to England in no way disappointed me, of that I am sure. (I might have disappointed him. It was impossible to know his thoughts, but I believe he found me prettier and fairly amusing, a bit brash.) If anything he was too perfect: clever, gentle, humorous—rather abstrusely—admired (a leader among his Cambridge friends), elusive. I did not wish it otherwise. If he had come down to my level, I might have been disillusioned. How I idolized him, man and boy.

But what hope had an idol against Maurice?

Waiting in the storm, my mechanical hands alone moving, my thoughts racing, I tried to make sense, work out lists of their virtues, subtract one from the other; and so, choose. What didn't make sense was this new turmoil that threatened to overwhelm my neat double-entry columns. Maurice was very sure of himself—it was the most remarkable difference in him after a year apart—but especially when he said, "Does Edward make you feel *like this?*"

Even the remembered words, in his absence, worked like a powerful drug. For when I let myself think about him, I forgot the gloomy crowded room, the roar of wind and rain, the needs of my companions, my own lurid fears. I sat quite still and closed my eyes, and let the lingering warmth lap over me, annihilating reason; a rising tide carrying me hopelessly out into a broad sunlit sea. . . .

I got up, knocking my knitting onto the floor and startling the aunt. Reality, responsibility, danger rushed in on me. Tom and Maurice had been gone fifteen minutes.

The shelterers, it seemed, had started to accept their surroundings. Two were standing up, stretching their legs, looking around them at the horned heads, pointing out the buffalo over the door. Some were stacking up their sacks and bundles to provide more room, while others were making the wounded man more comfortable with blankets and cushions.

I saw Nan returning from the downstairs cloakroom with the elder of the two remaining women; then others took their turn.

"Miss Liz, I just going to look at the man hurt him leg, and dress it a little. Please if I can take the candle them— is better light I need in this darkness."

"Of course, Nan," I said. "Could I hold it for you and help at all?"

"The man might shy, Miss Liz, to expose him mash foot to pretty young lady like yourself—ugly old brown woman don't trouble him so much."

But I could see how much more Nan was than that. When she walked in among them, they treated her with a respect that amounted to awe. The wounded man even tried to stand when she approached. Moreover, I could see that they viewed the aunt with something akin to fear. They would start up in alarm when she let out one of her piercing calls, and an old man furtively crossed himself. Her newest amusement was to hold St. Cinderella close to the lamp and watch the dancing butterfly of light reflected from her tin halo flitter round the room. The shelterers observed in silence, but when she started playing the bright spot over them, they cried out and took cover in their blankets, and Aunt Clarissa contributed a wild giggle to the confusion.

"Aunt!" I said, hurrying over. "Don't do that! Look, let's pretend that you have to shine it on the big looking glass only, everywhere else is out of bounds."

She liked this, and when I showed her how she was bouncing a second butterfly back onto ourselves and across the dark bookcase, she was quite entranced. "Only on the looking glass, now, Auntie dear, or you shall have to drape her with your handkerchief like a naughty parakeet."

Turning away from her, I listened intently to the tempest outside, and thought of Maurice and Tom. I found, as I had so often, that however hard I tried, I couldn't catch the tumult at a moment of increase; yet I was well aware that its force was growing steadily, and that we had no scale to mark it by or estimate how far it still might go. I remembered the first great buffet, when Nan and I were in the storeroom, four hours ago. Had it reached its peak? Could the house—could our minds—survive another four?

Lord Penn was waiting his turn for the lavatory; I went up to him and asked if there was anything more I could do for him and his companions.

"Thanks, Miss Liz—we shaping up pretty good—excepting only one man come without him teeth—can't even bite crust—so him feel hungry. If you have a little cornmeal and cowmilk, now, marm, is what he favor best—keep asking for it. Is a bit simple in him head, you know."

Grateful to have something practical to do, I took a glim

119

to the storeroom to look for meal. The worst thing about this time-killing, I found, was the helplessness; we had done all we could, and now it was simply a question of seeing who won, the house or the storm.

That, I supposed, was what Tom couldn't endure. Usually he was only too glad of a rainy day to sit and read, to drink and play cards, but here there was no relaxing—every time the wind reached screaming pitch, the note seemed higher, the pounding of the driven rain more fierce. Mountainous wave after wave kept breaking on the old house, and we would lift our eyes instinctively, listening. No wonder even Maurice had taken refuge in any small job he could lay his hands on.

Me, for example? I busied myself, measuring out a cupful of milk, bringing it to the boil on the Primus stove, pouring it from jug to cup and back again to cool it. No, I thought—or rather, felt—Maurice wasn't simply diverting himself with me. Or I with him? *Was* he no more than a port in a storm? Or the doomed romance on the sinking ship? My racing blood might be just adrenaline, I told myself sternly. Edward had explained about crises and adrenaline: it had come up when he was holding forth on the war poets. "Doesn't just take you over the top and into battle, you see, Eliza, but sharpens your vision quite remarkably. Think of the details of flowers, every rut in the mud so clear. Yes, and the other senses, no doubt. The smell of cordite, the roughness of serge—"

Or of a coarse damp shirt, and smell of skin and tawny hair, the softness after stubble of the inner lip . . . But all so quick—moving so fast—instinctive, direct, like animals, at the threat of extinction.

Edward could have explained it all, no doubt. He was so good at that. With Maurice, explanations came too late. He touched, and caressed, made alive; and words died.

I stirred the fine cornmeal into the cup and carried it in. Lord Penn took it from me and passed it over to the shy toothless man.

"Him say thanks, Miss Liz. Look, I have two dry ciga-rette lef' inna me pouch. Make I light up one fe you. . . . There now." He made room for me on the roll of matting.

"You think it's still getting worse, Lord Penn?" I asked. "How long before it eases a little?"

"The good Lord knows, missis, and Him alone. Could maybe slack off when morning come. But you know what them say: you can't hurry hurricane. Mus' crouch down and lef' him take him time." And I nodded as stoically as I knew how.

Round about us, people were discussing a "Great Light."

"What was that?" I asked, "the Great Light they are talking of?"

"Them refer to one big light we see as we come."

"And what was it, do you know?"

"Please, missis," the older woman joined in eagerly, moving closer to make herself heard. "No one know, please'm. And some people tell how them hear a bang, like when them blasting roadwork—but I never hear it at all, with storm and present trouble and rain and every*t'ing*."

Other voices were raised now over snatches of a running argument ("Is bamboo burn, me dear—" "Bamboo clump can fire off same way, bang!").

"Where was it?" I asked. "Could you see?"

"Couldn' rightly tell, 'm—some say is over the hill, some say is far off by Rookoom."

"And what did you see? Was it like a fire? Or like lightning?"

"Is hard to say, Miss Liz," said Lord Penn. "We cross-ing the pasture, heading fe Big House, and lift up our eyes and see Great Light—"

("Is bamboo, man, I tell you—")

"Light something like lightning flash, missis—but some-thing like fire."

"That's right, Miss Liz—bright like lightning flash, but then carry on like fire burning. Way over by Rookoom—"

"Is nearer than that, man," another voice joined in.

("And you never seen bamboo fire light up the heavens?")

"No, man—is maybe two-three mile off. And then, Miss Liz, we approach the Big House and we lose it. And even now we wonder, with the power of the night, whether we really see it at all."

"I can well understand that," I said. "It's a miracle that you reached us."

("Choo, man!—you never see big bamboo how it bright? Is bamboo clump, me dear—")

"The Lord is to thank, missis—" "Praise Him—" "Glory be!"

"Come now, Miss Liz." Nan was standing over me. "Is time you come and sit down peaceful and maybe sleep a little."

"How is Aunt Cissie?" I asked, reaching for the empty cup. Nan took it firmly from me.

"Is I will remove it, Miss Liz. You don' have to mess with cornmeal nonsense, you know."

"But I *like* doing something to help, Nan."

"No, Miss Liz. Is more than sufficient what you do already. Must rest now—"

"Please, missis—" A hand plucked at my elbow as I got to my feet; it was the older woman. "Please, if you have a little piece of shawl or cloth fe wrap up me head. The night air always trouble me, and me headcloth still wet up."

I found a stole of my mother's in my sewing basket, and Nan took it over to the woman, while I was made to sit down. So I pulled out the old striped shirt of Father's I had promised Maurice.

I had planned to cut back the worn collar and cuffs and trim them with broderie anglaise for myself, but now he needed it more than I—would be even more glad of it when he came back, cold and wet, out of the rain. And yet I knew he would be warm to touch and hold, just as I knew the bright streaks in his hair would show even when it was drenched. I must have hot soup ready for him, for him and Tom, when they got back. Soon enough—tomorrow—we would see, in the light of common day, if this was just a passing fever or, as Maurice believed, so much more: the first blaze of a huge slow-burning, long-lasting logwood fire.

And tomorrow Edward would arrive. Edward, I knew, would bring order and a sense of proportion to all this muddle. He'd help Tom sort out his finances—he was so good with money, knew all about economics, and discussed so confidently the political issues that passed over my head. He had even mentioned that his father—Father's cousin, influential industrialist—wanted to put money into the old property. How I'd been looking forward to Edward advising me about what training I should do, what plans to make, the first steps toward being useful and independent—maybe even as a wife who could pull her weight, be worthy of him.

Everything had changed. Could I ever leave Maurice now? Could I live away from that warmth and light?

I started opening a can of soup to bolster my faith in his, in their, safe return. The storm shook the house and it seemed to groan round us as if it could bear no more. All the eyes were rolled up, flashing in the light. Aunt Cissie cowered into her feather boa, squinting wildly at the corners of the ceiling. Something must happen, I felt; it can't go on, it can't get worse than this. Something is going to happen. Then it did.

It was not the rending of timbers or the splintering of glass. The roof did not go, nor the shutters; the iron bar of the great door did not bend and break. But it was, suddenly, to the great door that all eyes turned.

For there was a thud against it, a sickening impact, not of the storm, that jerked it inward for a second. Then another, but different this time—two sharp clear knocks that rang out even through the squealing tempest.

"Open it!" I cried. "It's Maurice." No one moved; no one spoke. "He's come back!" I rushed to the door and wrestled the bolts free and lifted the bar.

The two wings of the great door burst open with an explosion of inrushing wind, water, and debris. Candles guttered, spat, and went out. The oil lamp crashed to the floor and the kerosene caught fire. But in that instant before our lights were doused we thought we saw it; and by the creeping yellow flag of flame flattened by the wind, we knew we had seen it.

It was the body of Maurice that fell through the open doorway and lay bleeding into the pool of driven rain. It was the Headless Man.

ELEVEN O'CLOCK

I KNEW HIM by the sodden sheepskin over the red shirt; and in the ragged light from the burning pool of oil I saw his arms stretched out among the broken branches and shreds of leaves, one fist closed tight, the other spread out. I would know those hands anywhere. But of the black seconds—or minutes—that came next, I knew nothing, for the roaring wind was inside my head. It put out my mind, so there was nothing but dark.

Afterward, I became conscious of turmoil and panic around me. Struggling—screaming—no light anywhere— rain and flying debris beating upon us: it was madness itself, black, tumultuous, deafening, unbearable. I did not think or begin to realize what had happened, what was going on. I crouched with my arms shielding my head against the flailing hurricane, just to survive, to resist, like a stone.

Then all at once a strong steady light shone through the darkness. I perceived it through my tight-shut eyelids, opened them to its hard brilliance, and closed them again. I could hear Tom's voice shouting above the tumult —something about the doors—and felt movement round me. Suddenly, stillness; the roaring was distanced. They had shut out the storm.

I heard a babble of frightened voices and crying, but

then I think Tom shone his torch onto the floor, for there was a moment of shocked silence—no sound except the wind—and then a high-pitched screaming broke out. It may have been the aunt, or Nan, or me.

Tom was shouting orders, and there seemed to be a lot of activity, and I felt someone lift me up gently and firmly, taking my aching arms from round my head.

"Come, Liz," said Tom, holding me. "He's covered up now, with a blanket. You can open your eyes."

I did, and I wondered where I was. The room looked different. I stared round me but I didn't recognize it. Tom was there wearing bright yellow oilskins, flapping open; underneath, his shirt, black and clinging, slick as rubber. There were lots of people I didn't know, and Nan's face came close and peered at me, a big polished brown triangle, and went away again. Gradually, as there was more light, and by the beam of the big torch from the office glancing about, I saw that I was in the hall. The sofa and wicker chairs that belonged on the veranda were there, all keeled over this way and that; tables were lying on their sides and everything was decked with straggling leaves and branches. Then I saw where the body of Maurice lay shrouded, and the sickening hollow where the head should be.

"Maurice is dead," I said. "I must—"

But the room had gone quiet. There was no sound, not even of the wind, not even of my own voice. Total silence. It was such a relief. Except that I had been saying something; I felt it was important—but it didn't really matter. It was nicer like this, all quiet.

Nan came up and mouthed something at me, stroking my hair, my hand. Tom sat me on the sofa—it was the right way up now—and wrapped a heavy coat round me. He crouched in front of me, holding my shoulders, making me look at him. He, too, mouthed at me, and seemed to wait for an answer. Then he gave up, tucked my stone hands under the wrapping, and went away.

I watched him: he was waving his arms about, pointing,

beckoning. The people moved in and out of my line of vision, gathering up the mess of broken branches, catching the flapping chickens and retying them, spreading sacking in the puddles, lifting the fallen furniture. I watched Nan sitting beside my aunt—so strange to see Aunt Clarissa away from the turret room—holding her wrists, telling her something. It was all marvelously quiet, a dumb show for my entertainment.

I don't know how much time went by, but very slowly I saw the room I remembered taking shape. Except that it was darker: the warm circle of the oil lamp had disappeared, and a dim storm lantern was in its place. Somewhere behind me they had lighted candles; I knew that clear unsteady light. Maurice and I shared it at the side table, our heads close, talking softly, watching each other's hands and eyes and lips. . . . I could see a great pile of branches and rubbish by the office; that was not there before, I thought. And moreover, the people who had come to take shelter with us seemed to have rearranged themselves, so that they were more crowded now, and farther from the big door.

Perhaps I was mistaken—had they only just come in?—for they were as I remembered them then, wet and huddled and frightened, not talking, not even passing a bottle or smoking. Perhaps Tom was going to give them a cigarette now, and Maurice would go over and squat down and talk to—Maurice is dead. Or had I dreamed that? It *could* have been only a frightful dream, I thought, when the door flew open and he fell forward into the room and—

When did I wake up? Why had it all gone dark suddenly—but then *not* dark: a yellow flapping light along the ground, in my dream, showing me again what I thought I had seen come through that door. A dream within a dream —this time, beyond bearing. It had gone now, the flapping flames, the terrible vision, so I must have woken up.

And the silent scene they were playing round me, where did this fit in? I stared straight ahead, trying to concentrate, to observe closely and catch them out. Why, for instance, were they collecting branches into a pile? Perhaps they were going to burn down the office door. But Tom did not seem to mind, he even seemed to be directing them, but he must know that such wet green wood couldn't catch fire. He was so animated; yellow-jacketed, he seemed to blaze with life. He moved about quickly and decisively, exhorting, encouraging—he looked almost inspired. Now he was settling them, ordering them to sit down.

And why, I wondered again, were all the people huddling up here? Because the water came in under the door. And Nan told Maurice to mop it up; she was cross and he smiled at me over her shoulder; he was glad to be back, to see me, and I couldn't hold him because of all the sacks. Then he dropped them on the floor and sucked my cut hand. . . .

Yes, and that was after everything had gone dark, and Aunt calling "Hide!" I was so frightened—like being buried alive—and I could feel my hand slimy with blood. Then Maurice lit a match. His hands and his face were brilliantly alive in the darkness, and he reached for me and held me and I didn't mind the match going out. For I was alive again, my heart beating all through my body, close against him—his mouth hot on my hand, sucking it like a juicy orange—together under the shade of the Halfway Tree.

Once, riding out with Maurice, my horse shied and I had a bad fall. I must have been concussed. When I came to, he was bending over me, shading my face from the harsh sun and mopping my forehead with cool wet leaves. The light splintered dazzlingly through his red-brown hair, and I thought: I've broken every bone in my body, but I'm not blind. A great wave of well-being filled me unreasonably, as well-being does. The world seemed suddenly such a marvelous multicolored creation, and I watched the troubled marmalade eyes and the freckles and bright spikes of hair craze and mingle in a kaleidoscope as I lost consciousness again. Later, I remember, he brought me water to drink and I was able to stand. I was bruised but had not broken anything. My horse had bolted for home and I was anxious that Mother might worry. Maurice put me on his mule and got up behind me and we rode home together. From an upper window, Nan saw us coming up the hill; and that evening she told Father that Maurice was too familiar with me. I was thirteen, I think. Father said to me: "Nan came along with a technicolor tale about Maurice. . . ."

Afterward he often referred to Maurice as my "technicolor friend." I liked it; it fitted him. I could see why brown girls might be attracted to him, too: he had none of the pallor and physical narrowness of most white men, but the strong build and the warmth and openness of their own menfolk. He was warm against me as I leaned back on him riding up the hill to the house, his hands with the reins resting easily on my thighs. I gave in to his protecting care, to the invading weakness, to comfort that weakened me more. I closed my eyes and breathed in the leather and sweat, the smell of sheep dip as we passed the pen. Then it was time to get down; Nan, bossy and anxious, blaming my happy vagueness on my fall. Lying down later, I tried to relive the ride, substituting Edward for dear old Maurice, but it didn't work. Funny to remember it now, in the silent underwater world of the benighted hall.

And Edward was coming in his plane. Everything would be all right. But I wished I could imagine Edward making love to me. . . .

I must try to concentrate. Had I been asleep? I opened my eyes and watched the people moving their belongings. Yes, they must have moved up there to get out of the wet; that made sense. And they were keeping very quiet because they knew I was asleep and only dreaming all this. Was Maurice mopping up the water as Nan had told him to?

I slid my eyes round a little way toward the door, and the end of the huddled blanket came into view. "No," I said loudly, without making a sound; "No no no—" because I had no tears for Maurice, and no blood for him since I was only a stone. I was cold and white and deaf.

But not dumb, it seemed, for people looked at me, and Tom came over quickly. Now he took me onto his knee and cradled me. I felt the cool metal of his hip flask warmer than my cold lips, and the burn and seep of brandy in my throat. My hand ached; it was aching for Maurice's mouth—I hadn't dreamed that. Tom had seen and worked himself into a temper.

I tucked my head into his neck; warmth was coming back to me. As I revived I looked cautiously out under the curve of his chin, noticing disjointed details in the dim thick light: the uneven hem of Aunt Cissie's oyster satin dress, draggled with rain and leaves; higher, past the crowd of fugitives and their gleaming eyes, and up above the door—that was safe—where the buffalo brooded; its wide middle parting of white bone between the black horns was exact, symmetrical, so overdressed for the occasion; and quickly back, blinking to avoid the space below, back to what was near and familiar, Tom's shoulder, his chest, and the rent in his shirt, the button missing. Poor Tom.

Sounds crept through to me as though from a great distance—first just a faint roaring, and then, like blood returning to a damaged limb, the pain of the loud beleaguered room flooding in, a fearful senseless babble and thunder in my ears, and I cringed and covered them with my hands. Gently they were pulled away. ". . . Worry, Liz —you're all right. Rest quiet. Tom's got you. Don't worry. It's all right now."

"So loud—" I said, tight against him.

"Can you hear me, Liz?" He was looking down at me. His forehead, I saw, was cut, his cheek and neck smeared with blood.

"Yes, I can hear. But you've hurt yourself."

"I'm fine," he said. "Truly. I've got you." He held me and rocked me. "You'll be safe with me. . . . Now, Lizzie dear, I must talk to these people." He stood and settled

130

me back on the sofa, tucking the coat round me. "I'll come back soon. Someone's got to explain to them—they're all pretty shaken up," he said gently.

He moved away, stopping to hush and calm two men who were arguing loudly, and then went on to the others. The raging storm, tearing at the shutters, breaking over the roof and along the veranda outside, made it impossible to reach everyone at once, except to shout simple commands. Now that the shelterers were huddling together in small vociferous knots, it was like beating out separate bush fires. Tom moved confidently among them, and I could see as I watched that this new energy and authority was still with him. And though I wasn't able to catch his words, I could hear what he was up against; from the people nearest me, behind the sofa, fragments, emphasized phrases, reached me through the storm.

"Busha Maurice—zinc must a chop him—O Lord!—a hundred mile an hour—zinc sheeting—is same t'ing happen down Lambs River—is so them say—but the knocking —how the *knocking*, man—is how him knock on door?— dead man can't knock—is duppy, man—*duppy* knock— *spirit* knock—Lord Jesus!—"

Then Tom's voice, silencing the chattering and moaning:

"Come now, all of you, you talk of the Busha and how he died. Could only be flying zinc that killed him, as you say—plenty of zinc sheeting about—yes, and—hush now!— and what a terrible thing. He was a fine man. Now you good people know better than any how bad the storm is, how you can call somebody and search and still can't find them. I tell you, it is blowing stronger still when we go out. We get down near the stables and try to reach the engine house: we wanted to fix the generator so we could have some light in here, you see, for us and all you people. But in the dark I lose him, and in the noise I call and call and hear nothing. I find the electric wires all down—it seems like a tree is across them—and I start back, calling Busha Maurice continually, and I shine the torch so he

131

may see it and find his way. At last I get back to the house; I cross the veranda and I remember how I step on a zinc sheet that must have blown there. I find the doors open and the Busha lying dead inside—it seems it hit him just as he was reaching safety. A truly terrible thing."

He walked over to where the body lay; all eyes were on him, and I watched him over the screen of my hands, so that I should not see the thing at his feet. He must have stood behind it, with his back to the door, and he lifted up his arms and called:

"May the Lord God take his spirit; and may He watch over us in our trouble!" He bowed his head for a moment. Then he looked toward Nan, and beckoned her. "Come, Miss Nan, do what is right for him. You know best."

There was a murmuring round me: "Miss Nan know what is right . . . what is best. . . . Hallelujah!"

Nan took two candles in their small silver holders from the candelabra we had saved. She lit them; slow and stately, she carried them over to the body. Tom came and stood by me. All the people got to their feet and watched her—and I too watched, mesmerized as they were by ritual. She bent down and gently straightened the huddled legs and spread the blanket out smoothly like a flag. She placed a candle at either end, and then she spoke. Her voice was high and clear above the storm, a keening, measured chant, and the people crouched down, intent: her congregation.

"For the Lord sent down a Great Light—" "Yes indeed—yea Lord!" came a chorus of ragged responses.

"The Angel of Death came down in glory—" "Yea Lord!"

"He hold forth the deadly sword of flame—" "Deadly, Lord—"

"Cut down Busha Maurice in him prime—" "Cut him down, Lord—"

"Now Him satisfy and leave us—" "Lord Him satisfy already—"

132

"Take the Spirit and depart in peace—" "According to Thy Word, Lord!"

"Let the Great Light be Thy Sign, Lord—" "A Sign, yea Lord—"

"That it finish and done, Lord, Thy Wrath!" "Finish O Lord—Hallelujah!"

I felt Tom's disquiet as the responses grew in fervor and unison; and out of the corner of my eye I saw the aunt move. I got up quickly and put my arm round her. "They're holding a little service for Maurice," I said, fearing the effect her brand of mad rhetoric might have at such a moment, but she clasped her hands together and gazed obediently at the ceiling.

It was too much for Tom, however. He stepped forward and spoke loudly into a pause. He faced Nan across the body, but his words were for everyone.

"All right!" he called. "Busha Maurice is dead and gone now and we have prayed for him. But hear this: we too saw light over toward Rookoom, and I tell you: it was a bamboo clump burning—"

The murmurers were disturbed and displeased. "Is never bamboo—" "Is Angel self—in all Him Glory—come fe seek out poor sinner—"

Still Tom tried to hush them, walking among them now.

"Listen, all of you, it is lightning strike a bamboo clump and the hurricane fan it—way over by Rookoom. That is what you see, I tell you!"

"Lightning, no, sir—no bamboo can't burn so long in rain—is Angel self we see—Death Angel come down by Rookoom—Glory be!"

"Hush, everybody! No angel—"

"Preserve him, Lord—do not strike the young master down for these words—By Rookoom Him alight with Fire and the Sword—for even the Headless Man walk there—preserve us, Lord—"

"And who knock? Tell me, is who *knock*?"

Lord Penn's deep voice came from the shadows, and

there was a moment of silence filled only by the screaming wind. He had voiced the unspeakable fear beneath the growing hysteria.

Who knock?—Who knock?—preserve us, Lord—Thou who sendeth unto us the Headless Man—for a sign—for our sins—only him body come—preserve us Lord—when the Dead walk and knock and enter into our midst—yea, Lord—preserve us—from the duppy—from the Angel—flaming in Glory—His sword is terrible—save us, Lord—from the Headless Man—from the Spirit that walks—from the Walking Dead—"

Not even Tom could make himself heard now. Nan seemed to be in a trance, her head back, her arms at her sides.

Then a piercing shriek rose above the sound of wind and words. The older woman stood up; Mother's stole was still wrapped round her head. She was clutching her throat, and her eyes were white, rolled right back into her skull. She screamed:

"Hearken unto me, for the Spirit is upon me! The Dead knock and we open unto it. And I say unto you: now Head must find body, seeking unity. One body one grave. And the Head will come looking!"

TWELVE O'CLOCK

THE POSSESSED WOMAN fell back; unconscious, but she had said enough. At her words, the heaped-up horror of the night's alarms seemed to topple over into madness. A screaming babble filled the room, as wild and wordless as the storm outside, and I heard my own voice among it. That terrible warning swept away every control.

In the absence of the Flaming Angel Himself, the grandfather clock was probably the only thing that could have brought silence. It rang out suddenly like a gong—majestic, measured, inexorable—and it held them spellbound until the last stroke died away.

I had not been able to see it where it stood in the dark at the end of the hall, and its sudden metallic boom caught me quite unprepared. But, with the advantage of knowing what it was, I recovered from the shock after the second strike, and by the third, saw we might have a short breathing space. I was still standing by my aunt. I sat her firmly in her chair—"Perhaps you should powder your nose, Auntie," I said, the unexpected being what she best understood. I left her rummaging in her bag and crossed over to Tom. "We must have some sort of diversion—*quickly*—" I said in his ear. He nodded. "What about the old Gramophone in the nursery? Okay." Then I got round to Nan. I was careful not to look down, but made a wide circle, and as the last stroke faded I took her arm and led her away. "Miss Cissie needs you, Nan, to fix her hair after the door—after all that rain came in."

Deprived of their figurehead, the fugitives broke into small excited groups. The woman who had "got the spirit" was now lying still, breathing stertorously, tended by those nearby. No new spokesman emerged to voice their fears or lead their responses, but I knew from what I could hear that the grandfather clock's intervention had been a doubtful blessing.

It broke the spell, disrupted the rhythm and mood of the chanting. It had shocked them into silence. But now they began to talk again among themselves, and its significance had not been missed: it was midnight. "If Head come look for body, will come soon." Between now and the doubtful dawn, anything might happen: as soon as that last solemn note had died away, I felt—and they *knew* —that there was more than the hurricane out there.

I found I was shivering and weak after the burst of activity. I looked round. Tom had taken the storm lantern and gone. Drawn and silent, Nan was attending to the aunt's bedraggled hair.

"Put the cardigan on her, Nanny," I said, "and then we must find some solid food for these people. That's what we all need."

For me, it was vital that I should lay hold of and cling to normality. Somewhere in myself I had to find the strength to continue, and the answer, I knew, was in small practical things: tending the lights, stuffing up the cracks against the rain, preparing and serving food—sewing on buttons, if there was nothing else. For me, salvation lay, not in prayers and chanting, but in the trivial, the familiar: the passing of bread, the stacking of plates.

At the same time, the people who had taken shelter with us, and now were stretched to breaking by disasters in strange surroundings—might most naturally seek their comfort in superstition. With all our differences, we were simply thirteen frightened mortals shut in together, condemned to watch and wait beside a headless body through long hours of storm. And now it was midnight; fear walked abroad, and the darkest hours of watching were only beginning. Somehow we must be calm, must unite and endure.

First we needed lights round the room. Now that the oil lamp was gone, and the candles and the kerosene for the two lanterns were running out, there could be no pools of bright light as we had before. From now on we must make do with glims. I went to the side table and set to work drawing through the wicks with the pliers, topping up the oil.

But what hope was there of putting him from my mind? Everything I touched was Maurice's. These glims—which might well be the saving of our sanity in the long hours ahead—were his legacy. To make them with him had been for a short while to outwit the besieging storm; and the onslaught of wind and water had receded as we sat together in our ring of candlelight. I thought of his deference to Nan, his gentle humoring of my mad aunt, giving employment even to her restless hands, and to Nelly's idle ones; and then how he had returned to me, told me suddenly he loved me—undramatically, and yet with such force of conviction. The remembered passion of his look, his touch, was so vivid still that I bowed my head and closed my eyes. How *could* he be dead, my body cried, recalling him. How could I be warm from his kisses, and Maurice growing cold. . . .

I forced myself to concentrate, steadying the big can of oil and pouring it in a thin stream that would not disturb the little raft. I had no tears; Maurice's violent death, the sudden loss of him, was still more like a physical blow, the pain of exposed nerve ends still tingling from contact with the living man. I knew I must resist the pain of that blow, busy myself, find numbness in activity and, ultimately, in exhaustion. When the night is over, I thought, I'll come to terms with my loss. Then I may be able to weep for him.

137

I took the tray of little lights and placed them round the room, on an empty shelf of the bookcase, by my aunt—now neat and calm and wearing her pink cardigan—on the small table by the cloakroom door, and on the ground among the shelterers. They watched in silence as I showed them how to pull through the wicks when they burned down. They nodded thanks.

Tom appeared on the big stairs, carrying the old wind-up Gramophone. It had started life in the drawing room; Mother used to listen to Percy Grainger and Delius, or the English dance bands of her youth, and dream of home; Father liked to hear the horn concertos when he was around on a Sunday morning; and it was carried through to the schoolroom on wet afternoons. Then the electricity arrived, and a small secondhand record player; the old one was sent upstairs to Aunt Cissie for "I Dreamt I Dwelt in Marble Halls" and "O for the Wings of a Dove." When at last the shiny new machine was installed by Tom, it was all change: the aunt was given the small electric one, and the Gramophone of our youth was banished to the nursery.

Now we needed it: we always lived in a backwater, ten years behind the real world, but the storm was encamped about us, thrusting us yet further back in time, onto our own resources, into a sort of limbo, beset by many of the dangers and hardships of our bold forefathers. Looking round me, I felt we probably lacked something of their style.

One of the women had started a low keening hymn, and others were taking it up, joining in the chorus:

> At the Cross at the Cross where I first saw the Light
> And the burden of my heart roll away . . .

It was a doleful sound, and the sight of the Gramophone with its wide flaring horn gave me heart. There was not much choice of records—Tom had found only two in the nursery—but anything would be an improvement, I felt, barring the Funeral March.

"Look," said Tom, " 'Viennese Waltz Selection' "; and smiled at me as he unfolded the cranky handle. It was suddenly very comforting to have him there; and the bright swirling music swelled confidently through the tempest.

"That's better," I said. "Now I'd like a cigarette, please."

"These are our last," said Tom.

Nan was busy cutting bread on the side table. She turned round when the music started, and even by the light of the glim I could see that she was displeased. I went over.

"I'll light the Primus, shall I, Nan?" I said. "And then we can give them all some hot stew. We'll mix in this soup to make it go further, so even the toothless man—"

"Dance music don' right for a wake, Miss Liz," she said.

"Oh, Nan—isn't it gloomy enough without holding a proper wake?"

"Proper or not, Miss Liz, is a wake. No mus' be? Wake is to watch up by dead somebody through the night: is same thing we do. Is a wake."

"But, Nan—"

"I only telling you what is right, Miss Liz," said Nan severely, "what is right and the people them expect."

"But don't you have dancing at wakes, Nan? I've heard—"

"Long ears catch talk like tin gutter," she snapped. "Dancing take place at wake when the feeling is right, Miss Liz; with drum and singing, the dancing come upon you."

"But this is just music for dancing, Nan—"

"Is big-ball trash, me dear—big-band, big-ball trash."

"But you used to like—"

"Not for wake, Miss Liz. No, sir." She turned her back

139

on me, picked up two plates of bread, and went over to the shelterers.

Tom had been opening tins of stew and heard most of this exchange. He said, "I'll move it over to the bookcase. We can listen better there, and they can sing their dreary wake hymns undisturbed."

"I was hoping to cheer them up a bit," I said, "but they want a different sort of party, I suppose."

When I carried the saucepan of hot stew over to them, and a stack of bowls to ladle it into—Nan said they preferred to help themselves—the singing was going strong: *"Follow, follow, I will follow Jesus,"* with syrupy harmonies thickening the mournful tune.

Tom and I took our bread and stew over to my chair near the music. Aunt Cissie was eating contentedly; every now and again she would stop and dab at Cinderella and the Prince, nearby on a cushion, with a small spoonful. Tom turned the record over and sat down on a pouf, his back against the bookcase. Close beside us, the "Blue Danube" competed with the hurricane. The background roar continued, but the shrieking wind was masked by ardent violins.

"You all right?" I said.

"Fine."

"Don't want something on that cut?"

"It's only a scratch."

"The hero always says that when he's wounded," I said.

I was feeling light-headed, almost detached. Maurice was dead, and I knew I couldn't cope with my feelings now; I would founder. Tom was very much alive. Surreptitiously I watched him as we ate. He was calmer than he had been all evening, the young master in a rare moment of well-earned rest. I can see now that for him the long uneven duel was over, started years ago under Father's eye, but at the time I could only admire this new dynamic brother, decisive in action, companionable at ease. It was almost as if he had taken on something of Maurice's strength, like a young cannibal warrior eating the flesh of the tribal hero slain in battle, to absorb his might. Or so it said in *Coral Island*, I thought—but I did not ask him: he would not object to the idea, but he would resent the implied canonization of Maurice; he couldn't have altered *that* much.

Looking back, such thoughts amaze me—they show how unreal I found the whole situation; and I accept that I could only have endured it in those terms—an adventure story, a bad dream, a Greek tragedy, with chorus. It helped the waiting, the surviving, by turning it into a frightening game.

Nowadays I have the waiting, but without fear to divert me. The game is of Tom's making, and this one I shan't survive.

He got up and cleared away our bowls and spoons. At the side table he poured out two drinks. Nan was standing by, and I could tell from the set of her shoulders and head that she was busy disowning us and our unsuitable music. I saw him offer her a drink, and persist; saw her soften a little, accept, and sip at her tot of rum, the little finger crooked. Then Tom said something else to her, but he seemed to have gone too far. She drew herself up even taller, crushed him without recourse to further words, and walked away.

"I only asked her if she'd like a game of cards," he said when he brought me my drink.

"That was rash," I said; then, "Oh, God, *no!* Look— she's going to sit beside— She's going to do a proper wake."

Nan had established herself, with some ordering of skirts, on the threshold beside the blanket, her glass discreet but within reach. By the light of the candle I could see her lips moving. Soon the women joined her, and the wailing hymn that reached me in fragments through the storm was not one I had ever heard before. Its haunting minor key made me shiver and filled me with foreboding. I couldn't believe the unheard words were hopeful, for the melody told only of despair.

141

"As long as she doesn't get them all out there, swaying and clapping," said Tom.

"I doubt it," I said, confidently. "Anyway, two of the men are busy playing dominoes. . . . There seems to be an endless supply of bottles. What is it, d'you think? White rum?"

"I expect so. Not Bacardi though . . ."

How strange to sit there with Tom in the smoky light of the glims, with Maurice lying dead a few yards away, and a wake in progress, and a mad aunt, nine strangers, and two chickens—and the storm pounding and the old house shaking and groaning round us. And Tom was dealing the bezique cards, getting out the markers, putting on the Viennese waltz selection again. Yet I felt that this was exactly how to survive; there was no other way. And Maurice would have understood.

I picked up my cards. If only I could *accept* the storm, I thought, and tried to concentrate on whether I should collect kings or queens. If only there were a status quo to get used to. This is It, and we only have to go on enduring it. I wondered if it wouldn't be easier to be buried alive and wait to be rescued. Now the storm's note seemed always changing; if you gave way, you would just crouch there listening, becoming an expert on its minute variations, its pattern of attack. One or two of the fugitives, I could see, were doing just that. Then Tom declared two ordinary marriages, and I decided to collect aces after all.

The aunt was nodding in her chair and woke suddenly.

"You've been fiddling with it!" she said crossly.

"What, Aunt?" I asked.

"You've changed it again."

"The record, Auntie? Don't you like this?"

"No, girl. The roaring! It's different again! How can I be expected to sleep if you *will* fiddle with—"

Lord Penn had come over to speak to Tom.

"Please, Mars Tom, you hear the wind going round? Almost due west now it feel."

"It's been a bit west of north for some time, hasn't it?"

"But is west-west now. You think we should check on that side?"

Tom got up. "Yes, Lord Penn—we'll do it right away. The top rooms first."

They took hammer and nails, lit the storm lantern, and set out, and in a moment they were swallowed up by the dark.

I went over to see what supplies we still had, whether there was tea enough for everyone. Milk was running low, so I just made two small cups of black coffee and took one to Aunt Cissie. She was singing to herself now, and, leaning close, I heard, not a hymn, but a bright little twenties love song. It was curiously shocking.

"That was clever of you, Aunt," I said. "You heard the wind changing before anyone else did."

"I felt it in my water," said she in her best broadcasting voice.

"Time for us to go to the lavatory, Aunt Cissie," I said, and I took her there.

On the way back she stopped at the bottom of the dark stairs.

"Now I shall retire," she said. "Good night, my people!" She waved a royal hand toward the fugitives and they watched suspiciously, frozen in mid-action.

"No, Auntie," I said, leading her past them. "It's the hurricane, you see. It's better down here with us. Don't worry, it will soon go away and you can—"

"Always worst from the west!"

Sudden and loud as an alarm bell, her cry reached the nearest group and I could hear them take it up—"Worse she say—" "Always so from west—" "So them say—" "Storm worse—" "Lord preserve us—storm worse!"

I hurried her back to the Siege Perilous. "Come, have your coffee, Aunt, while it's still warm—and then we'll make a necklace for Cinderella."

I was relieved to see the light of Tom and Lord Penn returning. The storm did sound as if it was getting worse; there were hardly any gusts now, just a continual scream-

143

ing pressure that never slackened and gave no respite. I felt like running over to Tom and clinging to him. I wanted to cry out, I can't stand it! Make it go away!

But I held myself back: it was more important than ever, since it had become virtually impossible to make ourselves heard. Rumor alone could reach them, and the aunt's words had passed round. We could counteract such rumor now only by acting calmly, behaving normally. More than ever we must appear cool and orderly in all we did.

For they had stopped playing dominoes and had put their bottles down; half were singing—huddled together, swaying, like desperate survivors in a small boat. The others crouched silently, with eyes rolled up, listening to the merciless scream of the hurricane.

There came a moment when the wind's high note swung up into a deadly whistle only just within reach of human hearing, but suddenly beyond human endurance. Tom came to a halt halfway across the room from me. The singers clapped their hands over their ears. All eyes in the hall were lifted now to the groaning rafters. And still that high note crept up minutely like a tightening fiddle string, a turning screw.

There was a tearing crash above us—and everyone was on their feet; there was a slithering scraping sound, like a giant clawing wildly at the back wall of the house. Then came a deafening explosion. The huge ragged limbs of the bitterwood splintered through the far door, ripping the side off our safe little nailed-up box; and the storm roared in.

ONE O'CLOCK

THE TREE CAME into the room like a wounded beast, its torn foliage still roaring, its broken stumps as red as flesh. In the onslaught of wind and rain every glim and candle went out; only the lantern Lord Penn was holding survived. The air was full of screaming as a great wave of driving rain, thick with flying debris, broke upon us and scoured round the hall, carrying everything movable in its path.

Tom was yelling above the din. The beam of the big torch came on and played round the room. As it passed, I saw the aunt cowering against the bookcase; Nan crawling out from behind the rubble of storm trash and belongings that had silted up in a heap near the main threshold; the fugitives scrabbling, struggling, some hugging their bundles, some clinging to one another. Then Tom moved out from the shelter of the staircase and shone the light onto the shattered door and the monstrous treetop that had invaded our sanctuary.

There was something peculiarly alarming, almost obscene, about the jagged thrusting branches, each thicker than a man's thigh and still decked out with garish shreds of leaves streaming in the wind. It shifted out of its steep slant and settled down, reaching now a third of the length of the room; as it did, it caught the side table, which went over, and all the bowls and the unlit Primus with it. I crawled forward but Tom shouted, "Keep back, Liz! Come over here—bring cushions—" I picked my way across to him, staggering under the driving rain, stepping over a huddled body with a bottle, and I managed to gather up two cushions as I went. Tom pulled me close into the shelter of the wall by the broken door.

"Where's Lord Penn?" I panted, wiping the clinging scraps of leaves from my eyes.

"Getting the saw from the office. Lucky this happened before the wind had shifted right round—not full on this side yet."

"Can we patch it, then?"

"Got to fix up something before the storm really gets in or it'll take the place apart. Only hope there's not too much damage to the roof above—that'd really muck us up."

Lord Penn was there with the saw. He set down the guttering lantern in the protecting angle of the wall and the clock. Here the stinging tip of the storm's whiplash could reach us only as it curled back on itself, its main force spent.

"Good man. Liz, get some help. Let's go—and take it up high, man, as high as you can catch—"

When I returned with another of the shelterers, Lord Penn had climbed up into the prone treetop and was sawing hard at the uppermost branch where it passed under the lintel.

"Okay, Liz, hold the torch for him. You, get up there and hold a couple of cushions across the hole to protect him as much as you can—all right? I'm getting another saw—I left one in the pantry."

Sawing wet wood above shoulder level in a driving rainstorm is slow work; even the cushions, wedged and supported across the top part of the jagged gap, could not shield Lord Penn much, and often he stopped to turn

146

away, gasping and scraping leaves and sticks from his face. My job was only to keep the torch steady. I held one arm crooked round my forehead to take the brunt of the gale. Strenuous and monotonous, it was just a matter of endurance; and we were nothing more than patient, wet, exhausted animals patching up our nest.

At length Lord Penn called, "Look out, Miss Liz—him going now!" I moved; and he jumped clear and crouched back into safety, panting, as the great branch crashed to the floor. I took the chance to shine the torch round the room; people were hobbling about among the chaos, making their way across to the passage door and creeping through. I could not see my aunt, but her chair was upright, its back toward me.

Tom reappeared with the ripsaw; together they attacked the largest branch, the lowest of the four that had broken in. I set the torch on the ground, and joined the cushion holder, trying to shield them. It was crowded and awkward, for they had to cut as flush with the door as they could in order to nail new boards across the hole when they had done; and all the while the rain soaked us and the wind screamed at us and spat the chewed-up forest in our faces. Once, something bigger and harder struck the outside of the doorjamb with a sick thud.

"Sound like roof slate," shouted Lord Penn, grinning hellishly. "We lucky fe true!"

The big branch was nearly sawn through. We moved back, and he jumped hard on the lower section, and it tore off and fell the last two feet.

"Good! Just the two small ones now—shine the light!" Tom shouted.

I found Nan beside me.

"Is Aunt Cissie all right?"

"Yes, Miss Liz. She get back to her chair by herself and now she refuse to leave it. But I turn it round out of the draft and it give her good protection."

"And the others?"

"Them gather up slow, Miss Liz, shifting inna pantry fe take shelter."

Only in the broadening of her speech did she admit the presence of an emergency. Nature's terrors were there to be coped with, as far as Nan was concerned, and she was the familiar of far greater ones. I had seen real fear upon her when the crying came to us out of the storm. Duppies, spirits, avenging angels—these were the big battalions. As for me, I was scared by each fresh hazard, even by those dark things I thought I did not believe in; frightened even by the rituals, the spells, that were meant to guard us from them.

"I will hold the torch, Miss Liz."

I gave it to her, picked up the heavy sodden cushions again, and went back to my task. Tom and Lord Penn were using the two-handed saw on the last of the branches, as it now was, for the whole treetop had settled lower, twisting as it moved, after the removal of the heaviest part, and the trunk beyond two joining boughs must be cut through. It was only one, but it was much larger— and higher too, for the twisting fall had flipped it up, ripping out the overhead light fitting and adding a sprinkle of glass to the flying flotsam. I was glad Aunt Cissie had the stalwart back of the great chair between her and the broken doorway.

Tom had righted the side table, pulled it over, and climbed onto it to get a better angle at the great limb. Lord Penn was on the ground, working the other end of the saw, while the third man pulled down on the tree itself to hold the edges of the cut apart and help the blade run easily. I stood on a chair and strained across the gap beside Tom where the rain drove through; I wedged my cushion and held it, trying to shield him. Briefly—pinioned there in the dark wet welter of wind and lashing bitterwood twigs—it occurred to me that, for the moment, I was *not* afraid. Our worst expectations had come about, just as Maurice had warned; but it was a relief fighting

148

the storm face to face to reclaim the ground it had taken. No less dangerous, but the violent mindless activity was like a drug.

Here in my tiny world of insects and creeping words, I have actually prayed for a storm to take the lid off my shut room. I crave the excitement, and a quick death—*anything* rather than this slow, lonely fading. I know that somehow I must finish this; but it would all have been so much simpler if I had died then—I would have been spared the rest, the worst, that was still to come.

Tom preserved me. I had grown numb and lost all sense of time and danger. He shouted and grabbed me back against the wall, and the two men ducked away on the other side as the huge limb came crashing down. Its wide swinging tip caught the antlers of the wildebeeste and swept it, mount and all, onto the floor, where it lay with its big sad eye sockets peering out between the foliage. Tom lifted me down, still dazed, and I was surprised to feel him trembling as he held me close.

Now the broken door was clear and we could see the extent of the ragged hole. More than half of the tall double doors was gone, and the three dark red amputated stumps stood out against the dark beyond.

"Quick now!" Tom shouted. "Planks leaning up in the passage there—nails, good—hammers. Okay, Liz, look after the aunt—we can manage now—just so long as there's no damage upstairs."

"Shall I go up and see?"

"No, it's too dangerous—I mean, if the roof has been holed, well—anything could happen. I'm going."

"Be careful, Tom!" I cried.

"I'll just take a look and come straight back if I need help."

Lord Penn and two other men were already hammering the new boards into place. I flashed the torch round the room for a moment to find the other lantern; two scared faces looked in through the passage door, saw the hopeful signs, and disappeared to carry the word.

The tempest still poured through the narrowing hole as through a sluice gate. As I struggled to light the storm lamp, I listened, trying to make out if the wind had broken in on the floor above; but the roaring and the din of hammering were too great. The shelterers were filtering back one by one to view the wreckage and find their possessions.

Then in the beam of the torch—laid on the floor to angle up at the top shuttering as the men worked—I saw a large crack in the ceiling above the broken door; water was dribbling through, and, even as I watched, it seemed to come faster. Before I reached the stairs to call him, Tom was down again.

"Tom!" I shouted. "Water's coming through—from *above*—"

His lantern was out and I could not see his face.

"I know," he said. It was more of a gasp. "I should have taken the torch—I saw enough, though: bedroom ceiling above here—open to the sky—not big, but enough —bloody tree must have caught it on the way down. . . . Should have known, I suppose—nothing we could do anyway—no stopping it—shingles tearing away like so much straw, flying everywhere—hole must be getting bigger all the time—soon the wind'll lift the lot—" All this shouted, crouching in the lee of the stairs. Some of the fugitives were just visible by the door, watching and wondering, keeping out of the shrieking jetstream coming through the small remaining gap, and two of them were handing boards over to the hammering where the bright light was centered.

"How long have we got?" I asked.

"Can't tell—but not long. We've got to move to somewhere safer."

So. The final stronghold. But I did not say it out loud.

The hammering stopped; the storm was blocked out,

the hall was intact again, suddenly quieter—almost snug, in spite of the rainwater and the wreckage. Oh, God, I thought, if only we could stay put. So many people, so much stuff to move. To move *down there.*

Why did I have a dread of the old store? Certainly it was compounded by my loving brother's discovery of this very early on; he used it as the ultimate threat. "If you don't," he would say slowly, when all else had failed, "you'll be locked inside the bottom store. . . ." He did not need to enumerate the rats, the tarantulas, the shades of darkness—and that cold stuffy smell, which will forever be to me the actual smell of fear.

When I thought about it sensibly—as sensibly as I could —I used to wonder how Tom would get the keys to carry out this threat; Father carried them with him always—but still I never dared put it to the test. Twice—once when I was quite small, and once when I was older and, I thought, braver—I had been persuaded to go with Father to bring up the bananas; they hung in there, ripening in the cool darkness until they had turned color and were fit for their hook on the veranda, where we could all help ourselves, us and his precious birds.

The first time, I had only crossed the threshold and run out again—that was enough; and Tom observed this from the drawing-room window, and used it against me—seldom, but with effect. Now I remembered how, even in strong sunshine, the tall weathered door looked grim and final; how the iron key scraped and the chain clanked; and how the cold struck my bare legs and arms stepping out of the warm bright air into that gloom. The second time, Tom was with us, and he slammed the door shut behind us to scare me. Father, not seeing my fear in the semidark, not knowing me, dropped his voice into his boots and intoned:

> *To sit in solemn silence in a dull, dark dock,*
> *In a pestilential prison, with a life-long lock,*

Awaiting the sensation of a short, sharp shock,
From a cheap and chippy chopper on a big black block!

I lost my head and screamed; and found myself outside
in the sun once more with Father carrying me. I felt such
a fool that when he said: "Come and give it another try—
as if you'd fallen off a horse," I followed them in again,
biting my thumb and hugging my goose pimples. I even
managed a bold laugh—a little high-pitched—as Father
pushed the door shut to show me it was all right. I kept my
eyes open this time, and they got used to the dim greenish
light that filtered through the slit window, the Glass Arch.
But I did not look at Tom. I felt him watching me;
he was storing it all for later, for whenever he should
need to use it against me, to bring me to heel.

This was why I did not answer him now. I could laugh
at almost all the fears of my childhood, and at Tom's ruth-
less and ingenious exploitation of them. Some of the best
games had arisen, in fact, from his daring me to overcome
them; or he would weave them into adventures and we
ended up by braving them together. "Good old Lizzie!
Not so wet and weedy after all . . ." It was the final acco-
lade, for me.

But even now, to say, out loud, "It's perfectly simple—
we must all move down to the bottom store. We'll be safe
there." Safe? *There?*

Nan was relighting the glims, still unaware of the trouble overhead. Tom had climbed across the tree trunks to
Lord Penn, inspected the new shuttering, then turned to
talk to the men. I saw him point upward and shake his
head; I guessed that he wanted to organize an orderly
retreat before rumor got round and panic spread. But he
was losing time: already I was aware of a strong draft
down the stairwell, and now that the storm no longer
raged round the hall itself and the hammering had ceased,
I could hear—perhaps because I knew—a sound above us
that had not been there before.

The loud shuddering of the windows—that was the

same—and the whistle of the gale, the roar of rain, like surf pounding on the roof, the creak and groan of the beams and rafters. But now I could hear a fearsome grinding wrenching sound: a thousand nails twisting in wood, the aching extraction of bolts, pinions, pegs, and linchpins. Suddenly there was glass breaking, furniture falling.

Then we heard the roof go.

It went with a splintering squeal that was instantly drowned by the storm's full force roaring into the upper story, just above our ceiling. Everything above us seemed to be smashing and tumbling. The tempest howled down the stairs.

"All into the bottom store!" I yelled; and, clutching the lantern, protecting it with my body, I scrambled across the wrecked room to the door and started hustling people through it. "Go on!" I shouted, but they floundered about, calling on God and their possessions. "Come!" I said. "We will get all your things too—but come with me—"

I led the way through the passage into the drawing room. The lantern by me, I knelt down where I could see the brass inset handle gleaming through the scummy wash. Two others were with me, more following. When they saw me pulling at the ring, they crouched down to help, and we lifted the trap door and let it fall backward with a splash that made the lantern sputter. I picked it up and lowered it into the hole. It broke through cobwebs as it went.

The cold breath of the bottom store rose round me, almost tangible, making my scalp creep. By the weak light dangling just past the beams, I could see a stepladder disappearing down into the dark; nothing more. It did not look inviting. I pulled up the lamp and turned to the man nearest me, but before I could speak, he drew back, shaking his head.

"Here," I said, "take it and hand it down to me."

I shifted round and stepped cautiously into the opening, felt for the next step. Waist-high in darkness, I took

153

the lantern from him. Then, clinging to the ladder with one hand, I moved on slowly down into the cavern below.

It was a long way, seventeen steps. From firm ground I looked up at the dim faces round the trap door, then about me. I held the light high, and, hoping I looked more fearless than I felt, I walked round the store.

It was chill, but dry and comparatively clean; dust and rust and cobwebs in plenty, but the brilliant green bunches of bananas hanging from the ceiling, the rows of yellow oil drums, the folded sacks, bags of maize, heap of new straw and cornhusks on a firm mud floor—it was better than I had imagined, and I saw that there was room for us all.

I called up—and it was so much quieter down here—"All right, come down now. . . . It's good in here." When no one moved, "It's fine and dry—you people coming?" I set the lantern on the ground and climbed halfway up the ladder. The hatch was crowded with faces now.

"Listen, we all have to move down below," I said. "Nowhere else is safe now the roof has gone. One of you, go call Mars Tom and Miss Nan, tell them. Another go gather up everybody and bring them—you hear me? Good. Now —who will come down and show the others it is all right? Come now, one of you—"

The faces disappeared and a pair of legs dangled through. I backed down and stood away, and one, then another, of the dazed and frightened shelterers climbed slowly to the bottom of the ladder. I heard a call, looked up, and saw Tom's face in the opening.

"Are you okay, Liz?"

"It's fine down here," I called, "safe and dry—"

"Good girl—not so wet and weedy—" Tom said, smiled, and disappeared; and I heard his voice above the trapdoor: "All right, now, women first—yes, go back, you two, and bring anything you can carry. You others go on down. Nan? Is Miss Nan there? All the little lights we want—and any food that's left."

Now the younger woman was down and the older one was being helped through the opening; some bundles; then the man with the bandaged foot; then came a youth who had been struck on the head by a flying branch when the bitterwood fell.

It was an extraordinary scene in the light of the one weak lantern. I had set it up on an empty oil drum, and watched as they eased through the injured, nearly naked man. They held him caught up under his armpits, while the women received him from below. His head drooped sideways onto his bloody shoulder, like the *Descent from the Cross* above Parson's desk—the tired load of flesh, the straining arms and faces, the dark gold varnished lighting. The Son of God was never more mortal than then, Parson said: "It was a despairing moment for the faithful." And however hopeful and hearty I tried to be, there was the smell of mortality, of despair, in that rough cellar, itself more like a tomb.

Now the men were passing down belongings in a chain from hand to hand; mostly sacks and bundles, blankets, a net of breadfruit, a chicken—only one now, it seemed —coats, bottles, and other possessions that had lost their wrappings in the move: a fancy hat, a framed photograph, a parasol (irony), a marble clock—carried all the way from the Line. They sorted them from the general pile on the floor and stowed them in the shadows round the walls. They were muted and orderly; soon the central space was clear again, with room to sit down, and they began to make themselves comfortable. I looked round to find the best place for Aunt Cissie: *not* in the center, I thought. There was the pile of straw—it would be soft, but too low, so I arranged an old trunk I found against the wall with some sacking on it. It would be better when we had more lights, and now the glims were being passed down, one by one, and set out on the flat top of one of the empty drums.

"Please, Miss Liz—" Lord Penn was calling me through

the trapdoor. "Is trouble with you auntie, Miss Liz—seem like she won't move."

"I'll come up," I said.

I climbed up the long stepladder and went into the drawing room. Nan appeared from the passage, flustered and anxious.

"I can't shift her at all, Miss Liz—she too strong and stubborn altogether. Mars Tom with her now—Lord, no end to this trouble."

"You go down, Nan," I said. I took her lantern and went through. The hall door was heavy with the wind against it. Inside, by the light of Tom's torch, I could see the aunt sitting tight, gripping the carved arms of the Siege Perilous.

"I won't go," she said coldly through the wet wisps of her lashing boa.

The room about her, as far as I could see it, was like the lounge of an abandoned ship—wreckage and hurled spray and the floor awash—it only needed a runaway piano now, and the aunt looked as though she might strike up "Nearer My God to Thee." The hurricane roared through above, spraying shingles down the stairwell. Nearby, glinting in the moving torch beam, lay the stuffed birds and a litter of curved glass.

"It's not safe," said Tom, "but she won't listen. We'll have to carry her."

"Oh no, Tom—not that!" I said. "Let me try."

"Tell her she'll get bloody *killed*, for Christ's sake!"

"She doesn't understand about ordinary danger." Bending close, I said, "Aunt, I've been down to the bottom store and it's lovely—really. Dry, and much much quieter. It's high—like a ballroom—with beautiful green bunches of bananas for chandeliers—or like a magic cave, all safe and secret, away from the storm. And you've got a box to sit on all ready for you, and—"

"A *box*?" It was the *grande dame* who spoke. "For *me*? I won't go." She looked up craftily, sideways. "Not unless I can have my chair."

I glanced at Tom. "Will it go through the hatch? Better see before we promise anything."

"It'll go," he said.

"All right then, Aunt Cissie. Come along now."

I took her arm, and the torch; she carried her bag and my spent lantern; Tom followed with the chair. When we came to the trapdoor she peered into it quite undismayed.

"Does one go backwards, as in the royal presence?" she asked, a point of etiquette.

"That's right, Aunt—or on board ship," I said.

Lord Penn stood a little way down, ready to hold her, and Nan was waiting at the bottom. The plimsolls came into their own, clinging like long pale suckers to the wooden steps as she felt her way, and I heard a flutter of clapping from those assembled below—not the "Grand Staircase," perhaps, but certainly the "Cynosure of All Eyes." Then Tom passed the chair through, strong arms took it, and there was more clapping and a faint cheer. Morale was high at the moment.

Not mine; I felt my whole being instinctively rebelling against that final incarceration, as it seemed to me. Our world was contracting with each progressive stage, and at this point I felt even the abandoned, windswept hall was more bearable than the hole that gaped for us.

"You go down," said Tom. "I've left something behind."

"So have I," I said.

I lit the storm lantern once more, and Tom went ahead with the torch. We looked into the pantry to see if there was any food left to take, or a candle that had been missed, but there were only empty tins and dirty mugs; one eerie "plop" from the dripstone, unfilled. Life was coming to a halt. Tom turned back into the passage, but I lingered a moment more, holding up my light and gazing round the sad familiar room. It seemed a whole lifetime since Maurice stepped in through the doorway and took hold of both my hands. I looked at my watch—as we had, together, and by this same lantern, clinging so close

157

in the rising tempest: eight o'clock, it had been. The storm seemed exciting then. Now that storm had killed him. I followed Tom toward the hall.

Water was coming into the passage under the door, which shook with the wind on the other side; I pushed through, protecting my light as best I could. Rough eddying gusts, trapped and circling wildly, buffeted me as I made my way across to Tom. He was shining the torch beam into the corners and seemed to be hunting for something.

"It's nearly two," I shouted. "How long can this go on?"

"Can't tell," he shouted back, "but it's moving round."

"What are you looking for?"

"Nothing really—just seeing if everything's—" The words were blown away as he turned back, peering among the fugitives' leavings, turning them over with his foot—sodden sacks and blankets and clothing that had been laid out to dry.

I had something to do. I moved toward the great door, where Maurice lay forgotten in the panic, deserted even by his own wakers. Only the chicken that had escaped kept him company now, perched high above on the buffalo's skull, rocking and clinging in the wind. The chairs and sofa had shifted down the room with the gale and lay in a tangled heap, a rough barrier on the weather side. Beyond it, on the broad threshold, the blanket covering the long low landfall of the body was hardly disturbed, pinned down as it was by broken boughs, and heavy with rain. I straightened it a little, removed a branch, and two shingles caught against the feet, and took the heavy brass doorstops to weight it down at either end. The candles had gone.

The torch beam settled on me, dazzling me so that I could not see Tom's face beyond it. He shouted something like "Hurry." I set my lantern down beside the body in the lee of the piled chairs, near where the head would be, and stood up.

"Hey!" shouted Tom. "You can't leave that! We *need* it! For God's sake—what use is it to—"

"I will not leave him alone *and* in the dark," I shouted back.

He gave up and turned toward the passage, and I followed. At the door we stopped for a moment. I clung to his arm as a soaking gust from the broken roof swept howling down the stairwell and made us stagger. He shone his torch on the staircase and slowly upward. Leafy branches lay across the banister, rain poured down the treads, and for a moment I had a glimpse of a bosky woodland waterfall, of jeweled water and brilliant moss.

Then we closed the door on the wasted room, the shredded lilies, the lonely dead. We went to the drawing room, climbed through the hatch, and closed it after us.

TWO O'CLOCK

OUR FINAL STRONGHOLD was not large, but high—nearly twenty feet high—so that when Tom switched off the torch to save the battery, the light of the glims didn't reach the distant ceiling; the ladder and the banana chains dwindled up into the dark. The space we were in was about twelve feet wide; at its length one could only guess, as it stretched back into the hill. Behind the ladder the floor became uneven and swiftly degenerated into ribs of rock that sloped to meet the roof somewhere in the darkness beyond.

A snaking stone promontory extended from this dark hinterland into our living area. Bundles lay against its sides, and on the last jutting ledge, chest high, Nan had set two candles. By the glint of silver at their bases, I recognized them as those she had used for the makeshift wake upstairs. As Tom and I stepped down and looked around us, she put a match to them, and the tall flames shed a wider radiance on the store and the rough sloping rock behind them; and in that special candlelighting silence, we heard something skitter and scrabble yet farther into the dark interstices of the old store. I thought it must be a rat, but found myself wondering whether the tarantulas might not be that big, and we all stared up the incline, where ridged shadows wavered with the wavering light.

This was the backbone of the island, the final vertebra of the range whose proper, spectacular end was Rookoom, and which traveled all the way up through the precipitous Cockpit country to the Blue Mountains themselves. The very tip of the coccyx was that rough ledge, that little altar, on which the candles now burned. All that is wild and unknown starts here, I thought, and reaches back into the dark, into the past—into a future just as hidden. All we had was the slender moment, two pale candles burning down.

Most of the shelterers were sitting on the earth floor; some had pulled over yellow oil drums. Glims were set out on others, one beside Aunt Cissie, who held herself very straight on her imported throne, placed against the wall. Already it was getting close and stuffy with packed bodies steaming dry and the oily smoke from the floating lights. The only air down here came through the narrow slit of the Glass Arch. We were now on the lee side of the hill, the storm whistling past beyond the thick door. The padlock outside had been removed, I knew, and Lord Penn had shot the inner bolts, so now it no longer rattled—only quivered when the eddying wind struck it; and then the dust crept along the floor. Standing up, I could feel a welcome draft from the little window.

It was a loophole set high in the massive wall; there was another on the short twisting staircase of the turret, and they were clearly designed for defense—during the slave rebellions a century and a half ago—angled in from a bare three-inch aperture to a wide arch and sloping sill. This one had been cased in a crude basket of wire mesh, to contain the broken glass of the household and yard. With so many bare feet and wandering domestic animals, it was a sensible institution, like a giant razor-blade disposer; narrow slit into broad container. The shards and splinters caught the light: broken bottles and jars, but mainly window glass—a heap of dirty ice. Now and again it tinkled faintly, shaken by a strong gust.

161

But in the well, the glims only shivered in the dying movement of the air that reached them. Despite the initial relief from the bedlam of the hall, such stillness and quiet was curiously unsettling: not only did we find ourselves actually crowded now, but we had lost the privacy, the separation, imposed before by the storm's racketing. The fugitives conversed in harsh uneasy whispers as if they had found themselves in church, and, as in church, they seemed to be waiting for something to begin. Tom and I tried to talk normally, making ourselves comfortable on the box I had prepared for Aunt Cissie. Nan came and sat on a sack of grain beside her. All the parts of the pop-out book had been blown away or lost in the last onslaught, and I wondered how we were going to amuse the aunt if she would not sleep. She looked alert as ever. The squinting eyes darted about unsynchronized, exploring independently the unfamiliar room: the bright bananas hanging on their chains; dark shadows softened with pale dusty cobwebs; the big door, its row of hooks carrying coils of wire and rope and a forgotten straw hat frosted with the fine white powder that drifted down from the stone walls; the bare rock sloping away into the heart of the hill.

"Come now, Miss Ciss"—Nan always found work for idle hands, like her lord and master, Tom used to say, though not in her hearing for fear of blasphemy—"make Nan a nice doily from this paper."

The newspaper she had found was old and yellow, but she took out the clean inner leaves and folded them ready for tearing.

"What else have we got, Nan?" I asked. "Did you manage to bring down any supplies?"

She got up and showed me her cache: a small milk can of water, two tin mugs, the half-empty bottle of rum, a loaf of Chinese bread, and three tins of corned beef. Tom's gun belt, dappled with rain, was hanging across the milk can to dry out.

"With Primus gone, Miss Liz," she whispered, "what

good to carry down rice and peas and tea and all that need to cook?"

"Quite right, Nan," I said, lowering my voice like hers. "This should keep us. Not enough to feed everyone, of course—"

"Them have food in them bundle, you know, Miss Liz," she hissed. "Them won't go without, don't fret."

"Well, we needn't worry now, certainly. Perhaps later on we should pool what we have and divide it. I think that now we ought to get some sleep."

None of the shelterers looked at all like sleeping. A bottle had been retrieved from the jumble of belongings and was being passed round. The two dominoes players were laying out their pieces on the dusty floor between them, pulling a glim closer. There was little talk, and that low and nervous. Most of them sat hunched, glancing about them like Aunt Cissie, but always avoiding those bulging shifty eyes.

They would take time to settle down again properly, I thought; sleep must overtake them eventually. At least they were dry and safe and calm—an uneasy calm, but one that I must learn to abide with. This was something like the status quo I had wished for, the being buried alive. I must reassemble my own scattered resources, and adapt myself to this the next stage in our ordeal of survival. I looked round almost automatically for something I could do; but of course down here, reduced to what I had on, I looked about in vain. The bottom store made the besieged hall look like an entertainment arcade by comparison. Here we had no books, no cards, no sewing, no Gramophone. There had not been time to gather them up—and if there had, I doubt we would have found them in the wind and rain and broken branches. It wasn't safe to linger and search, once the wind had broken in; very soon, we knew, the drawing-room roof must go too, leaving the house above us open to the storm—as deadly as the outdoors where Maurice had been struck down a couple of yards from shelter.

Maurice. And what would *he* do now? It was a reflex action to turn to the little light beside me. In a way, I realized, he was still with us, his glims watching over us; the orderly store, the bright tins of coconut oil—even our presence here—were all thanks to him. But my mind shied away from tenderness—to think too clearly was to court pain—so, in my mind, I thanked him, and then I clicked it shut and stood up.

"Can I have your lighter?" I asked Tom. "I'm going to see to the glims." He had his two silver bullets lying in the palm of his hand, tilting them to catch the light, and as I spoke, he started to toss and catch them. I took the lighter and put it into my pocket. "I forgot the pliers," I said. "You didn't bring—"

"Nope—sorry," he snapped. That companionable ease was gone. He'll settle down soon, I thought, but I felt lonely.

"I can manage," I said. "Just a matter of snuffing them first so as to handle them."

I started on Aunt Cissie's glim; it was sputtering. I snuffed it, eased the oily wick through a little, and relit it. Once the scrap of vest was shortened, I could see that the oil above the water was ample; but I wondered what we should use for wicks when these ran out. Surely among all the bundles we would find some rag that would serve. I moved on to the next. Two of the glims set down among the shelterers had already been tended; I could see by their light that the young man was having his cut forehead dressed, and was sipping from a tin mug. But the glim on the floor by the dominoes players was burning low.

"I'll fix it to give you a better light," I said, squatting by them. They watched me pinch it out. When I rekindled it, one of them said in a drowsy voice, heavy with spirits:

"What a night, eh, my friends? One night we won't never forget."

"Night of the little lights and the Great Light," said his companion, gazing into the flame.

"Night of strange happening," said the older woman.

"Strange strange things them happen this night," murmured the first.

"Mark my words"—the woman again—"no good come of wake when it disturb, when it cut off, bam! before it properly finish."

"Cut off like German self cut off, my friend—so, bam! —before him time finish. Here, missis, make I wipe you hand fe you." The smiling drowsy dominoes player offered me his kerchief for the oil that shone on my fingers and dribbled down my wrist.

"I've still got one to do," I said, "but thanks." I took the handkerchief, passionately grateful, in the midst of this morbid exchange, for the simple normal gesture.

"Please, missis, is what happen over there?" One of the other men sitting on an oil drum leaned across and touched my arm, and as he moved into the light I could see that his eyes were frightened.

"Over where, friend?" I asked.

Without looking away, he gestured toward the back of the store with a movement of his head.

"Up yonder, please'm. Is what it lead to?"

"Nowhere," I said, "there's no opening back there, no other trapdoor—nothing. Why?"

He dropped his eyes and plucked a piece of corn trash from the floor.

"Never mind, missis."

Others were ready, waiting to fill the pause, and spoke out louder, capping each other.

"Him 'fraid fe Busha head, missis—" "Hush you mouth!" "How it can get in, missis, and follow us—" "Hush man—" "But is true—" "Is Head—"

"Hush up!" the man said, half rising, but still in a stage whisper. "All o' you 'fraid so-tell, 'fraid same like me—is not I one—" He scowled and sat, his head bowed, shredding the corn straw between trembling fingers. There was a moment's silence, then I stood up quickly.

"I'll show you there's no other way in," I said. "I'll get the big torch and shine it for you. It feels strange down here." I kept talking as I fetched it from Tom's corner ("Want help?" he asked grudgingly, but I shook my head). "It only feels strange because it's not much used, this old store. So you get cobwebs and a rat or two, I expect—the thing is, it's strong and safe."

I stood among them and shone the beam into the corners and up the rock slope, but I could see that the battery was going fast—the light was weaker and yellower than before. I stepped out of the circle of shelterers, over the fringe of bundles and a few paces up the rough incline. The people were mostly standing now, watching but not speaking. There was only the edgy click of Tom's bullets; and then we heard a distant shuffling and a faint fall of stones. One of the women squeaked; the others said, "Hush nunh, woman?"

Then someone observed: "Even electric power torch can't catch so far. . . ."

"Seem like darkness go on back and back—"

"Torch can't catch—"

"Seem like is no end. . . ."

I took another two steps up the ridge of rock, feeling for footholds and raising a pale dust as I moved. I called back, "Now you can see, can't you?—it's going away to nothing?" I shone the light at the rafters and down again. "It's nearly joined with the ceiling, see?" But my voice sounded hollow and echoing in the space; even I was surprised by the extent of it, and was loath to climb farther, however logical the conclusion.

I was spared by the torchlight waning abruptly and noticeably.

"Torch going die out, Miss Liz,"—Lord Penn's voice— "come away now."

I turned round carefully and, shining the dark yellow beam downward, made my way back along the incline.

166

"Not even power torch can last in that deep darkness!"
—the older woman added, a little too shrill.

"It's not that," I said briskly, "the torch was nearly
finished anyway. It's lasted well—all through the mending
of the door, remember? If you like, I'll take a candle up
there and show you—"

"No, Miss Liz."

Nan, who had been watching silently all this while,
suddenly swept forward, stepping across the dominoes
and legs and bundles, and reached up and took my arm.
"Come down, chile. Is sufficient foolishness—you must satisfy with it and rest quiet."

It was a humiliating end to my bravado: I felt not only
that she was letting me down—like the torch—but also
not a little surprised at the stand she seemed to be taking;
and the little band of shelterers clearly felt rebuffed.
They looked around at one another, then one of them
summoned up his courage and addressed the wise woman
directly.

"Please, Miss Nan, is what happen back there?"

The older woman chipped in, "Please, Miss Nan, you
really think we safe from *everyt'ing* in this place? At
night?"

Then I saw that Nan had by no means finished: the
change of style had merely been surprise tactics, to get
attention, to cut us all—and especially me—down to size,
for presuming even to speculate on such matters without
referring to the fountainhead in our midst. She turned
to them, very tall and dignified; from my rocky perch I
couldn't see her face, but the candles on the promontory
threw her huge shadow onto the door beyond.

"Questions!" (I could imagine the turned-down smile
of pity and disgust, also used when gutting fish.) "You
think I don't know is why you people scare up so? You
talk talk 'mongst youself and look for answer. But meanwhile something look for *you*." It was quite still in the
well of the store; even the silver bullets had ceased their
clinking. "You think it going creep in through some little

167

hole and find you?" A low mutter: "Lord, let it not creep and find . . ." "I tell you: the Dead don't need no hole fe creep through." She paused dramatically. Under the distant hurricane, the only sound was the wind moaning and sucking at the door. Then: "If the Head going come, I tell you, it will come!" Softly: "Let it not come, O Lord. . . ." "*Safe*, you ask me? All right—you going listen to me now?" A rhetorical question. "Good people, I tell you: No bar-up door or pile-up rockstone in this world can keep it out!"

A woman cried out in terror: "Sweet Jesus, guard us now!"

Whether Nan wanted to get me back under her thumb or the limelight for herself, I do not know, but she had done both. The people were once more her cowed congregation. And as for me, my mouth had gone dry with fear. Ridiculous as it seems, writing this in daylight on the turret window seat, it was a very different matter in the benighted bottom store, my childhood nightmare factory. The frightened eyes in the weak light, the barely whispered responses and final shriek, the double pressure of the rocky darkness behind me and the storm leaning on the door, and Nan's tall menacing shape brooding over everything, were altogether too heady a mixture, overcoming reason.

At once, even familiar things half perceived out of the corner of my eye—the lumpy grain sack, the twitching white chicken, the piles of ragged bundles—seemed sinister and threatening; I crouched down where I stood, covering my face, and the torch fell from my hand and clattered onto the floor.

Nan turned swiftly and gathered me into her arms. I hid my face in her shoulder and let her lead me toward my seat. But I heard, behind me: "Lord! The poor chile take bad—" "Look 'pon how she hide up her eye them—" "Lord Jesus—she mus' see something bad—" "Lord preserve us! Is what she see, you think?" "Is what her eye catch? . . ."

168

Tom, who had—as I now realized—sat silently through-out this whole scene, suddenly got to his feet. As I reached him I turned from Nan's comfortable shoulder and looked at him. His eyes were close and nearly level with mine, and they were *scared*, for the first time in that long terri-fying night. He glanced round the dark edges outside the ring of light, and back at me; then visibly suppressed his fear—for my sake?—and said with exaggerated nonchalance:

"What *did* you see, Liz? Something nasty in the ba-nana shed? Or was it just the usual creeps?"

If I hadn't seen his panic a moment before, I would have thought him callous.

"Nothing," I said clearly, so that the others could hear me. "I'm just tired and overwrought. I didn't see *any-thing*, for goodness' sake—there's nothing *to* see."

He turned away and faced the fugitives. "All right," he said. "Enough of this fanciful talk, now. There is not one single thing to worry about—this is a good strong store—see how the walls are thick, and the timbers go right back into the rock—the master showed me himself. Noth-ing can harm us here." He blustered a little, riding over the murmurs of "Duppy can harm," "Head can come," "Lord Jesus—safe nowheres!"

"Rest easy, you people, and get some sleep; after your time of trouble you all need sleep."

There were mumbles of agreement and others of dis-satisfaction, but fear carries better than reassurance—it is pitched higher. And as Nan, with hooded eyes and pursed lips, handed me a mug of water, I heard: "Sleep, him say—hunh!" "Is how we going sleep when It still search—" "Hush up now—hush up!" "But is how we can sleep? Lord Jesus what a night!"

There was still another glim, I remembered, and roused myself to tend it. Nan pushed me back.

"Is I will fix the glim, Miss Liz," she said, stroking my hair.

"Thank you, Nan." I realized dimly that she was safer employed than idle. "Nan," I said, "would you tuck some

169

of those spare newspapers under the door while you're up? It'll stop the dust blowing."

Enviously I watched her at these little tasks. Things had come to a pretty pass, I thought, when I had to deny myself the numbing busyness I craved, in order to keep troublemakers quiet; and that, I could now see, was what Nan had become.

I know it took me time to accept this. It was a long painful step forward out of childhood, away from the comfortable blind acceptance of authority; and all the harder with Maurice gone, and Tom apparently out of reach—retreated, it seemed, into his own private stronghold. The Fearless Three had often resisted pressure from above, would have, now. But I found myself alone. Instinctively I turned to Nan in that moment of pure terror, only to realize afterward that she had staged it.

At first it was just a sense of loss that Nan was no longer reliable, but it grew into a recognition of her as something new to contend with. More than just a dark horse, an unknown quantity in the survival stakes, she seemed— now that I was calmer and had time to think—a positive threat to our equilibrium. Perhaps we should have been sterner at the first breath of superstition. At that time it had seemed important to be tolerant, to accept it within reason as the fugitives' own way of enduring our common peril. Once already it had got out of hand, and Nan had been a prime mover. She was so powerful among these people that her behavior was crucial. I had hoped, at worst, for a spirited prayer meeting, as the hymns promised; but now she seemed to be encouraging the darker side of religion, uniting her followers with fear, not comfort.

What changed her? It was almost as if she had reverted; as if, never quite tamed or entirely domestic, she had— under stress—returned to the wild. And I was suddenly afraid of Nan.

Aunt Clarissa was not among the awed whisperers, nor was she one to mumble her complaints. Now, with that

170

unerring instinct for timing, she gave tongue when least expected, and, as usual, the subject matter was provocative.

"When the Head comes in, I trust it will have its halo on."

It was a cross caw, produced with all the affectation of a county dowager bemoaning that people don't dress for dinner anymore. But its effect was even more startling.

Nan scrambled up from the newspapers she was folding —"Quiet now, Miss Ciss!"—and three of the shelterers were on their feet, knocking down an oil drum. But Tom was already standing over the big chair; he had Aunt Cissie by the shoulders and was shaking her.

"Shut up, you bloody old hag—or I'll shut you up!"

Nan and I pulled him away and he was trembling.

"Look here, Aunt," he said, low and fiercely—that change of pitch I most dreaded—"if you don't stop your morbid squawking, I'll put a big black sack over your head—see?"

The aunt had cringed down into her boa. Now she straightened up, preening herself haughtily.

"Oooh, naughty temper!" she crowed. "Little Tommy's jumpy about something—aren't you, dear? What is it, we wonder, that makes Tommy jumpy, then?"

I felt him straining against us and said in his ear: "Tom darling, you've got to ignore her. Come and sit down." Nan hushed the aunt and I tried to calm my brother, sitting by him, holding his arm and talking quietly to him. "She's mad and she's bored and she's overexcited, Tom—she can only be humored. Frightening her is no good, you know—she rather likes it, I think."

"Only trouble—always trouble—a man of violence—" Nan moaned. "Lord Jesus—wha' fe do? . . ."

"I need a drink," said Tom.

Nan settled Aunt Cissie with the silver hand mirror and her makeup box. The fugitives' alarm died away to a quiet grumbling; and Tom had quite taken the wind from their sails. Now the nervous glances were for him.

171

And I too was alarmed by his outburst. One by one I felt abandoned by my companions. But I suppose we were being isolated by our own deepest fears. The dark storm was dividing and conquering.

Yet, for a while, upstairs, Tom had been such a comfort, nursing me and coaxing me back to sanity—to reality, anyway. Action suits Tom, I thought, like Hamlet: a pirate ship, breached defenses; it's only the waiting in between that undoes him. But I wondered if there wasn't something else, something that sat brooding on his spirit.

I poured some rum and water into the mug for us to share. He was calmer now. I was so weary, I leaned back against the crusty wall and closed my eyes.

"Here, Liz—you can have a shoulder," he said, and I settled myself against him.

I woke with a start out of a dream of drums on the Line: Tom and I were in Father's big bed, listening to them, a distant throbbing, but quick and urgent; and Tom knelt upright—he was wearing his gun belt and the big knobby pistols—and said, "Something awful must have happened: hear the rhythm?" and I woke up. His arm was round my shoulders, my head had slipped down onto his chest, and it was his heartbeat that had woken me.

I put my head on his lap, and dozed and dreamed again —this time, of Cousin Edward. It was only a glimpse: I was waiting at the foot of Rookoom; it was very hot and still, so that I felt I could not breathe. Nevertheless, I had to wait—I seemed not to know why—and I was full of dread. I didn't know what to expect, or what might be about to happen. Then Cousin Edward stepped out from the forest alone—he had no horse—*and I saw him in black and white.* That was what was strange about him. That was what frightened me so that I woke with a cry.

"What was it?" asked Tom, holding me. I told him.

"And it was all in color till then, you see—no, it was *still* in color: the trees there, those tall spindly figs, were dark green, and the grass piece bright green and tall—

summer— But Edward was like a little cut-out photograph—quite flat—all black and gray and white. . . . God, it's hot in here—I need some air."

I stood up and stretched, and went over to the Glass Arch and breathed the cold damp draft that whisked through the slit from the storm outside. Shreds of leaves brushed my skin. The glass creaked and a long sliver shifted and settled lower in the heap, tinkling faintly as it went. Where is Cousin Edward now? I wondered. It felt as if I had not thought about him for hours. Maurice and I had talked of him. And Maurice had driven him from my mind, had made even Edward's sacred *Punch*es seem irrelevant, and they had ceased to divert me. And I had tried to imagine Edward's face; that didn't work either. I've lost them both now, I thought, listening to the wind roaring up the wooded hillside, our favorite playground. How many of our special trees would be down, I wondered, when we emerged from our safe hole?

I thought about the times when Tom and I had played the Orpheus game, using that same hillside for his ascent from the underworld. I was always made to trail behind, crying, "Sweet husband, turn and look upon me—just once, I beg!" "Come on, Liz—I bet you're not making a really *despairing* gesture—" "What's the point if no one's looking?" Then of course he would turn round when I least expected and catch me throwing a stick for the dogs; and we had to do it all again—fine for *him*. "You're making it more like Grandmother's Footsteps!" I'd grumble, longing to be Orpheus myself and carry the old broken badminton racket as a lyre—which had started the whole idea.

Edward let me be the hero once, though. "You mustn't turn round whatever I say, remember. Keep going up towards the light. Hide your face in your cloak—anything —but don't look at me."

"But I haven't *got* a cloak."

"Pretend you have, Eliza." He swept up the imaginary folds in a magnificent gesture over his left arm, bowed his head onto it, and stretched his other hand behind him in balletic rejection. I set off up the hill with my lyre, my own imaginary cloak flowing from my forward arm, renunciation in every line; behind me, the sad imploring wail:

"Wait, oh wait! I am too weak from my sad sojourn in the dark land. The shadows of Hades are clinging to me, Orpheus, dragging me down! Lend me your hand—one touch, my love, I beg, or I will fail and fade away—"

He was awfully good at it—really moving—and I longed all too genuinely to turn and take his hand. Suddenly I heard a crash and a sharp cry.

"Ow! Oh, God—I'm hurt! Stop it, Eliza—pax! Come back and help me!"

In a flash I was kneeling beside him, and he was on his feet and running back down the hill. He stopped and turned at the edge of the ruins, and called out very sternly to me where I sat, stupefied, as if I had been slapped.

"I told you not to turn round, Eliza, *whatever* I said. Don't you *see*? I've lost my chance. Now I'll be dead forever."

"But I thought you'd really—"

"Precisely. You let yourself be fooled by the Dead, didn't you? Silly girl."

It was the harshest he had ever been. Later, playing records, I tried to exonerate myself a little.

"Wasn't it cheating a bit to be yourself, and call 'Eliza'?"

"But the Dead are terribly crafty, you know. They'll cheat like mad—after all, they've nothing to lose, everything to gain: everlasting peace, no less. Well worth a touch of the foul play. Never trust the Dead, dear girl—transparent liars every one."

He was in a good mood again, talking hard as he flipped through the records; and, wanting to preserve it, I was happy to play along.

"So is that why the Dead—" I did not like the word, "why ghosts appear to people?" I asked.

"Yes, Eliza. Traditional ghost stories, at any rate, usually show them seeking peace through human intervention."

"Yes—but was Eurydice *tricking* Orpheus?" I persisted. "I thought she *loved* him."

"So much, dear girl, that she wanted to drag him down with her into Hades. I think it was all a big con, Eliza, and Pluto and Persephone were in on it. Eurydice was dead—she'd never have made it to the top, into the light of day; she'd have melted."

"A *con*?" It was all so disillusioning, somehow.

"The con was that Orpheus thought she was real and alive. Now here's Gluck's version. . . ."

I remembered this incident one day in the turret, reading our old *Myths and Legends* from the nursery, which my brother sent up to me for good behavior. (Its endpapers were yellow and spotted with age. I used them up last week, writing very small—I hope legibly. Since then I have persuaded Nan to let me draw, so I have wax crayons—very clumsy. I'm clumsy anyway, being so feeble now. My moths and ants have to manage on their own.) But it was only in remembering it, so long after, that I understood those words of Edward's, and it all fell into place.

"Well, I just hope the plane's been grounded," I said to Tom as I turned away from the Glass Arch window. "It's still tearing around out there—hard to tell down here on the lee side, but I wouldn't say it was even beginning to blow itself out."

Tom was juggling his bullets again. I wished he would stop. "If the still center passes over us at least we'll feel it's going somewhere," he said without taking his eyes off them. Someone, probably Nan, had salvaged his pistols and belt when the storm came into the hall and brought them down with the provisions. Now he reached over for them and stood up to buckle them on.

"Are those to drive away the duppies?" I whispered.

"Always loaded and at your service, marm," he said, grinning suddenly. "But only two shots, come to think of it—I didn't bring any ammo down with me."

"You've got your silver ones, though," I said. "Would they work?"

"Oh, they'd work," said Tom solemnly. "Right size and all that—very effective, in fact. Ask old Nan. Yes indeed, they'd work." Smiling again, and dropping into dialect: "Dem don' tell you, Miss Lizzie me dear? Silver bullet can stop even duppy in him track—is so dem say."

"Hush up, man," I whispered; but the shelterers were not listening. Some of them had at last curled up to sleep. Others were sharing out biscuits, and I saw yet more bottles being unwrapped from their protective sacking.

"Are you hungry?" I asked Tom. "We've got some bread and a few tins."

"Save the tins," he said, "but let's have a bit of bread. And some more to drink."

I gave some bread to Nan, and she poured herself a mug of water laced with rum. Aunt Cissie was nodding forward over her bejeweled bosom; I put her bread on one side for later.

Seeing perhaps that their hosts had little left to offer them, the people were beginning to look among the nearest bundles for a proper meal. It was now a quarter to three by my watch; the small bowls of stew we had provided were two hours ago. Some slept on, but the others started to move about and sort out their supplies from the rest of their possessions. Nan was right; they had not come unprovided—though most of the food turned out to be raw material: a net of green breadfruit, yams, bags of dried peas, and, of course, the chicken, quietly settled now in spite of its tied legs, and nodding like the aunt into its ruff of bedraggled white feathers. But there were also two tins of luncheon meat, and bread, and some short sticks of sugar cane. One of the men, when pressed— "Come now, Jamesy, is what you have to offer, man?"—

176

produced a tin of herrings in tomato sauce, with opener attached. Once he had declared it, he became generous, stepping over to offer some to us and to Nan. Tom refused —he seemed very jumpy again, leaning forward and watching them as they unwrapped their provisions and laid them out—but Nan and I dipped our bread into the sauce, scooped out some fish, and pronounced it good.

"Wait now, Jamesy me dear—" The older woman got up. She was not to be outdone. "I got just the thing fe set off you herring: one sweet and lovely cook breadfruit I roast inna me fire when them come tell me of storm. Wait make I fetch it fe you—I know it lay down somewheres hereabouts." She did not find it in the nearest bundles. "Is where it hiding now?"

I felt Tom's shoulder quivering where it touched mine— from contained laughter rather than from cold, I guessed.

"Not all the bundle them bring down you know, Miss Queenie. Some still remain cover up with furniture and branch and everything."

"Don' come with that, Lord Penn me dear. I tell you I see it carry through trapdoor—it must set down somewhere abouts—a fine sweet roast breadfruit, just *wait* fe eat up—"

At this tantalizing prospect one of the men joined her in the search.

"Is how it wrap, missis?"

"It wrap in crocus bag, me love, tie up with string. Ah now, this here one of mine." She straightened up, feeling the sack. "Lord, how it wet up even now! Oh no—this one me yam bag. . . . Wait, but some Chinee bread is into it, I recall—you can't find me breadfruit then? Never mind now—I will seek it again." She had looked round and seen the herrings disappearing. "Must make do with bread till we find better, eh?"

She began untying her bread and yam bag; no one was taking much notice of her now that the promise of breadfruit had receded. But I watched her and so did Tom; she was so fluent, so self-absorbed, so busy. She it was who had gone into a trance during the chanting; she showed no ill effects now, fossicking inside her food bag.

"Look now, you see—Lord, is what a way it wet up though!—see, we have some bread—Jesus Christ! Is why the bag wet up so?"

"Everything wet up, woman," (it was the cool druggy dominoes player) "is occupational hazard in hurricane, my friend." Everyone laughed.

But the woman dropped the bag with a shriek.

"Lord Jesus—is what this 'pon me hand? Don't tell me is rain now—Lord have mercy—is same t'ing wet up me bread."

She scrambled into the circle, holding her bread and her hands to the light. On the white side of the loaf was a dark stain and her trembling fingers gleamed stickily.

"Is blood! I tell you is *blood!*"

"No, missis, is sauce from the herring them—look, see my hand same way."

"Then how it get 'pon me bread?"

"Is finest epicure way fe eat herring, man."

"But how it get on this bread, eh? I don' get any herring yet, you know—nor sauce neither!"

"All right then: it leak out the tin and catch you bag. Wipe you hand, woman, and sit down, nuh?"

Now the man with the herrings was indignant.

"Nothing don't wrong with this herring tin, friend—don' tell me no sauce leak out of it—no, man, don' com wi' that—"

"I tell you, is *blood!*" cried the woman, waving her hands under their noses. "The whole bag wet up with it."

"Seem like someone bring fresh beef inna them bundle."

No one answered. Tom was standing now, leaning back against the wall; the bullets clicked softly.

"I tell you is something *must* leak out." The woman clambered back to the pile of belongings beyond the edge of the light. "Is a shame, I tell you, a shame fe go mess up poor woman bundle. Someone bring in a nice piece of beef go leak 'pon me bag—'pon me bread. But him don't fool

178

me—not at all—*I* know him won't speak out—oh no! Him might have fe *share*: nice piece o' beef fe each one of us and can cook up little bit over candle them. . . . And I going find it—so help me! I tell you, if joint of fancy beef come bloody up me bread, *I* going have a share of it."

All the while she was picking through the sacks in the gloom, mumbling threats and promises. The others went on eating, dealing out the Spam with a penknife.

"Find you breadfruit, woman," said someone. "Fresh beef can wait till morning fe cook up proper."

But she persisted. "All right now, something here, wet again. No—seem like is bottle leak out. . . . And something big inna this one and wet again—"

She lifted it higher to get the light on it. It was a long dirty crocus bag of rough burlap, with a dark patch in one corner. It looked heavy.

"Make I see what is into this one now." No sound from the silver bullets.

The sack was roughly knotted. She set it down, untied it, and peered into it.

"Light don't too good here. Let we bring it over." She climbed back into the circle where two glims stood flickering on the mud floor, dumped the bag beside them, and peered again.

"No must shake it out and see, woman? It favor breadfruit—see if this time we get lucky—"

Now everyone looked round, eager and expectant. One leaned forward impatiently, grabbed a corner of the sack, and tipped it up; and Maurice's head rolled out.

THREE O'CLOCK

AND THAT was how the head found a way into our stronghold.

There was only one scream, from the woman holding the sack, and then she fell back, unconscious. No one spoke; but from the circle of fugitives came a huge intake of breath that seemed to draw them up and out like the blossoming of a dark ragged flower, and the thing at its center was hidden from me.

Oil drums were overturned, and glims crashed to the floor and fizzled briefly in their water. Sleepers, stumbled on, woke and cried out, breaking the spell. A low babble—"Lord Jesus Christ . . . It find we, Lord . . . Preserve us, sweet Jesus!"—filled the darkened cellar, not hysterically, still contained breathlessly by awe. Some drew farther back and covered their eyes—"Hide you eye! . . . Hide up you eye—don't look Dead in Him face!"—and the circle broke to reveal the center again.

For a moment I gazed at the waxen profile outlined by the glims that still burned beyond it on the floor: I saw the drooping eyelids and the glint of cornea beneath. Beside me, Aunt Cissie started to her feet, and I looked round and saw Nan unfreeze, make a sign across her own brow, lips, and heart. Then she gently turned the aunt's face away, cupping her hands round the pale frizz of hair; but her charge jerked back again, eyes staring, and let out a piercing cry, ripping the tight atmosphere apart, and everyone was screaming, a pandemonium of terror unleashed.

I was an observer, cold and uninvolved, quite unable to reach out to my aunt, to hide my eyes or block my ears, to move at all. I did not even wonder; I accepted that the head had found a way to us. Hadn't Maurice said he would come back? I gazed at the familiar profile, the slightly parted lips, the dark tangle of hair, the man I loved.

Then Nan's skirts moved across my line of vision, heavy swishing drapes; I remember thinking, now the house lights will come up, and they'll lower the safety curtain. . . .

What will the last act be like?

Nan raised her arms and called out something through the high screaming. Gradually it broke up into babble and wailing, then that too died down. The people were crouching back against the walls, and most of them had their arms up over their eyes. Only the candles on the rock and a single remaining glim now lit the center of the room, and on either side of Nan's skirts I could see remains of the interrupted feast: broken bread, and a pool of liquid seeping darkly into the mud floor. Rags and open bundles were scattered around, and beyond, pale in the gloom, the chicken flopped and scrabbled.

Only one other person hadn't moved. Tom was there behind me, standing close to the wall. I didn't look at him; I knew he was there, quite still, alert, watching.

Nan spoke, and the last whispers fell silent.

"Which one do this?"

No one moved or uttered.

"Who bring this thing?"

Murmurs: "Who bring it?" "Who would do this thing?" "Preserve us, Lord—" "Who could do it so?" "Lord Jesus —like breadfruit in crocus bag—" "Jesus help us—who do it?"

181

Frightened eyes glinted in the shadows, turning to one another and back to Nan. But no one stepped forward into the small arena or looked toward the light on the floor and what it shone upon—hidden from me by the broad wedge of skirts.

Suddenly the aunt brushed past me and I saw her by that light, bending forward and peering, before Nan could stop her. Her face held nothing but curiosity—not even wonder. The ropes of pearls and heavy trinkets swung forward as she hung over the head that had come without its halo. The gaping crowd looked on in silent horror, following the line of the feather boa as one end slithered loose and dangled, shedding a few shaggy snowflakes that circled slowly downward.

She straightened up, tossing the boa back round her neck in the gesture of a haughty mannequin. Then, turning those broken doll's eyes up to the heavens, she pronounced her verdict, and it came out as flatly as an election result.

"You see, it made its own way here. No one brought it: it came by itself."

"It come by itself—" "Find its way—" "It seek we out!" The muttering rose.

There was a sudden high screaming from the woman who had found it, as she returned to consciousness. It was monotonous and piercing, unbearable in the enclosed space; and all at once I felt panic tighten my own throat and press at my temples. I squeezed my eyes shut and still the two tall figures, one black, one white, burned on my brain; still the regular, harrowing cry went on, screwing up the horror of the frozen tableau notch by notch.

Then like an exploding white flashbulb in my head, I saw the naked truth, the contradiction of my aunt's oracular words. I heard it spoken clearly, in the clipped White Slug voice of the young Edward: the voice of Reason. And, as Maurice had said, it was always right. "Of course it couldn't come by itself, Eliza. Someone must have picked it up outside and hidden it in a sack and carried it in—a relatively simple operation in the dark, really. . . ." And the two voices continued in counterpoint, one mindlessly screaming, the other coldly reasoning.

(Ever since that night those voices have stayed with me. Usually they only twitter and whisper and can be ignored, interfering perhaps with full concentration, as half-heard words will. But when I am very tired or anxious or ill or trying to hurry—when I am frantic to conceal something as I hear my brother's footsteps on the turret stair, or wrestling with the shutters to see the car that has come up the hill—even hoping maybe to attract attention before Nan comes to lock them in place—then, at times like these, the two voices tear my head apart: cold reason talking low and evenly, very clipped, almost leisurely, measuring out the syllables of good sense. Its message is always: What good—? Why try—? Surely you can see that—? The other, high as a bat's squeak: Hurry—hurry—you *might* —you *could*— Hysterical and eternally, pathetically hopeful, plucking nervously at straws and spinning fool's gold. I suppose I have complained of them; I have heard Nan say to him as they pass on my threshold. "She got her voices bad today, Mars Tom." It was because I tried to puncture my eardrums with one of my hair grips that they took away even those; my hair is brushed back and tied with a short white ribbon. Surely I must have known that these are voices even the deaf can hear.)

How I longed in those chaotic moments to retreat into the total silence that had settled over me like a great bell jar when I saw the Headless Man; when I had been safe and set apart in the same way as the stuffed birds so snug in their glass dome, looking out at the noiseless world of the hall. But, as I had seen, even those bright birds now lay wet and trampled on the floor, their protecting glass scattered about in curving fragments, a ghostly eggshell.

I opened my eyes. The two tall figures, one in silhouette, the other radiant in the light, from pale hair to canvas shoes, still held the floor, and the screaming had dulled to a sobbing giggle, shushed by the murmuring congregation. The black Sibyl raised her hands, timing her pronouncement. The light throbbed and quivered, coming and going with the pain in my temples, the roar of the wind pulsed in my ears, and the shadow of that towering shape seemed to lie heavily over me, a suffocating black cloud.

I struggled to my feet and turned my face away to catch the cool air from the little window. At this moment the storm that raged beyond the thick walls was clean and welcome, more benign for all its fury than the things within that swarmed and pressed and threatened to choke me. I made myself breathe evenly and deeply, and thought about the time when I stepped out with Maurice into the great cool torrent of air. Oh, *Maurice*—and I tried to imagine his face, but I kept seeing only the frozen landfall of that still profile and the new-moon glimmer of dead eyes.

I breathed deep; I thought of flying through the storm; and somewhere buried inside me—deep as I sucked in the free fresh air, deep as the instinct to survive and look forward—I knew Edward was on his way, coming to the rescue. . . .

But all I heard was the noise of the storm and the moan-giggle behind me; then Nan's voice, not loud, but low and intense:

"I say unto you: the mad can see through into the light of Truth. Since no one bring it in, the Head must come by its self strange power—is so Miss Ciss have spoke. For it seek its rightful burial, to rest in peace."

There was a murmured response: "Is sacred truth—" "It come seeking—" "Lord keep us now!" "Mus' bury together—" "To find peace—" "One body one grave—" "According to the scriptures—" "Hallelujah!" "So German can rest easy . . . rest in peace . . . Glory be! let him rest in peace. . . ."

High, clear, and impersonal, the aunt's voice cut across

the brooding antiphon, and her words made theirs seem as cozy as a nursery rhyme.

"Peace? But there's no peace for the poor murdered man."

There was silence in the dark store; for a long second only the sound of the roaring wind beyond the door and a thin creak of settling glass in the wire bucket. Then: "She say murder . . . But zinc sheet kill him. . . . She say *Murder* . . . Machete could chop him same way . . . *Murder* . . . Is why him head walk . . . Lord keep us . . . Could chop self same way by murder . . . Lord Jesus, let it not be. . . . But the Mad see the Truth. . . . She say Murder. . . ."

Nan spoke again:

"You simple people! Is why the Head look *here*? Is why it seek *we* out when body lie elsewhere? True, it look for rightful burial—but first it look for justice! Hearken when the Mad speak! This Head come seeking its murderer. And whosoever murder this man is here right now within these selfsame walls!"

A ragged cry answered her, and it held a new note—the fierce throaty noise of fear turning ugly, the glimpse of a scapegoat in reddened eyes. "Murder—it seek within these selfsame walls—it seek justice—or have no peace—Lord Jesus—for the killer is here—preserve us, Lord—seek the killer—seek the killer and find him out—"

The hungry roar filled my head. I found myself crouching down on the earth floor, my eyes squeezed hard into the crook of my arm. The roar caught a rhythm and became a repeated cry: "Who kill him? Who kill him? Find the killer! Find the killer!" Over it, like a descant, the woman's voice rose: "Miss Nan will show the way! Read it for we, Miss Nan! She one know the right way—glory hallelujah!" The others took it up: "Seek and find! Show the way!"

Through the earth floor I felt movement—the people shifting, gathering in closer, tightening the circle. I heard

185

the flopping of Aunt Cissie's shoes near me, the creak as she settled in the high chair, then a soft keening that I recognized as her version of "The Daring Young Man on the Flying Trapeze." I didn't, I couldn't, move toward her. "His movements were graceful, his action divine . . ." Suddenly I was revolted by her.

Aunt Clarissa's part in the ghoulish charade was innocent, I know. And now I understand her better. A disturbing influence, not evil, just excitable and mad, stirring and thickening the dark brew of that fearful night. But at the time, and to me, she was more. To me, the fair figure bent over Maurice's head had taken on the loathsome pallidness of some night creature that had crawled out from between the rocks—uncurled and swaying, stooping to fasten on its prey.

The floor under me shivered with the soft insistent drumming of many hands. It was far more fearful than even the worst moments of the storm, earlier, when the lantern had blown out, and alone in the pitch black I had felt the house shake under its onslaught. That had been terrible indeed; but here, contained in this narrow breathless confine, was a new threat—a pressure was growing like yeast culture, thriving on the heat and the dark, feeding on fear. And now the ground itself seemed to desert me, as in an earthquake—but shaking rhythmically, the heartbeat of terror.

Above this, only a soft humming came from the people. As the rhythm grew, became more insistent, this sound broke up into short grunts, almost a word, as the closed humming lips broke open on the beat: "Imm-eh imm-eh imm-eh"—continuous, steady, hypnotic. I crouched, doubled over my knees with my arm locked round my eyes and my other hand trying to block my ears. But it was like hiding from a drumbeat while lying on its skin; the hard-packed earth sent the pulse through my whole body, invading me and reaching into my mind.

186

Then through the grunted "Imm-eh imm-eh" I heard another sound, of labored breathing—a long snarling intake, slowly exhaled as a groan. It was as loud and deep as that of a man; but voices cried, "Spirit come! She have the Spirit!" and I knew they meant Nan.

The chant dropped to a whisper as the deep slow breathing filled the well, like the snoring of a nightmare slumber, someone trapped in darkness deep down below the reach or the release of words. It was a devilish sound; something nameless had been raised, still sleeping, from beneath the earth, beneath the ribs of rock, the ancient burial place of disused gods. Now half-formed words I did not know struggled and were born from the exhaled breath, painful wrenching gutturals tearing a shape in the thick air. No chanting now, only the drumming, quickened to a hectic pulse beat, and the storm roaring beyond the door. And the breath turning into utterance.

The words came. They came from Nan, her voice now low and hollow, a voice from beyond the grave; and the sound made me shiver in the heat.

"Ask Itself!" she said. "You must inquire from the dead man who kill him. Ask the Head Itself! Let the Dead speak!"

I jerked up, wide awake. I saw three or four people rush forward into the small illuminated clearing. Nan was standing rigid with her back to me, her head straining backward; as she sank slowly to her knees I could see that her eyes were closed, and the cords of her neck glistened with sweat. Then her head lolled forward. She spread her hands on the ground and leaned on them, panting.

Beyond her the figures crowded in, casting huge shadows on the walls. Their faces and arms and bare chests gleamed as if anointed with oil. Two crouched down by Maurice's head, in a ring of chanters and drummers. Now the empty drum pans were set up; their muffled gong beat, pounded out softly at first with fingertips and heels of hands, was still far louder than before. "Glory be!"

187

they cried. "She show us the way. . . . The Head will lead us. . . . Let it speak! . . . The Head will lead us! Let it speak! . . . Set it up—let it speak—set it up—make it speak!"

The two crouching by the light took hold of the dark tangled hair and raised the head reverently from the ground, while two others stood by with the candles. Urged on by chanting, they set it up on the rock altar with the candles before it. Ready hands brought sacks to cushion it, wedging it upright and smoothing the starting hair. It looked out between the flames under lowered lids; below, the severed neck was wrapped round with colored kerchiefs. A woman tried to hang a bead necklace about the throat, but the head was too big, and the circlet stayed looped in the wild locks like a tinsel crown.

The glim on the floor was knocked over in the eager press; the other, set beside Aunt Cissie, had gone out. She seemed to be asleep, nodding forward in her chair. Only the two candles lit the scene before me; and now the worshipers drew back in a crouching semicircle to survey their new oracle. "The Head will lead us! Let it speak!" And black hands fluttered on yellow oil drums, catching and stressing the pattern of the words.

It is hard to describe this now—both painful and difficult. Not hard to remember; I can close my eyes and watch the frames flick past on the screen of my shuttered lids. Often at night I daren't close them: it is too real, and I rise up weeping and sweating and crying for Maurice.

The difficulty simply lies in being precise and objective, recording who was where and how it could have happened at all; why Tom or I didn't step forward and halt it; whether we were too afraid, or too involved. I'm sure Tom was afraid—he stood silently in the shadows; much of the time, I think, like me, he closed his eyes against the horror. But could he have stopped it if he chose? Covered the head, relit the glims, confiscated the rum bottles, put back the oil drums in a neat row against the wall, bullied and jollied the chanters to lie down and sleep in

188

another neat row? Could he have silenced Aunt Cissie? Calmed Nan and persuaded her out of her dangerous folly? Even supposing he had pulled his pistols on the lot of them—fired a shot over their heads—he might have increased the frenzy instead, and drawn it upon himself: the crowd was looking for a fitting sacrifice.

And me? There had been those moments of absolute detachment after the head rolled from the bag, when almost coldly I had observed my own reaction, the reactions of others, the angle of light, the degrees of darkness. Empty of emotion, swept and garnished, I was ready then for seven devils to enter into me: they rode in on the galloping drumbeats when I hid my face and covered my ears. But if I opened my eyes and kept them locked on Maurice, I found I could endure.

His brow was broad and serene, the thick hair swept back, caught by the bead necklace; the bright foxy streaks snaking up through it were like small tongues of fire in the candlelight. Now that they were above me, the eyes were more visible; the glint of irises showed beneath those thick lashes, and the candle flames, flickering in the troubled air, were reflected by the large black pupils in borrowed animation. His lips were slightly parted. There had been a thread of blood from one corner of his mouth. Someone had wiped it, and the smear carried the line of a half smile upward across his cheek. The other cheek was scratched and bruised and there was dark clotted blood below his ear and jaw. The neck disappeared into a purple kerchief—the same that I had borrowed earlier from the dominoes player to wipe oil from my hands. Then, where the eye demanded a chest and shoulders, there was only a pair of wake lights, and the rock falling away. Look up —at the lights glimmering in his pupils, at the forehead that was broad and smooth.

Maurice's serenity filled me with an unearthly calm. I saw how the ruddy sunburned skin had paled to a waxy gold, like a gourd put away in a store to harden;

the streaks of sunbleached hair, a crown of turning leaves. It was the image of a benign woodland god. Nan and the two women knelt below the rock; the others had drawn back as if in awe at what they had done. The head was the center of our shrunken world not only by virtue of the concentration of light upon its face, but because, even in death, it seemed the source of color, of life. Nothing in its expression suggested revenge: Maurice looked amused, drowsy, about to speak.

His people awaited his words. "Who kill you, boy? Who kill you, boy? Busha Maurice, who kill you, boy?" they chanted softly; and the drums picked it up:

"Busha Maurice, who kill you, boy?

"Busha Maurice, who kill you, boy?"

The volume of chanting and drumming swelled, a long cumulative crescendo until the store was filled with it and it bounded back from the stone walls in a fiendish babble. As it swelled, Nan rose slowly to her feet, a priestess high on rhythm and power. Maurice and the light were hidden from me, and I foundered in outer darkness.

I seemed to lose my sense of time. The next thing I remember consciously was becoming aware of a catch in the rhythm. I concentrated to listen, and I saw the drummers' eyes roll up, and Nan's head angled, oddly, listening. The difference was not in here, but outside. The storm was changing.

A heavy shower of driving rain battered against the door, then the wind seemed to waver and weaken, and attack again. Nan raised one hand and the drumbeats lost their pattern and died away to "Hush man hush." They crouched, listening, looking up.

The gale was buffeting now, great gusts like repeated blows, no less powerful than before, but varied. It had lost the steady roar we had grown accustomed to. The aunt sat up straight and said:

"What is it then? Has someone arrived?"

No one answered her.

"I think I might have been told," she said peevishly,

reaching for her velvet bag. "I shall have to tidy myself if it's someone important."

The squalls came and went, and the screaming wind seemed louder, but only by contrast with the short respites, for the pitch was a little lower as it came tearing round the buttressed corner of our refuge. Was it no more than a shift of direction? But Nan, her hand still upraised, her finger pointing heavenward, cried out above the gust:

"Change, I tell you! Storm change! The Eye of the Tempest is coming!"

"Storm eye come . . . Still center come . . . Hallelujah!" Murmurs from the shelterers, and movement.

Tom took a pace forward, started to speak. But something stopped him.

It was a sound that did not make sense. It was not in our dungeon, nor part of the tumult outside. It echoed hollowly through to us from the windswept, rain-scoured drawing room above. Nan's hand fell to her side and everyone in the store froze to listen. It came on, clearer now, and there was no doubt about it: firm heavy footsteps overhead, walking on our ceiling.

The tread was slow and steady, across the floor and then back again, and all the eyes followed them. There was no faltering or unevenness in those powerful gusts, no staggering or falling. Then they faded and ceased, and we heard only the swish of rain.

In the brief lull, Nan's hoarse rapt whisper broke our silence.

"Only duppy can walk in storm." The words were whipped away by the next noisy onslaught, but the shrill wailing of the older woman could be heard through it: "Lord Jesus! Duppy walk fe seek out him killer!"

Under a babble of voices, the drums started again, not loud, but frenzied and insistent; then words took up the rhythm:

"Who kill you, Maurice, boy?
"Who kill you, Maurice, boy?"

Outside, the wavering storm slackened, then returned, then suddenly died away into silence. It was the still center.

"Who kill you, Maurice, boy?

"Who kill you, Maurice, boy?"

And faint but clear, beyond the great door, out of the stillness, a voice calling: "Tom!"

FOUR O'CLOCK

AT FIRST no one moved. The fugitives crouched over their silent drums. Their eyes were on the head; then they swiveled back to one another, to the door, back to the head, to Nan, questioning. And Nan turned toward Tom.

He had fallen to his knees, with his hands over his ears, his eyes tight shut. Nan did not raise a finger nor say a word, but her face was terrifying. Nan's displeasure was always fearful to behold, but this was not the fierce wooden mask I knew. This was coldly knowing and triumphant. It only shocked me, then; but now I can see that it spoke, not of instant death but of blackmail for life.

I alone observed it. He was blind. The aunt was patting her hair and gazing expectantly at the door. The others could only see Nan's stern accusing back, as she faced Tom. For a moment I thought they might seize him and tear him apart. They had invoked the Dead, demanding a victim; and they had been answered. What made them hesitate then?

Two strange marvels—and they were caught between them. The mysterious voice that had answered their question: to the many whose eyes had been closed in fear, in religious ecstasy, to all whose senses were reeling, the source of the voice was the head of the murdered man. But with the footsteps above and now the sudden unearthly

193

stillness, a recognition of something new, something outside, had reached even the tranced and the drunk. Their first guess—if they were not past guessing—would be that the body we had left lying in the big hall had got up and walked; but it could not speak, of course, for it lacked a head.

At the same time, closer and more immediate, was a blurred vision of the culprit they so ardently sought and that their terror demanded: not just one of them, but a white boss convicted by black arts—no less marvelous than a head whose body stalked across the ceiling and whose voice came to them out of the eye of the storm.

For a moment their wonder held the balance. If Nan had so much as lifted her hand and pointed her finger at Tom, I think they would have turned and rent him. But then the balance was tilted the other way. The voice called out again:

"Eliza! Eliza!"

There was only one person in the world who called me that. I was at the door before anyone could speak or move.

When I heard the voice the first time, only the sense got through to me, its meaning. It came as the answer to a question. Strangely, I didn't wonder about its source, though I am certain now that I knew it wasn't Maurice's voice, that it came from outside, that someone—one of Tom's friends wanting shelter? a neighbor? and yet someone uncannily strong—had walked through the storm's buffeting across the roofless drawing room, had come round to the bottom store and called out. My only clear thought had been for Tom: not, So he killed Maurice, or even, Did he kill him? but, Will they kill Tom now? And then the voice came again.

Now there was one idea in my head, one fact in my world—quite as marvelous to me as any supernatural verdict.

"Edward has come!"

I shouted it as I wrenched back the two great bolts that

194

secured the door. I swung it open, felt the air of the huge cool night, and saw the world outside.

We were on an island, cut off from the rest of creation by the spinning wall of wind and water as surely as if we had fallen through a fault in Time. This wall was dark and muddy at its base, glinting like metal where the moonlight touched it, and growing more translucent as it climbed. Overhead, the sky was clear.

It was, I suppose, about an hour before dawn, and the moon, which had showed briefly between the clouds as we watched from the veranda railing, was now in the western sky, riding the rim of the hurricane. It shone full and yellow as a smoky lamp on our threshold and across the earth floor. Outside, it showed a scene of destruction I was not prepared for.

The big breadfruit tree that would have hidden the moon had gone; beyond it, the forest had been minced; only the lie of the land remained the same. Two royal palms on the slope stood straight and slender, like pillars of a lost civilization; their feathery crowns had been lopped off clean. Behind them, and in a deadly circle round us, the storm stood, motionless as a top, glassy with velocity, hemming us in. Inside, nothing stirred. It was extraordinarily still. The only sounds were the distant roaring and, nearby, the drip and gurgle of rainwater. After long hours of the blustering shrieking wind, it was silence.

The small grassy terrace before us was a junkyard; and in the midst of this wreckage stood an airman. He wore a flying helmet, goggles, and boots, and he stood quite still in the waning moonlight, a black and white photograph from the Great War.

He moved forward one cautious step, and spoke.

"I'm sorry I can't introduce myself," he said, very clear and clipped in the strange quiet. "I don't know who I am—I must have got a knock on the head when my plane came down. But would you be Eliza?"

"Yes—I'm Eliza," I said. "And you are Cousin Edward. You've come. I knew you would."

The nightmare was over. The intolerable pressure of those hours and horrors inside that sealed tomb was lifted suddenly and completely: no more than opening a door and seeing Edward surrounded by space and stillness. I felt as if I were floating. I wanted to run and shout and cry, and yet, when I found my voice, the words came out simple and flat, as though I were altogether overcome by shyness now that he was really here. I stepped forward to meet the light—air—liberty—and the Hero in person.

But behind me Tom's voice suddenly cracked out: "Stay back, Liz!"

I was amazed; I stopped and turned round. Tom was standing in the doorway, holding his dueling pistols leveled at the airman. Behind him, Nan and Aunt Cissie, and the rank of shelterers, some crouching, some standing, filled the open doorway—bunched close and all wearing the same fixed stare, caught in a long exposure. Then the aunt moved; she dug into her bag and pulled out her silver hand mirror. In a dreamlike gesture, she turned her back and watched the intruder's reflection in the glass.

I shook my head with exasperation and disbelief. What had got into them? "But, Tom—but see, Aunt—Nan—it's Cousin Edward! He's *arrived*!" They seemed to be in a trance. "It's *Edward*!" I said. "He must be tired—come and welcome him, Tom! Nan, get him something to drink—"

Tom said nothing, just watched the airman along his pistols; but Nan slid round him and came up close to me. She put herself between me and the tall stranger, and took me by the shoulders.

"No, Miss Liz," she said in a hoarse stage whisper. "Is not Mars Edward, me dear: is duppy. Is a ghost, I tell you. Is *dead man*, Miss Liz." The frantic hiss gave her words a terrible subdued force. "Leave it alone, Miss Liz. Don't look on it."

The watchers heard: behind me there was a long satis-
fied sigh of justified fears; the receiving and acknowledg-
ing of the monstrous truth. It was like the harsh breath of
some night prowler at my back, and I turned involuntarily.
Those that had moved forward into the moonlit doorway,
I saw, had their hands over their faces; yet their eyes
glinted between their fingers. Technically, I suppose, they
were not looking on the Walking Dead.

I had no time to pity them, to demonstrate their folly.
Behind the rigid bars of their fingers they were locked
fast in superstitious fear; the Obeah woman spoke and
they trembled. And I had trembled too, shut in with their
hysteria; I had been mesmerized by their newest god in his
crown of beads. But now I was liberated. The sky was open
above me and Edward was before me, supported by invisible squadrons of good sense and pure reason, and all
the armory of the civilized world beyond the whirling
wall.

Suddenly I felt angry that they should so cling to their
panic and persist in hiding their eyes from the truth; so
paralyzed that they could not even give help to a weary
traveler. I was ashamed of them all, gawking in the
doorway—and most of all of Nan, whose business it was
to throw off her foolishness and make our English cousin
welcome. I shook myself free from her restraining arm as
she tried to shield my eyes from the sight of him, and I
stepped past her and went toward him.

The airman stood alone and uncertain, like the last survivor on a field of battle—a tall frail ragged figure that my
aunt might have torn from a folded newspaper. The moon,
behind and above him, rimmed him with pale light, a
blurred outline, soft edge; and as I drew near I saw that
his nylon flying suit was tattered, almost shredded in
places. His helmet straps dangled; a gray scarf was
wrapped loosely round his neck; he wore a crisscross
harness over his chest and shoulders; his hands in leather
gauntlets hung stiff and awkward at his sides; and one

197

flying boot, unzippered, gaped open. I could not see his face in the shadow and hidden by the glinting goggles, but strands of fair hair streaked his forehead and trailed onto the helmet, caught in a buckle.

"Edward," I said. Still he did not move. "Edward? It's wonderful to see you. You're home, and safe." I held out both hands to him. But he drew back from me one shaky step.

"Careful," he said. "I feel very odd—battered, you know, Eliza. Positively fragile—This Way Up." He laughed, and raised his hands and patted his arms and chest, touched his head, then shook it slowly and wonderingly. "I feel—well, quite amazingly shaken about—as though if I took off my headgear and goggles—unstrapped my harness—I might just come apart. Utterly pulped, as it were. Understandably, I suppose—that was some flight."

It was Edward—how could they doubt it? Those cool self-deprecating tones, the pure crisp accent, the way he laughed, the way he used words, the words he chose—why, I had seen him only six weeks before at the May Ball, and said good-bye to him by the light of another moon and early dawn in Cambridge. He had been black and white against the greensward of the Backs and the misty river; neat—even the morning after—in evening dress; promising he would come flying down from Miami to see us. And he had.

I wanted to touch him, put my arm round him and lead him gently to the house, help him off with his helmet and goggles and see again the face that had eluded my imaginings. But there was an odd distance between us; it was as if we had been apart a long time, and he had grown away from me. More clearly, I sensed his uncertainty. He seemed puzzled and withdrawn, absorbed in a wondering daze. What a fool I am, I thought: his plane probably crashed—and me standing here gaping, and Nan and Tom behaving so oddly. Poor Edward—he's suffering from fatigue.

"You'll be all right now," I said gently. "You're home now."

"Well, it's funny," he said, lifting his head and looking up at the house. The light caught his face: Edward's mouth and Edward's chin, smudged and gray with exhaustion. "I know this place. This is where I was aiming for —wherever it is. And whoever I am . . . But it's changed— and I don't remember the front door being there—"

"It isn't," I said; "it's the old store; we were sheltering from the storm. The rest of the house—"

"Yes—the storm. I was flying in the storm. Very rough, it was. . . ."

"Did your plane crash?" I asked.

"I think it must have crashed. But I knew I'd get here, to this special place—the place I was aiming for. There was an odd-shaped hill—I saw it through a gap in the clouds and I knew it—knew I'd been there. . . . Yes, and I suppose the plane went down then—or perhaps I gave up"—he laughed shakily—"and here I am." He turned back to me and seemed to gather his gaze and his mind on my face. "I know I was looking for Eliza. You're Eliza—" slowly, tentatively. Then he looked past me. "And you must be Tom. Funny—I can remember the things I was concentrating on, flying. But the rest is a bit patchy—who I am. . . ."

He sketched a shrug and spread his stiff gauntleted hands palm upward, miming despair. Everything he did was in slow motion, as if he knew the moves but had forgotten the timing.

But he had remembered me. I felt joyful and triumphant, like all the faithful rolled into one. Still, I must not rush him; I knew that.

"You are our cousin Edward, from England," I said carefully. "It's all right, Edward—we've been expecting you. I knew you'd come—you said you'd come."

"Did I, Eliza? Tell me." I saw his cheek wrinkle as he smiled at me.

But Tom—I hadn't realized he was so close—stepped

roughly between us, pushing me back with his shoulder, still covering the airman with the absurd antique pistols. He kept a decent distance from him, watched him, but it was to me he spoke.

"I don't see why we should think he's Edward." His voice was low and rapid. "He can't offer any proof—won't even take off his disguise. I don't believe him for a moment. *What* plane? And who could fly a plane in that wind anyway? He's just a looter, Liz—that's all. Only too easy —finds out who lives in the big house, our names, and wanders in—"

"But his clothes—" I whispered.

"Just fancy motorcycle gear—or army reject stuff— doesn't fool *me*."

"But—for God's sake, Tom! Are you *mad*? You *can't* turn him away on a night like this!"

"Just what looters count on, don't they?" (Still Tom did not speak directly to him. The airman had not retreated, had not moved. Only his eyes moved, unhurried yet unpredictable as fish, in the depths of his goggles.) "Count on you taking them in without any questions asked—all good pals in a crisis. . . . *Who is he*, for God's sake?" he hissed suddenly, both angry and frightened. "It's just too damn easy to say he doesn't know—got a bump on the head —very convenient—he can't prove anything!"

"I can't remember anything." The level clipped tones were reasonable and slightly amused. "Pretty odd sort of guest, I admit; no bags, no name, no box of chocolates for the lady of the house—all wrong. . . . But the place is right—" His voice faded to a whisper then came back again. "I was determined to get here. That I remember. And they all said—when I was refueling—they all tried to stop me" (fading again) "to stop me getting here . . . but I had to." Then stronger, but still with that puzzled wondering note—the voice of a man wakened from sleep and telling of a dream—"I knew I could make it . . . though there were times when it felt like—I don't know—

200

just willpower keeping that plane in the air. . . . Yet I was so certain I'd get here—"

He seemed to lose the thread, looking round him vaguely and swaying a little. I pushed past Tom, but the airman was speaking again.

". . . Telling me to keep on flying, forcing me to . . . Eliza. And I knew she was waiting and I mustn't let her down. That was you. And here I am." He smiled and made me a little bow; as he straightened up he put his hand to his head as though to steady it.

I could not bear it. He was clearly at the end of his strength—and Tom keeping him standing there with the pistols leveled at him.

"Tom—stop it!" I clung to his arm but he elbowed me away.

"Keep clear!"

"But, Tom! It's *Edward*!" I cried. "He's exhausted and we must help him! He's got amnesia, can't you see? Can't you *see* it's Edward? His voice—his hair—his build—" I remembered that Tom hadn't seen him for four years. But the voice had not changed; and it was the voice, even weary and wandering, that was unmistakable. And the reserve was Edward's. Usually it was his special form of defense; now he seemed to be holding himself together with it. I did not press him with questions or sympathy: if he had attempted to recall, to describe, his experience of the hurricane and the crash, it might have quite undone him.

I mustn't be too impulsive or precipitate, I told myself. He isn't like Maurice. Shut off; switch to Edward—tall and tattered, proclaiming by his very presence here a weird, even an exotic, elegance: nothing could be more out of place in the midst of this conflux of wild and evil forces than the pale shabby figure before me, product of Eton, Cambridge, and the University Flying Corps; punch-drunk with disaster, still on his feet, still cracking rueful jokes about guests and chocolates. Marvelous alien.

He needed time and care, not hurrying, not smothering. And not threatening.

"Look, Tom," I said, turning and lowering my voice, trying to reason with him. "He's dead on his feet, can't you see? You can't let him collapse in front of us. And, Tom, you know the Great Light the people saw, and you saw—it must have been the plane crashing! So he's got here from somewhere near Rookoom, through all those hours of storm."

"The plane came down at the foot of Rookoom. That's right." The airman's voice made me turn round; it was the voice of the young Edward, precise, unemotional, and pitched higher. "I remember Rookoom now, that hill coming through the clouds. It's a considerable distance from here; but I thought someone might see the fire and come out to help."

"No one could come out, you fool!" Tom addressed the intruder directly for the first time. "For Chris' sake—no one could even *walk* in a storm like that!"

Nan spoke, and the fear in her voice was sharp. For her the horror was real, the danger imminent; nor was there any comfort in Tom's arsenal.

"Is truth I tell you!" she cried. "Only duppy can walk in storm—it blow clean through them body! Is a dead man, Miss Liz—don't harken to it! Miss Liz, I beg you trust me—is *dead man*, I tell you—maybe even is Evil Spirit talk same way favor Mars Edward fe come trick you and harm you! Come away, chile—"

But I had outgrown Nan. She had gone too far that night, and she had lost me. Her power over frightened people I had seen, and felt; it had almost driven me out of my mind. But the nightmare in the bottom store had brought about a sort of catharsis in me. Now I felt only pity for her. No terror: that was over. A cold clean breeze had come from the northlands, from the snow-trimmed Gothic strongholds of reason I had so often built in air when I dreamed of Edward. It swept away the choking cobwebs of those last hours and took with them a whole childhood of dusty fears.

I pitied the benighted Nan, Tom hiding behind his pistols and his preconceptions, my poor mad overexcited aunt, and the frightened band of survivors huddling on the threshold. But I was emptied of fear. I have not felt it since. I turned my back on it and them, and looked only at the airman. I had been obsessed with the demands of survival: perhaps that alone had kept me sane. Here in front of me was the real survivor.

"It's Edward," I said, and my voice seemed suddenly clear and firm against the distant roaring of the wind. Then I spoke only to him. "Edward, my love—" and came nearer. "Edward—you remember now, don't you?"

The mysterious pilot made a cautious step toward me, as though he was feeling his way. Out of the corner of my eye I saw Tom back round and take up a position with the intruder clear in his sights, and where I gave no cover.

"Keep back, Liz!" he said, and his voice was low. He wasn't playacting now.

But Edward had taken a step toward me and nothing else mattered. I went up close to him and put out my hands. Slowly he lifted his and took mine into them. The leather gauntlets were cold and stiff. I pressed them to reassure him, to warm him, to reach through to the warm hands inside. I felt an answering pressure. I shifted, drawing him round a little so that the moonlight fell on his face; but his head was bent intently toward me, and I saw only that he was smiling at me, that the eyes behind the goggles were pale green, ill-defined, and I knew that the lashes were pale. I hadn't been able to remember his mouth earlier, conjuring him over the *Punch*es. Now I could see that it was long and thin-lipped in a thin-skinned face, and his cheeks crinkled in brackets round his smile. A skeptic's mouth; even now he had an air of not quite believing in us—as though we might be a bunch of ghosts, haunting the ruins of his childhood paradise.

"I remember you," he said. "I remember you dancing with me. And there was another lady, rather prim and smart—was that Miss Asprey? It's all so muddled. But I remember you."

He let go of my hands and touched my cheek with a cool leather fingertip. Even my clasp hadn't warmed him; the hand I still held was as cold as ever. Warm Maurice is dead, I thought, and cool Edward is here. Involuntarily I shivered and closed my eyes for a moment at the touch on my cheek.

"I came here to take you away, Eliza," he said. "Will you leave it all and go with me?"

"Yes, I will," I said. I had always dreamed of this, but the words sounded small and distant, and I felt very tired. My bandaged hand throbbed. My body ached with weariness, crying out for solid comfort and strong arms and warm embraces, as for a bed. I want Maurice, my nerves and muscles whimpered. I want to sleep. Maurice, why did you die and leave me?

Here in the quiet turret, listening to the distant sounds of herding cattle, chickens clucking and complaining on the hillside, and the pea doves' call "long-day-come," there is a louder, nearer sound that does not change. All through the slow hot afternoons when every other noise is still—even the crickets, or in the hollow night, empty and silent—even the tree frogs—this closest sound goes on, a steady sad heartbeat: Maurice, Maurice, Maurice. It will be quiet as soon as I die.

"Yes, Edward," I said. "I want to go with you, away from here."

My destiny, my goal. For a little while, Maurice had altered all that: my ambition melted; my world was the area closest to him.

Now Maurice is dead, I thought, there is nothing to stay

for. I held the gauntleted hand in both of mine, like a royal subject swearing fealty, and looked up into the minnow-green eyes moving behind the glassy wall; but the stiff glove came up and hid them from me. For a moment he rested his forehead on his knuckles, then seemed to draw himself up and summon his strength.

"Good girl, Eliza. Now then, I must greet your family. That's the right thing. First I must do that, and then I will take you away with me."

"No," I said, coming back to reality with a start. "No—first you must rest and recover. Don't be put off by all this—they're not really hostile, only frightened. You must rest for a little and I'll look after you. You've been through too much, Edward. You probably don't realize it, but I can see you're quite done in. You need—"

He was shaking his head slowly. I thought he was just dazed and groggy, but he said: "I must take you away with me now. We mustn't delay."

"But the storm—your plane—"

"I'll tell you something," he said, drawing close to me. "You aren't safe here, Eliza." He put his stone hands on my shoulders. "And there's not much time, you see. Come along, my girl—damsels in distress can't argue with the knight in shining armor, you know." He smiled again, and then put his hand up to his jaw, supporting it. "Let's have a word with your people now. Come, my dear."

He took my hand and led me toward the doorway, ignoring Tom; but the pistols swung round and followed him.

I felt helpless and numb, as though I saw myself sleepwalking and could do nothing. Part of me blindly obeyed Edward as I had always done in the past. The other half knew that he would soon pass out with shock and exhaustion; then Nan would come to her senses and help me look after him—and Tom would not shoot a sleeping man. I walked beside him, my hand in his. I could smell the soft leather and the green sappy scent of the vegetation that streaked his boots and clothes. There was no hint of sweat or of warm skin.

Nan had retreated to the doorway. As we approached, she drew back against the wall beside it, turning her head away. The airman stopped and raised his hand to her in a slow-motion salute.

"Good evening, Miss Nan," he said.

The crowd on the threshold had moved back as we came closer and now faded away into the dark corners of the store. I saw Aunt Cissie totter a few paces and sink onto her chair. We stepped in through the doorway. The candles were still burning; the circling storm seemed far away, here inside the thick walls. Eyes watched from protecting blankets, peered out from behind hands or between fingers. No words—not a cry, not a moan. They watched, secretly. And the head watched, looking out across the candle flames.

The shabby airman stopped, and I saw the goggles swing slowly round the store, reflecting the unreal scene. Then he led me slowly toward Aunt Cissie. She was cowering into her feather ruff; but when we stopped in front of her, she straightened up and went through an arch little double take, as though we were embarrassing acquaintances insensitively refusing to be cut dead. She patted her hair and simpered up at the visitor.

"Good evening, Aunt Clarissa. I hope I find you well."

He bowed and took her cautiously extended hand. I saw her draw it back quickly, but good breeding prevailed. She covered her discomfiture with conscious charm, and answered him graciously.

"I flourish, thank you, dear boy. I fear you may have had a rough journey."

"It had its up and downs."

She tittered—her silvery social laugh. Then she leaned forward, holding her silver looking glass flirtatiously like a fan and mouthing the intimate question from its protection.

206

"Tell me, my dear, how does it *feel?* Being—well, you know—on the Other Side?"

"I feel a little worn, Aunt Clarissa. Not entirely myself."

He smiled politely; then, catching sight of the fugitives in the shadows, he addressed them, and raised the stiff gauntlet to his helmet in his mock salute.

"Good evening, everybody."

The shelterers, watching him narrowly from cover, did not cross themselves, did not breathe. Officially they weren't there.

Solemnly and slowly we moved round the small arena lit by the two candles. My hand, firmly held in the cold leather grip, felt strangely numb, an invading chill that seemed to reach up into my head. I knew only that I didn't need to think anymore. Cousin Edward had come for me, and he would know the correct behavior. He always had. Even his elders and betters used to defer to him on matters of conduct and protocol. "Is it because you *like* it?" I asked him once. "Yes, I find it—well, elegant." He laughed a little awkwardly at his excess. "But actually, Eliza, I think it makes life easier." *"Easier?* More complicated, it looks like—" "Yes, but sometimes one *needs* complications. Think of—say—the chieftain's widow, saved by the minutiae of the elaborate funeral. Or when you have a Situation, Eliza—you know: the meeting of rival potentates—or any tricky encounter in everyday life—you're saved by the rules, aren't you?—like a decent suit of clothes to cover up your real feelings—or even to keep you together when you feel unstrung. . . ."

The airman halted in front of the rocky promontory, where the two candles burned low in their shining holders. Face to face with the golden image of Maurice, and a yard away, he stood quite still for a long moment. Inside the store, it was quiet. Outside, the distant roaring was closer, and the faint radiance of moonlight slanting in as far as his battered flying boots was suddenly blotted out. I was dimly aware of rustling, of awe and bated breath in the darkness round us, beyond the ring of light. Then the airman stretched his hand out across the candles and closed the brooding eyelids.

"Poor Maurice," he said. He bowed his head, and turned and led me away from the altar.

Crossing the threshold, we were met by a milky tide of returning light that washed round our feet. Tom and Nan stood on either side, pillars of salt. The moon was fitful now, as the ragged rim of the storm whipped clouds across its face. The hurricane's gigantic pewter funnel was shifting, sidling closer. Wind shivered in the torn trees, and there was a brief flurry of raindrops, cold and drenching.

Tom, behind us, came to life. I heard the double click as he cocked the heavy pistols.

"Stop!" he cried out, "or I'll shoot!"

The airman did not turn his head or change his even, inexorable pace. He was taking me toward the path that led round to the lower garden and the drive.

"Don' go, Miss Liz!" Nan screamed over the rising gale. *"Mars Tom! Don' shoot—"*

There was a noise like a double thunder clap. Under it, close to me—and more like a shock wave than a sound—I sensed the impact of the bullets. The airman was a pace ahead of me and to my right, and, as I felt the sickening blow through his arm and hand, I saw two holes torn in the back of his flying jacket.

He seemed not to notice. He went on walking.

I twisted round. Tom had fired from point-blank range. Now he was crouching on the ground. One pistol glinted on the grass, and he was fumbling with the complicated loading of the other. Behind him Nan stood, her hands over her mouth as if to suppress a scream, her eyes staring past me at the torn jacket. All the people were there, crowding out of the door. Those in front had seen what happened and tried to retreat. Those behind struggled and strained for a better view. One short phrase panted from them, a low fearful hubbub: "Is the Living Dead— is the Living Dead—"

Tom's manic gibbering was louder:

"Wait—just you wait—bloody zombie—not getting off with my sister—damn White Slug—dead but he won't lie down—okay—okay—how about this then?" He was laughing and shouting through the whipping wind; he cocked the pistol and, steadying it with both hands, took careful aim. We had reached the path and soon would be in the shelter of the house, out of the treacherous moonlight, past the corner.

Only Nan seemed to understand what Tom was doing. She threw her apron over her face, and that was my last sight of her as I turned away, drawn by the cold firm hand that held me.

Tom fired again, and the airman let me go; he fell forward on his knees, hugging his chest with both arms. A howl went up from the watchers, and whirled away on the wind. I bent over him, trying to get a hold round his shoulders, my hands slipping in the rain and sudden dark. I felt people catch at me from behind, pulling me away, and I lost him.

"Lef' him, Miss Liz—lef' him, chile!"

"It's all right, Liz, I'm here—you're safe with Tom."

Then murky moonlight again—and I saw the back of the flying suit with its three black holes, like the key slots of some sophisticated clockwork toy, lurch up from the ground; and then the bent head uncurled. The ragged pilot started forward again, slower now, and swaying from side to side, as though he needed rewinding. As the hurricane came swinging in close, we saw him quite clearly for an instant: a pale puppet against the dark roaring curtain of wind and water.

"Let me go with him!" I screamed, fighting off the hands that held me. "Let me go!" I tore myself free and ran forward.

The airman did not falter as he stepped through the

whirling wall. Holding his arms still wrapped round tightly, and moving with that stiff rocking walk, he was received into the dark silver millrace and was gone.

"Edward!"

The hurricane thundered close, emptying my mouth of sound. I could only gasp and gape as the rain broke over me like an Atlantic roller. Then I bowed my head and followed him through the storm cone. Across the boundary.

FIVE O'CLOCK

I FOLLOWED HIM into a wild topsy-turvy world on the other side of the looking glass. Spinning air took my feet from under me, earth and water flew overhead, and trees carried their roots upward. This was the hurricane I had not met or even guessed at, safe and terrified within stout walls. I was no longer frightened now; I accepted it. It was the new element—an emulsion of earth, air, and water—and it obeyed different rules. There was direction, but no gravity. If I let go and went with it, I would fall forever, it seemed, for it had no top and no bottom—only continuous powerful movement. It was most like a swift river, but as much solid as liquid, and containing just enough air for me to manage without gills.

As soon as I could open my eyes, I caught sight of the airman ahead of me. He was visible in the maelstrom only because—as I realize now, trying to describe it clearly —he obeyed none of the laws that governed me and the headlong cataract around me; not buffeted nor deflected from his set course; often briefly obscured, but steadfast, like a weak torch shining up through rough waters.

I fought to get closer, but the fierce current of the storm flowed diagonally across his chosen path, and threatened to sweep me down into the void where the steep hillside must be. I crawled, I clung like a spider in a bath. Horizontal progress was vertical for me. I held on to bushes, to lashing branches, to the flattened grass—streaming by like river weed—when there was nothing else; while, a little way ahead, glimpsed and lost and found again, the airman walked upright, with that slow even pace, hugging his arms to his wound. He did not seem, as far as I could make out, to climb over fallen limbs or push past those that blocked his way. I did not see him duck when a large leafy bough ripped through the air—but I was cowering flat to avoid it and I saw little.

The ground sloped steeply away beneath my feet, and the screaming darkness thickened. I feared I might lose him, and plunged down the incline across the main flow. I slithered and fell several yards; the wind was so strong, the rain so dense, dragging me sideways, that it broke my fall. I was slashed and bruised, and carried off course; but I saw the flying suit glimmer below me and I pitched myself forward again. I fell, was caught in a web of creepers, then fell again—a long way this time, but the palpable air seemed to take my weight. I scraped past black rocks and silvery trunks of pimento trees and landed in a heap of branches. When I could stagger to my feet and disentangle myself, I felt my way forward. I found I was on level rough ground strewn with big stones; I guessed it must be the long shoulder halfway down the hill, where, years before, the Slave House had been built.

Here the current of the storm, which had flowed across me on the slope, scoured along the length of the promontory where I stood, and I realized for the first time that it was blowing from the opposite quarter of the compass to that from which it had sprung: it had reversed after the eye passed over. Now we were caught in its other edge. I saw too that the sky was a little lighter, or rather, since the sky was hidden, that the mess of elements I crawled and swam and fell through was more translucent; and it wasn't the angled, intermittent glint of moonlight, but a general lifting of tone, as though a measure of bleach had been added to the monstrous boiling.

Sheltered for a moment in the angle between the slope and level ground, I was able to stand upright and gasp for breath, and look around me. The storm lashed the tall trees above my head, and I felt I was cowering under the arch of a huge waterfall that rushed outward and on down the hillside to fill the pastures below. At the bottom of the steep drop beyond the Slave House, where the forest met the open land, there was a sinkhole—a wide gaping fissure in the rock, the mouth of a bottomless pit. It served the Big House and property as our largest tip, the ultimate dustbin. All bulky or dangerous waste was thrown down it: old mattresses, carcasses of diseased cattle or sheep, drums of outdated weed killer. Grandfather used to tell how his father had unloaded a complete four-poster bed down the sinkhole, after discovering his sister and the head pen keeper coupling behind the curtains—an unlikely tale; but no one disputed that the sinkhole was immeasurably deep. It was fenced against animals; as children we managed to get close enough to toss in the chosen gift—sometimes a whole chocolate bar—if we thought the gods were particularly displeased.

Now I felt that the plug had been pulled, and our whole universe was being swilled down into that black opening. Everything leaned or flowed that way, and as I stumbled out into the mainstream again, I was caught from behind by the full force and carried along with it. I could not see my wounded pilot, and I feared for him. He would stagger bravely and blindly on and be swept through the fence— if it was still there—and over the edge. Edward knew of it —but the amnesiac airman—?

I let myself be sucked along, tripping over stones and bumping into tree trunks, falling and getting up again, using the headlong hurricane as best I could to make up lost time. All at once I saw the dark mass of the Slave

House ahead, and the flying suit lighter against it, only a few yards away. But the leaning forest hid him from me again, and a gust hurled me flat on my face. I crawled on toward the ruins and collapsed in the shelter of a broken wall.

"Edward! Wait for me!" I cried; but only the stones heard me. Even on them—from my worm's-eye view—the miniature forests of shaggy moss bowed toward the magnetic pit, center of the world.

I raised my head, scraped back the wet hair and leaves that blinded me, and looked through a dim opening beyond my parapet: it was the shadow of an old doorway. A heavy flag of creepers slapped against it and streamed through into the room beyond; and I glimpsed the airman again.

I got to my feet and, leaning back on the wind and steadying myself in the doorway, I burst through into the ruins. It was comparatively still between those high dank walls. Above me, against the diluted sky, a wild fringe of ferns and lianas flowed with the tide. Below, there was only a circling backwash that eddied among the mounds of mossy stone blocks and puckered the pools of water. The airman was gone.

Splashing through puddles to the other side, ducking under a low arch, I came out into the open again. The storm struck me, barbed with splintered vegetation. It carried me forward, stumbling across old foundations, clinging to passing bushes; and I found myself only yards away from the edge of the last slope, where the wood dropped steeply down to the pit.

Ahead of me, tall trees—slender struggling figs and pimentos rooted in rock—leaned out over the void, streamlined by the gale: pale stems straining and whipping wildly; and paler, but unmoving, and quite unruffled, stood the pilot.

"Look out, Edward!" I shouted. "Mind the sinkhole! It's right ahead below you!" I clung to a small sapling and wedged my knee against the last low ruined wall. "Edward! Wait!" I yelled. "Stop! Wait for me!"

He had stopped. He stood quite still and I saw him straighten slowly and lift his head; but he didn't turn round. A fierce drenching blow, sweeping along the promontory and over the drop, deafened and drowned me. Desperate for his safety, I let go, and was carried forward. I came up against one of the trees, and lay hugging it, gasping, clearing my eyes.

The frail shabby figure was still there, a few feet away, standing upright in the flattening torrent. I saw it unfold its arms and raise them slowly like stiff wings; saw the head tilt back so far that the bulge of the goggles glinted up at the sky. Then waves of blown spray and leaves and vines obscured everything. It cleared again and the thick muddy light, filtering down through layers of churning cloud, touched the spread arms, the raised head.

I saw clearly the dangling helmet strap, the bullet holes, the tattered flying suit, the clinging rags of greenery; saw the rents and tatters spreading like a dark lacy growth, the shredded leggings come apart. As I looked, the divisions of the gauntlet, the lines of shading between the fingers, traveled and branched down the arm, met the shoulder harness, which seemed to rot and break like a spider web; and then the whole chest and body started to dissolve before my eyes. It did not explode or fall apart in separate limbs. There was nothing horrible about it; instead, it was marvelous and strange, a filmed record of fatigue. The figure before me did not even grow misty. It was simply consumed by a racing disease—the proliferation of raggedness, the meeting up of rents and holes. It was most like watching a sheet of newspaper eaten by sparks, a random charring that linked and spread until suddenly I saw daylight through his chest; then smaller chinks all over him; and he grew so thin that he was nothing more than an ancient lace curtain with the dawn light showing through.

215

It sounds slow, now that I read this; it sounds as if I might have reached him instead of sprawling there observing his dissolution. But it was as fast as fire, and although my impressions were precise—so that I could draw it now, choosing a frame here, a frame there, to illustrate each phase—yet all I glimpsed was between breakers of driven rain, torn leaves. And afterward I was able to convince myself that I could not have seen it happen; that conditions were right for illusion, that the torrent of leaves had finally obscured him, that he had disappeared over the edge and his body lay in the unfathomable pit below. This was a tragedy I could accept: the shining knight came for me, but was overwhelmed by the hurricane, swept down and swallowed up in the limestone shaft. Poor Edward, muddled and exhausted, weakened by his wounds, stumbling down the hillside to his death.

But he had not stumbled, nor were his wounds the weakening kind: they had been instantly fatal. And however often I run it through, the film track never shows him slipping or falling or being caught and swept over the last edge by the storm. I see driven leaves spattered and clinging but never hiding him; see him grow as ragged as they, fraying, holey, a leaf in winter, wearing thinner as I watch. Flayed by the elements myself, I observe the airman put through a high-speed weathering process. Edward's Undoing. What a piece of work is man; and what a rare privilege, as I appreciate, to watch the unpainting of that masterpiece, till only the dirty gray scumbled canvas remained.

The last thing that hung in the air after he had gone was the spattering of torn leaves, suspended motionless against the whirling backdrop: a ragged green line where his head and shoulders had been; then they too were released and spun away into the melting pot.

I do not remember standing up—I don't think I did, or the storm would have carried me over. I must have crawled forward in a last despairing rush to catch the dissolving outline in my arms, trap whatever remained, not let him leave me. But my hands closed only on shredded vegetation, and scrabbled, gluey with sap, at the ground where he had stood, and where I fell unconscious.

Without a body there is no wind resistance. No longer buffeted nor straining against the current—carried high and fast, breathless—no breath—looking down on a toy house on a hill, gliding round close enough to see the torn-back roof, open sardine can—bottom kitchen intact, turret still standing—the fallen tree disappearing into the back of the house, like a huge hand reaching in for the body that lay there. Then away in a wide circle through the careering sky—high above a six-pointed mountain and the dark scorched hollow at its foot, the glint of a fuselage between torn clouds. Chasing down through unresisting trees that melt away as I sweep through them—no yellow snakes, no witches, no legendary Rolling-calves—just virgin forest and black rock and streaming vines dissolving in my path. Out along the grass piece, flattened like water below me and flowing round a man's body spread-eagled, arms stretched out hopefully like wings. But you can't fly on a riverbed. He should have known. Land and landmarks that are familiar, though they look so different from above—a map read through torn tissue paper. The rock where my horse shied. And he took me home on his, held close, sharing one saddle. . . . The cow pen, the big pond. Then up again so high this time, spiraling free, that I can see the whole valley and beyond the Line. I see that order has gone out of Nature—the lawless sky—the mighty ranks of the forest quite undone, and the hills just so many heaps of mashed spinach—the world my oyster, the valley my plate of greens. And now so high that I hang motionless above the world and see the moon setting beyond the turbulent rim, and, far on the other horizon, the first red streaks of a shepherd's warning sunrise. The storm boiling far below me—I can see its inner circular motion and its wider curving course leaving a track and a spin-off like a whisk through thick cream. Above me the sky a clear dark blue.

And I knew that I was dead, for my body wasn't there. I was floating free. How sad, I thought—brooding over the troubled earth from which I had escaped—that I won't be able to tell them the Great Truth I've discovered: that the spirit does go on, at least for a little while, a bright observant breath, expanding in the blue air . . . growing thin. . . .

But Great Truth is a trick of the dark and doesn't survive the coming of day—even if you can read all that you scribbled down, the charred remnants of those words of fire.

And now pain summoned me back to my body: it had not finished with me yet. I fell, horribly, precipitously, felt myself caught and battered in the raging tide and hurled back to earth, aching, struggling, gasping for breath; mortal again. Something was crushing my back and squeezing the air from my lungs, and, when I fought to breathe, smothered my face and choked my straining mouth with the usurping earth-air-water. I dragged my head up a little and wedged my chin on my arm. Clammy greenery like thin rubber coated my nostrils and clung to my tongue. I spat and coughed but a sharp pain in my chest burst and splintered in bright burning fragments through my whole body. One skewered my brain and blacked it out.

Images flashed onto the dark safety curtain; at first only the points of light that swim behind closed eyes. They aligned themselves, resolved into a pattern—glittering loops, my aunt's necklaces swinging out as she bent admiringly over something. Her plimsolls perhaps. Pale suckers, pointing outward as on a medieval tomb. Then drifting away, slow-moving fish. Fish flickering in a deep aquarium. Pale forgetful eyes—floating apart, splitting up into little minnows—lots of little minnows, a shoal, all swimming the same way—a bead curtain. But not hanging properly—no

218

gravity—a horizontal bead curtain—flowing past—and the beads *hurt*—

My eyes were open. I had twisted my body somehow under the huge weight and could see the driving rain. And a tightly clenched hand holding a rag of dark cloth—no, holding dark shredded leaves. My hand, bandaged, dark with blood. A branch very close, wagging across, filling my small view, scratching my face. Twist sideways, hide my eyes. A glim—several glims, weak and fizzy. Two still candles. Broad golden brow—silver new-moon eyes—bruised cheek, sick sunset—ragged bloody stump of neck—black blood, white bone—thick red stump welling blood over a dark red shirt—no head—burning yellow oil and flowing red blood—Headless Man . . . *Stop the drums!*

I was crouching and shuddering, in heavy driving rain. I had got myself free of the tree that had fallen across me —may even have protected me a little. My chest ached as if I had a broken rib; my shoulders and head and arms were scraped and sore. I could taste blood in the rain that streamed down my face. But worse than these was the pounding pulse in my ears that had roused me: I was filled not with panic but with a sense of urgency, as if I had overslept and now might be too late. What I must do I did not know—or for whom I feared. Maurice was dead; I remembered that—and suddenly I wanted to get back to him more than anything else, to make sure his body was safe in the broken house. He was all alone, and I must go to him.

I pushed my way out through the branches and headed back toward the hill, butting into the gale, passing the ruins. The wind was strong but gusty, the earth settling back into its rightful place; and the lightening sky confirmed this, reaching down deeper into the dregs. Rain beat on my face, or turned a slicing edge as the wind caught it. I went uphill into the torrent, like a homing salmon, and fought my way against it. But it's hard to recall: I was numb with exhaustion, revived only by the

219

strong cold blast in my face, and a single purpose driving me mindlessly toward my goal. It was as though I had been through a sort of evolution in the hurricane: it had changed and absorbed me into it, making me one with it: I too was now a senseless force, direction my only law.

It was, I calculate, nearing six o'clock as I climbed the hillside; nearing the twelfth hour of that long night. Somewhere beyond the storm the sun had risen, and above the lashing treetops the clouds boiled a pale dirty red, like thrashing waters after a shark attack. Down below in the shadow of the hill, I moved upward through a twilit devastation, skirting fallen trees I couldn't climb over or crawl under, slipping on steep rocky paths that had become waterfalls: the last great Trial—fighting my way through to my headless sleeping prince.

Anyway, there is only one more thing to tell about that night—two, if you count my discovery. But one incident, perhaps the hardest to face, as I might have prevented it. If I had not followed Edward. If I had not lingered so long in the dark stupor; if I had been quicker climbing the hillside; if I had not gone straight to Maurice's body. If I had thought *at all*.

But I did not think. I hardly felt; driven by instinct, my mind and body were subdued to one task. I only knew that every foot gained, every obstacle overcome, every hazard survived, took me nearer to Maurice. I remembered, I projected, nothing, creeping toward the reddening sky like an animal that scented blood in the wind.

When I came over the edge of the drive, I was in the midst of the violent sunrise. It was all around me, caught in the ragged clouds that hid the hilltop and disclosed the house above me only in snatches, and shockingly changed —scalped and stark. The force of the storm, from which the slope had in part protected me, knocked me back to my knees; and on my knees I crawled to the mounting block, and over it: it was harder but more direct than the steps, the right course for a Trial to run.

The flight that led up to the veranda was completely blocked by a section of roof, and I had to take the long way round by the office. Once in the lee of the house, I could walk upright, stopping to cling to one of the wooden pillars when a wave of rain broke round the corner and caught me; and I dimly observed that the force of the storm was weaker, and so was I.

I tucked my aching hand into my shirt front to keep it high and ease the throbbing in it. I looked round. The climbing stephanotis that Father and Maurice had trained along the length of the terrace and over the top-veranda railings now lay in a tangle among the debris of branches and shingles and zinc sheeting, like a discarded garland after an orgy. I could smell the crushed white flowers, heady and sweet, among the sharp scents of sap and raw wood; and I remembered how, when I saw them in English florists—costly exotics, bent round a loop of wire into a sad formal wreath—that scent made me homesick. (Sometimes now, through the cracks of the turret jalousies, I catch it carried round on the wind from the front of the house; so it didn't die. They pruned it and trained it back. It will outlive *me*. I'm so absurdly weak now I seldom leave my bed. *Surely* they would let Parson come and see me before I die? Could I trust him with this? There isn't much choice.)

The hall door was still closed and barred from the inside, and the drawing room, though half roofless, was boarded up tight. I faced into the rough wind again, and made my way round the outside, hugging the walls, until I came to the backyard gate—still fastened; Maurice and I had found it banging in the rising gale. The landscape of the yard was so altered with the fall of the bitterwood tree that I almost lost my bearings, and had to stop, nailed against the wall by sharp rain, and wipe my eyes.

I thought I would be able to crawl in through the rent made by the large branches that caught the house; but when I had climbed over and under them and got close to the tall door, I found of course that it was blocked by boards. I peered in through a slit, feeling like some face-less stranger at a window, a revenant barred from its rightful haunt.

What I could see of the hall inside looked unfamiliar, cluttered and shadowy; the shapes I remembered, even in the half dark, seemed to be missing, and humps of wreckage filled the open spaces I had known so well. Even the lighting was different—different from my last view of the room in the dead of night, and of course from its normal early morning look. (If I came down about six o'clock, both doors would already be standing open, and maids starting to mop and polish, and there would be a distant smell of roasting coffee.) Nor was it the lighting of a rainy day, when the doors were closed and the sole illumination angled down the big staircase from the landing window. Now, what light there was was smoky and red, like a fire, and came in from above.

And so must I. I backed away through the whipping twigs, chose a likely branch, and climbed a little way to get a better view. Above me, the longest limb, a continuation of the main trunk, slanted up into the boiling pink mist that clothed the whole hill—"cloud-capped towers, airy palaces." My palace was airy enough now to let me in through the roof itself.

Slipping and clinging, straining for handholds, gasping and resting, I crawled up the quivering arch—a flying buttress indeed, shaken by onslaughts of rain and wind but sturdy enough to crush in our wooden lid, and sturdy enough to carry me. Halfway up, the clouds hid the ground and I could see the broken edge far above me only in glimpses. The storm had become finer-grained, a harsh abrasive fog that looked like pink cotton wool but felt like spun-glass fiber. The force of the gale had certainly dropped or it would have snatched me from my perch; but the blundering drenching gusts shook and blinded me. I clung helplessly and bowed my head onto the streaming bark in despair.

222

Then I became aware, perhaps because I had got above the noisy leaves, perhaps because of the lulls between the onslaughts, of a muffled banging. I had heard it once from below and thought it was part of the roof slapping against a wall. Now it was nearer, and, looking round the curve of the great limb, I could see that the lower part of one of the landing shutters had torn free inside the broken window. If I moved to a small branch leading that way, I could reach it. I eased myself into a fork and clambered along my new, narrower path. It bowed with my weight and tossed alarmingly in a strong gust; but now I could reach the sill. I pulled myself onto it, standing flat against the window, clinging to the sash where the glass had fallen away, and kicked in the remaining fragments of the lower panes and glazing bars. Then I slid my legs in and dropped onto the half landing.

High above me and right across to the top veranda, the roof was open to the raving sunrise. Before me the stairs, blocked with branches, led down to the ruined hall. I climbed over the banister to get round them, saw that the drop was clear, and lowered myself to the floor below.

I picked a way among the wreckage. The big oval looking glass had fallen and broken. Seven years of bad luck. Long splinters from it, reflecting the distant sky, looked like chinks in the floorboards, fissures opening up into the seething hellfire below. I saw my knitting, and a record sleeve, caught under a leafy bough; Aunt Cissie's coach and horses. The roosting hen was still there, a ghostly blur cradled in the curve of a black horn. I had to move the sofa to get round the pile of tumbled wicker chairs and sodden matting; and there in the rosy gloom beyond lay Maurice's body.

The lantern was out. The brass doorstops had kept the blanket in place, but a blown branch lying across the legs had rumpled a corner so that one foot was in the open. I lifted off the branch and smoothed the coverlet. I felt no horror as I had before. I felt very little except that I had arrived at the place where I wanted to be. I would stay with him now and watch by him till it was all over.

Kneeling beside him, drawing some sort of animal comfort from his nearness, I wished there was something I could do, something formal and appropriate. Edward would know exactly what to do on such an occasion, and he was flying down to see us. I knew that. It sustained me. Meanwhile, I had no candle to light, and my prayers were all dried up. But I could find some flowers. I went and searched among the rubble by the bookcase where the veranda pot plants had been set in a row. There was not much left of them now, but I found a half-open orchid, and a battered red lily dangling from a shred of stalk.

I took them back to Maurice and laid them on the rough blanket. I wanted to put them in his hand, to fold his hands properly, and put the flowers in them.

Must be careful not to smear him with my damp blood-stained bandage. Lift the edge of the blanket. His left hand, cold and heavy, the fingers stiffly spread; then his right, set hard into a concrete fist. Uncurl it—that's better —what's this you've got then? Clutching a button and a bit of cloth. What you needed, my darling, was a rabbit's foot. Now this hand will not warm me again, cosseting me like a pet cat, kindling me like a fire.

The rag and the button, obviously so dear to him, though they didn't save him. I peered at them. Then I stood up quickly, tipping the flowers from my lap. I moved into the stronger light from above, turning the shred of cloth, spreading it out to examine the pattern. A piece of shirt material, dark with a small paisley design; gray mother-of-pearl button: the shirt Tom was wearing. His shirt was torn, button gone.

Struggling on the stormy veranda. Tom on top. Held by his shirt front, tearing himself away to get a clear stroke. The swinging machete blade—sparking as it hit through to the stone. The Headless Man. See if she still likes the look of you now, Jerry-boy. Hump the body up against the door, steady it there—knock—and as it opens, duck back into the shadows. But the head—can't leave it here—hide it in a sack—where, though?—behind the clutter in the dark hall—carry it in safe behind the torch dazzle —bury it in the morning. No sweat.

You is a violent man, Mars Tom me dear. Vengeful and violent. Always trouble. Lord preserve us this night.

My numb brain cleared. Understanding dazzled me: so my urgent mission is revenge, for my brother killed my lover, and he must not escape. Tell the world. Cry for justice—cry for help.

Help at hand: Lord Penn—Nan—Cookie and Lena and Lena's boyfriend and all—sheltering from the hurricane. And Aunt Cissie? Safe—sheltering in the bottom store. I went to the door that led to the passage and the drawing room. Methodically I cleared away the branches and rubble, and opened it. And as I went through it I felt something disturbing in the air—no, under my feet. Thudding. Louder, as I passed the pantry and reached the drawing-room door. Drumming.

Inside the big elegant wrecked room, half open to the sky, the drumming and shouting coming up through the floor drowned all other noise. Its nature had changed. It wasn't just that I was on the outside this time. Once or twice we had heard it take on this desperate quality as it drifted to us in snatches from the hills or over the Line, though usually a prolonged session had no particular dimension; the drumming was loud or soft as the breeze carried it; no beginning and no end. We would become aware of it, listen to it, sleep and wake and still hear it, through the night; and, in the morning light, I would wonder whether I had dreamed it all. But this rhythm that thundered under my feet was climactic. It was a countdown in secret numbers and a strange tongue, but a countdown nonetheless; for the end was approaching, and must come. Power from accumulated compression, certain implosion: Black Hole.

I heaved open the trapdoor and the noise and heat

struck me like a blast furnace. I dropped back, my hands over my ears, then crept to the edge again and looked in.

The bottom store was so dark, lit only by one glim on the rocky shelf and a pale slit of morning from the loophole window, that it took me some seconds to accustom my eyes. It was strange, too, to look down from above on the tall narrow room, the foreshortened figures.

Dark, with a ragged edge of bright hair where the light shone up through it, a glint of beads above the livid golden brow, the head was the only still spot in a seething snakepit. They were dancing wildly, leaping and twirling, arching back so I could see teeth and white eyes and glistening chests; and they all brandished flashing knives —not knives, long splinters of glass from the Glass Arch. Even the drummers were writhing and jigging, with glass daggers between their teeth. I could see now that their hands were bleeding and there were blood smears on their clothes. But they were beyond pain. They were chanting—panting—"Offer up the White Fowl! Offer up the White Fowl!"

Was there a way of stopping this madness? By descending the ladder into it? Where was Tom? Where was Aunt Cissie?—was Nan looking after her? Where was Nan?

Leaning lower into the opening, I could see past the deep beams. I could see the wall and Tom lying against it, tied with ropes. I saw him shouting, struggling to get to his feet, and falling back. I found Nan; she was standing apart, near the rock; her arms were at her sides, her head back, eyes closed, her whole body strained and rigid in a cataleptic trance. Then I saw the aunt. She zigzagged into my field of vision, a light-colored angular figure running crazily hither and thither, tripping over her tatty finery.

The heavy hectic rhythm was so rapid now that it had become a syncopated drumroll; the chant, a pulsing scream.

"Offer up the White Fowl!
"Offer up the White Fowl!"

Unstrung and unattended, quite directionless, the aunt panicked. She flapped and fluttered along the fringe of the whirling mob and was sucked into its midst. I saw her ridiculous white feather boa bobbing on the piling dark waters of the dance. The chant became a hunting cry. The drumming stopped, and I saw the wave break, engulfing the fair bobbing head in a frothy explosion of flashing arms and glass knives and white feathers and blood.

Often, now, I start out of sleep terrified, in the certain knowledge of some disaster I've narrowly failed to avert. Nowadays it's the only real fear I ever feel: the horror of dreams. Like early this morning—one of the worst I remember; I suppose writing this stirred it up. Or I waken with my cheek on the hard edge, the carved sidewall of my bed, slowly and with growing realization of panic and remorse. For that is how I woke again in the drawing room, hanging over the trapdoor, my cheek hard against the wooden rim.

My hands were stiff from gripping it. Rain was blowing onto my face, and the wind slapped the heavy wet curtains against the jalousies, under the open sky. The lurid glow had gone and it was gray morning light. I could hear the retreating storm.

I turned my head painfully and looked down into the pit. There was no movement now; a scene of silent steaming carnage. Broken bottles, feathers, blood, and a bloody cross on every forehead. They lay sprawled elaborately like a painted massacre. But they weren't dead; now and then there was a moan, weak stertorous breathing. A limb twitched, a hand convulsed, a glass knife clinked onto the floor against a yellow oil drum.

I could not find my aunt or Nan. Tom had gone, and it was by the light from the open door I saw it all, could feel the draft reach me faintly through the rising fumes and heat. Weak sunlight warmed my back; it crept into the drawing room, coming and going between showers. I saw the light also brightening in the store below me; and a white chicken, the one intended for sacrifice, moved about slowly, making its way over to the doorway, stopping to peck where a split sack of corn had bled a golden pool onto the floor.

AFTER

My hands holding on tight to the polished edge of wood; but I feel carving now, explore it with blind fingertips of one hand, still gripping with my thumb. Left hand aching, clenched round a bandaged cut. Aching from being clenched round something small and precious, clutched like he clutched it. A secret, set in cement.

A rug over my knees, and a straight, padded back that I lean against. I can feel crawling velvet through my shirt—find myself shuddering at the touch of the aunt's special chair. And so they put a blanket round my shoulders—they don't understand; talk among themselves. But I do not speak. I am not questioned. I turn my head away from the hard rim of a glass; watch them sideways to see what they're up to.

People were moving round me: the maids, the yard boy, faces I knew, all looking at me. My chair set near the open front door—the dogs lying by my feet—steady gentle rain washing the veranda and Portius in a sou'wester sweeping up the rubble. He smiled and bobbed his head shyly at me, but he didn't speak to me.

Without turning round I couldn't see the room—the hall. Too tired to do that. With closed eyes I could hear all the layers of sound: Nan's skirts near me, Tom giving orders, brooms knocking and swishing, hammering, sawing, squeaking nails, clatter of stacked shuttering boards. Farther off, calling and clinking of pans from the cookhouse. Smell of coffee. And still farther, the tractor down in the yard; and the chainsaw starting up. An ordinary morning.

But too many people about, I knew, for that; and their voices muted. No shouting. Laughter in the cookhouse quickly hushed. Pen keepers on the step, reporting to Tom: damage to the sheep pen—to orange trees—to the timber plantation. Two steers dead and one of the mares hurt bad, "will has to destroy." Tom's voice, promising to go with the shotgun and finish her off. Men have to be able to do that sort of thing, I suppose. I wondered if it would trouble Tom: in cold blood, by daylight.

"But please it seem like a plane come down over by Rookoom and one dead somebody inna grass piece t'row out of it or maybe walk a little ways away. . . . We carry and lay it down a yard cover with couple saddlecloth and tell Chippy, say, now is t'ree coffin not two. . . . T'anks— t'anks, Mars Tom . . . Yessuh, Cookie promise we hot drink and all comfort—for the shock—is so Cookie say. And managing nicely with tarpaulin to make up fire fe cook and dry out everything inna bottom kitchen, she say, before we go down again. . . . Yessuh—fe go help Chippy with the coffin them. . . . But Lord Jesus, Mars Tom, what a whole heap of destruction in this one night, eh? and three poor soul strike down!—Yessuh, we going do it now. . . ."

Tom's voice too low to hear. That was deliberate. Now he was behind me, talking to Nan.

"Can't we manage? . . . Yes. Let the maids and Zaccy and Portius have their lunch. And they can take the dogs down with them. . . . Bring the coffee now, Nan. . . . Not bad in here . . . and with the stairs tidied up—"

The sweeping and clattering stopped. I watched the rain. The zinc sheet had been cleared away earlier, I suppose.

"Good, Nan—bring a cup here and see if she will take some."

Knowing what I knew? My throat was parched but I would not touch their coffee: it could be poisoned. I wouldn't stay. I was going to walk down the drive and get into the car and drive to Montego Bay and catch the next plane to England. My uncle, Father's brother, will help, I thought. Edward's father. I will be able to break the news to him of Edward's plane crash and tell him all I know. And tell him of Aunt Cissie's terrible death and of Maurice's murder.

I squeezed my lips and shut my eyes and turned away from the fragrant coffee; from Nan's wheedling "Come then, Miss Lizzie me dear—"

"She still can't hear. She's too shaken up."

"Or cussed same like her aunt before her—poor soul—may she rest."

"Enough of that, now. And no idle talk among the servants. The people from the Line who took shelter here won't tell of it."

"Them all leave now?"

"Seems like they just crept away. I took out the chair and locked the store. When the coffins are ready we'll go down."

"But is where German Busha body now, Mars Tom?"

"Hush, old woman. It's down there too."

"Lord, Mars Tom! You one carry it all that way?"

"No—the trapdoor."

"So poor Miss Ciss have company. . . . Lord Jesus! What a terrible thing—" I heard her sniff. "Is same like I lose me own baby, I care for Miss Ciss so long. . . . Come, me dear," at my ear, "have a little nice milky coffee now—"

I kept my eyes and mouth shut. Soon, when I'm rested, I'll just get up and go, I thought. I shan't talk to them.

"We better take her fe lay down, Mars Tom. Seem like her mind quite gone, poor little soul. . . . Come now, Miss Liz—let Nanny put you to bed."

I felt her take my elbow firmly and try to raise me, but I held on to the arms of the Siege Perilous.

"Come now, me dear. . . . Stubborn favor jackass same

231

like Miss Ciss—Come, Mars Tom, come take her fe me. Mus' loose her hand—"

I clung tightly, but they pulled my fingers free.

"Lord—what is this she hold so tight? Let Nan see, chile—"

I remembered vividly how once, in the pantry, she had prized open my hand; I was trying to save a tiny bright green moth. She got it away from me and washed it down the sink. So I clenched my fist tight and hung on. Tom took my wrist and bent it back. He pressed his hard thumb into the ragged bandage and I cried out with pain; but he bored up under my clenched fingers and forced them back.

"What's this then, sweetheart?"

"Look like is you own shirt button did tear off, Mars Tom."

"Where did you get this, Liz?" Tom took my head roughly and forced it up. "Look—" His strong fingers pulling my eyelids open. "Look, Liz—how did you get hold of this?" The shred of cloth and the button dangled close. I didn't speak. I would not say my lover's name.

"Don' hurt the chile, Mars Tom! She don't comprehend—"

"She comprehends all right—don't you, Lizzie dear? Silly girl—being a little mule just gives the game away. Couldn't you have thought up something? A neat little lie to cover your confusion?"

I watched him. He wasn't afraid of what I knew, or of my hatred. He was so sure of himself. He let me go, smiling. He turned away and spoke quietly to Nan, and she nodded and went out. I remained standing. I felt stronger. It'll be strange, I thought, just to walk out through the door, probably forever. I took a step, but Tom's arm was round me.

"Careful now, Lizzie dear—you're very weak, you know. We'll look after you. The turret is fine and dry and quiet. You'll be quite safe and snug up there."

Nan was back, and she took my other arm.

232